Gambling on Death

A Mortician Murder Mystery-Book 2

A. E. Howe

**Books in the
Mortician Murder Mystery Series
(in order):**

Return to Death
Gambling on Death
Memorial for Death
Search for Death

CHAPTER ONE

Lee Lamberton was escorting Randall Ward to the front door of the funeral home. Ward was seventy-six years old and unsteady on his feet, partly because of his age but mostly because of his grief. Lee walked at his elbow, ready to grab the man if he looked like he was going to stumble.

Lee was irritated that the man's children hadn't come with their father to help make the final arrangements for their mother, but he wasn't surprised. They were all pretty much useless. Bobby, the oldest at forty-nine, hadn't held down a real job in years. He'd had two wives and three kids and now spent the better part of his days at various bars in Gainesville. Marty, the middle child, was a little better and usually tried to do the right thing. Unfortunately, she seemed unable to find a man who knew how to keep his pants up and his fists down. The last one had abandoned her in Illinois and she was trying to find a way back to Florida in time for the funeral on Thursday. Then there was Taggart, the momma's boy who weighed at least three hundred pounds, and had the only decent job of the three, managing the Supersave grocery store.

"Tag's too broken up over his mother's death to come with me," Mr. Ward had told Lee.

Lee had kept his mouth shut. *If you can't say anything nice,* he thought, repeating the old adage to himself.

Now Lee opened the door for Mr. Ward and saw the glow of blue lights down the street. It was just after dark and a cool November wind had brought a light rain. The wet street and sidewalks reflected the flashing lights.

"What's going on down there?" Mr. Ward asked.

"Looks like the police are at Dobbs Appliances and Electronics," Lee said. "There's at least one police car and a couple of sheriff's deputies." Lee's curiosity was piqued. "Here, let me help you out to your car."

"I can make it," Mr. Ward said.

Lee politely ignored him and walked with the older man down the steps and over to the tan Chevrolet Impala parked in the driveway.

"Don't worry about anything. I'll take care of all the details, just as we discussed," Lee said, closing the car door once Mr. Ward was behind the wheel.

"Your dad and I were great friends," Mr. Ward told him.

"Your friendship meant a lot to him."

As Randall Ward drove away, Lee thought about his father, who'd passed away almost a year ago. Lee wasn't confident that he was doing a good job filling his dad's shoes as the owner of the Lamberton Funeral Home. *Co-owner,* he reminded himself. His sister, Kay, had inherited half of the business.

"What's going on at the appliance store?"

Lee turned to see Kay coming down the front steps, pushing a lock of plain brown hair behind her ear.

"Something big," Lee told her as they both watched the flashing lights and dark silhouettes moving between the police cars.

"Well, I'm going to go find out." Kay headed off down the sidewalk.

"You shouldn't be a rubbernecker," Lee said, falling in beside her.

"I'm just out for a stroll on a fall evening. No harm in that," Kay said, making a beeline for Dobbs Appliances and Electronics.

"A little early in the evening for a burglary," Lee speculated.

The appliance store was in the middle of a row of small businesses. On one end was an antique shop called Diamonds in the Rough, while Florida's Best Furniture Store sat on the other side of Dobbs Appliances. As Kay and Lee got closer, the number of law enforcement officers standing around made it obvious that whatever was going on was more significant than a burglary.

"Armed robbery?" Lee offered. "Though a Monday night doesn't seem like primetime to rob a retail store."

"There's Jerome," Kay said, pointing to a young black deputy who was using his flashlight to search the sidewalk and the storm drain.

"Can we help you find something?" Lee asked the deputy when they were twenty feet away from him.

Jerome Carter looked up, recognized them and looked around guiltily.

"Y'all shouldn't be down here," he told them. "After all that mess back in April, the sheriff is still giving me a hard time about working for you." Jerome sometimes drove for the Lambertons when there was a big enough funeral to warrant multiple family cars, and he would also act as security for funerals and viewings.

"What's going on?" Kay asked, ignoring his admonition.

"Someone stabbed Hubert Dobbs," Jerome muttered.

"No! Who would stab Santa?" Lee said, upset by the news.

"Santa?" Kay looked at Lee.

"You were too old to care by the time he started, but I remember every year on Friday nights between Thanksgiving and Christmas, Dobbs would play Santa. Had a really cool North Pole display set up in the store. Dad would walk me down here. Man, that's awful."

"Was it a robbery?" Kay asked Jerome, impatient with Lee's nostalgia.

"Don't know." Jerome shrugged. "We got a call about half an hour ago that the front door was wide open and that it looked like someone was on the floor in the back room."

"I don't remember much about the Dobbs family," Kay said with a thoughtful look on her face.

Last spring, six months after their father had died, Kay had returned to Melon County after spending years away. She'd left the town of Lang fifteen years ago to serve as a nurse in Vietnam. When she finally returned, it was with the intention of forcing Lee to sell the failing business and split whatever money was left. The last thing she'd wanted to do was to become her brother's partner, but the murders in the spring had complicated everything and now here she was.

"It was just Dobbs, his wife and daughter, Alison. He and his wife got a divorce when I was in sixth grade and the wife moved away with their daughter. Alison was in my class," Lee said in a wistful way that caused Kay to look at him.

"A childhood crush?" Kay smiled.

"Oh, gee, no. But we were kind of friends."

"So what's the chance we'll get the funeral?" Kay asked him, her mind turning quickly back to business.

"I don't think he had any relatives in town," Lee said in an inquiring tone, looking at Jerome.

"I can't be giving out confidential information." Jerome sounded offended.

"Come on. The sheriff's office leaks like the *Titanic*.

Remember that we pay you too," Lee reminded him.

"I hear you." Jerome sighed. "If I hear who Dobbs's next of kin is, I'll let you know."

"Even better, if they come by the sheriff's office, give them one of our cards," Lee said.

"Get out of here before someone sees you," Jerome said, looking up the block at the other deputies milling around the front of the store.

Lee and Kay headed back toward the funeral home.

"We need to talk about the Curry funeral," Kay said with a hint of rebuke.

"I think it went well," Lee said, pretending that he didn't know where this conversation was going.

"Oh, the funeral went great and the casket was lovely. Too lovely for the amount of money they paid," Kay said.

Lee focused his eyes on the cracked sidewalk and kept his mouth shut, because he knew that every answer that came to mind would only dig the hole deeper.

"You don't have anything to say?" Kay gave him a chance to answer before continuing, "We had this conversation after the Riggins funeral. You can't be giving free upgrades."

"I admit that I shouldn't have upgraded old Man Riggins's funeral flowers. But with Mrs. Curry's daughter…" Lee sighed. "She really wanted the frillier casket liner, but didn't have the money. That girl suffered something awful over the last couple of years. I just wanted to do a little something for her. After the medical bills, they don't have anything. The truth is, we may end up eating all of the costs anyway."

Kay shook her head. "I appreciate that you have a good heart, but you need to have a good head for business too."

Kay knew she couldn't give Lee too hard of a time over this. She'd heard everyone talking about little Amy Curry's battle with cancer during the viewing. Still, the funeral home was a business, not a non-profit.

Once they were back at the funeral home, Lee said, "I'm going finish up with Mrs. Ward."

"I hope you didn't promise Mr. Ward any free upgrades," Kay said with a stern look.

"He said his wife didn't want him spending a lot of money on her funeral, so he didn't want anything fancy."

"Where's Lester?"

Lester Andrews hadn't been around to annoy her all evening. He worked for Lee as a gopher and apprentice funeral director and, while he did good work, Kay found his personality highly irritating.

"He had to go get his stuff from a friend's apartment. He's been crashing there and the landlord found out."

"Don't tell me, he's going to be staying here for a few days." Kay had gotten used to Lester's comings and goings, but that didn't mean she was happy about it.

"He told me it'd just be for a couple of days this time."

"He camped out in the guest room for a month this summer."

"If we paid him more, we could deduct it from his salary."

"Just a couple of nights," Kay said, wagging her finger at Lee, who nodded. "And we need to scrape up another funeral for this weekend."

Neither of them said it out loud, but both siblings were wondering if Hubert Dobbs's funeral would end up with them.

Lee went into the embalming room where Mrs. Ward was laid out on the stainless steel table, covered from her neck down by a sheet. Lester had undressed and cleaned her before he left that afternoon. Lee tilted the table and went to work, replacing her blood with embalming fluid.

Two hours later he was doing some touch-up work on the body when there was a knock on the door that led to the back of the house. Before he could get to the door, it opened and Jerome came in.

"Mrs. Ward was a nice woman," he said, walking toward the table. "She was my history teacher in eleventh grade. Shame she didn't get to enjoy her retirement. Always told us she wanted to travel the country."

"One thing the funeral business teaches you is that we need to make hay while the sun shines," Lee said, gently gluing her eyelids shut. "So who murdered Mr. Dobbs?"

"I got called out to a domestic disturbance half an hour after you left, but they're still over at the shop looking for clues. You want my opinion, this is going to be a real head-scratcher," Jerome said, walking over to the refrigerator in the corner of the embalming room and pulling out a beer.

The *pop-fizz* sound of the pull-top ring caused Lee to look up.

"You know, you and Lester shouldn't keep beer in that refrigerator, and you certainly shouldn't eat or drink in here," Lee admonished as Jerome tipped up the can of Pabst Blue Ribbon and downed half of it. "Aren't you on duty?"

"Nah, just signed off." Jerome dropped down into a chair. "The case has been assigned to Wade Sutton."

Lee raised his eyebrows. "I know Sutton's brother. We went to school together. Tommy always called his older brother a lunkhead."

"Sutton hasn't gotten any smarter."

"How'd he get to be an investigator?"

"Easy as pie. He married the sheriff's sister-in-law."

"That'll do it," Lee said, giving Mrs. Ward's hands a light dusting of powder. Jenny Mathis, who ran the beauty shop across the street from the appliance store, would come in later to do her hair and face makeup. The beautician took care of most of the ladies in town while they were alive and, for the last twenty years, had done their final makeover before they were lowered into the ground or sent into the furnace at Hilltop Crematorium. It made things easier on the family, as she already knew the preferences of the deceased, so there was no need to ask a grieving husband things he didn't know.

Jerome nodded toward Mrs. Ward. "She'll be missed. I remember, about a year ago, I got a call about a little kid walking around this neighborhood by himself. I'm talking a toddler, here. By the time I got there, Mrs. Ward already had the kid cleaned up and eating candy. She even helped me find where he lived."

Finished with his preparations, Lee neatly folded the sheet so that it came to just below Mrs. Ward's neckline. He never covered a face after getting a body ready for viewing. Then he nodded to Jerome, who got up and helped him roll the trolley into the cooler that was large enough to hold six bodies.

Once the cooler was closed, Lee got his own beer and he and Jerome went outside to sit on the darkened front porch. Down the street, they could see a lone car parked outside the appliance store.

"Looks like they left someone to watch the place." Jerome was trying to decide which deputy it was, but the department's unmarked cars were all either white or brown and it was too dark to make out details.

When Jerome got up to go, Lee asked him if he'd be able to drive the family car on Thursday for Mrs. Ward's funeral.

"I got you covered," Jerome assured him.

Lee spent the next couple of days making sure everything was ready for Mrs. Ward's viewing on Wednesday. There were the usual last-minute problems, including damage to the coffin when it was delivered on Tuesday. Luckily it was just a broken rail and the company was able to overnight the replacement part.

"Let me do it," Lester said when Lee started cursing for the third time as he tried to install the replacement rail.

"Fine!" Lee said through clenched teeth and tossed the screwdriver to Lester.

"I need to do something to earn my keep." Lester caught the screwdriver and leaned into the coffin. Fifteen minutes later, the rail was on.

"No one likes a show-off," Lee said, though he had to admit that Lester was handier with tools than he was. "What's Ruby making for tonight?" Lester was also the favorite of Ruby Bowen, the funeral home's eccentric cook and housekeeper. On nights when they had a viewing, she served dinner early.

"Country-fried steak, green beans and cornbread." Lester recited the menu like it was holy scripture.

"Let's get Mrs. Ward into the coffin and wheel her into the viewing room," Lee said.

It took an hour to get the coffin, flowers, chairs and accessories set up to Lee's satisfaction.

"This looks nice," Kay said, handing out a rare compliment. "Ruby wanted me to tell you that dinner is almost ready."

"Do they know yet who killed the guy at the appliance store?" Lester asked Jerome as he joined them around the kitchen table.

"I haven't heard anything except that they don't expect to solve it quickly," Jerome said, straightening the tie of his dark suit and pulling out a chair for Kay. Lee had asked him to come and help with the viewing. It never hurt to have extra hands for directing the mourners or for handling an emergency.

"Robbery gone wrong is what some folks are saying around town, but there's more to the dinner than the biscuits. I heard a rumor that Dobbs was a ladies man," Ruby said, setting a platter of country-fried steak on the table. The housekeeper had a habit of jumping from subject to subject during a conversation so that it was hard to follow what she was talking about half the time.

"He looked like Santa Claus," Lester said with a shake of his head.

"He *was* Santa Claus, at least at Christmas." Lee forked a piece of steak and brought it over to his plate.

"No word on any relatives?" Kay asked, watching the men fill their plates.

"They notified the daughter, but I didn't hear any more than that," Jerome said.

"Not to be callous, but we don't have another funeral lined up," Kay pointed out.

"Have they even done the autopsy?" Lee asked.

"Like they tell *me* what's going on." Jerome laughed. "Be different if I got along with Sutton. I'll see if I can find out where things are," he said grudgingly.

"We sound like vultures," Lee said.

"Vultures got to eat too," Lester said, putting a piece of steak in his mouth as though illustrating his point.

"Yang seems to be very interested in the murder." Ruby was talking about one of her two obese tabby cats.

"Oh?" Kay asked. In the six months since she'd moved back to the funeral home, she hadn't been able to decide if Ruby was crazy or *really* crazy. Ruby's personification of the cats wasn't unusual, but she seemed to be taking it to an extreme by suggesting that the animals were taking a personal interest in a crime.

"He brought home a dead bird yesterday, a robin."

Everyone but Ruby was wondering what significance there was to the bird being a robin.

"Robin almost rhymes with Dobbins."

"His name was Dobbs," Lee pointed out.

"I don't think Yang makes much of a distinction between the name Dobbs and Dobbins," Ruby said as though it was proof that Yang was particularly clever. To Kay it was proof that Ruby was particularly nuts. Not that Kay or anyone else sitting around the table was going to suggest firing Ruby. Her cooking alone made her worth every penny of her salary and her rent-free apartment above the carport.

"I saw a Corvette in the Supersave parking lot," Ruby continued, apropos of nothing. "Anyone want another piece of steak? It will only take a moment to fry up more."

Lee kicked Lester under the table when he saw him look up. "Thanks Ruby, but we need to get ready for the viewing," he said, ignoring the disappointed look on Lester's long face.

The viewing drew a large crowd and kept them all on their feet for several hours. When it was over, Lee sighed with exhaustion. Jerome had already left to get ready for his next shift with the sheriff's office and Kay was in the office, reviewing the books. He looked over at Lester.

"Let's go ahead and get everything ready for the funeral tomorrow."

"Mr. Ward didn't look so good," Lester said as he picked up two of the flower arrangements.

"With those kids, can you blame him?"

"Kids? They're older than me," Lester said.

"And to the amazement of all, you're more mature than

they are."

"It's a little surprising." Lester was well aware of his own talents and faults.

They moved the flowers into the cooler and pushed the wheeled bier with Mrs. Ward's now closed and latched casket over by the rear door, so it would be ready to load into the hearse in the morning.

Lee said goodnight to Lester and turned out the lights in the viewing room. As he walked by the office, he could see that Kay had left the door open. She was hunched over their father's desk, comparing two columns of figures. Lee started to turn and head upstairs, but then he knocked gently on the door frame. Kay looked up, keeping a finger on each of the spreadsheets.

"How do the numbers look?" Lee asked, although he had very little interest in the books, which was the reason Kay had arrived six months ago and threatened to close down the failing funeral home.

"If you don't consider depreciation, then we aren't losing money anymore. However, I won't feel good until we've replaced the money that you ran through before I took the reins." She sighed. "That wasn't meant as a jab."

"I've admitted that I'm not a businessman."

"People like the job you do."

Kay wasn't used to handing out compliments. It was one of the reasons she'd never felt comfortable as a supervising nurse. She'd often get home from a shift and realize that she'd been critical of some insignificant flaw in one of her nurses instead of complimenting them on their skills. When she'd started working with her brother, their relationship had been so adversarial that she'd tried to spread more honey and less vinegar into her conversations with him. It wasn't that hard since he was very good at embalming and directing funerals. Growing up, she'd never been able to embrace the funeral service like Lee or their father. The tensions had culminated when she'd headed off to nursing school, then shipped out to Vietnam.

"It's odd to think that, without the murder of your old boyfriend, we might not have reached an agreement to carry on with the funeral home," Lee said.

"I'd like to think that Rick's murder had some meaning." Kay gave Lee a crooked smile. "But if you don't stop giving away stuff, we'll be right back where we were six months ago."

"Yes, boss," Lee said good-naturedly, giving her a quick salute before heading off to bed.

CHAPTER TWO

Thursday morning started out smoothly enough. At eight o'clock, Lee, Jerome and Lester made the short, two-block trip from the funeral home to Lang City Cemetery to set up the tent and chairs for the graveside portion of the service for Mrs. Ward. The weather promised to cooperate, with clear skies and an expected high temperature of seventy-eight degrees.

Back at the funeral home, they loaded Mrs. Ward's casket into the back of their two-year-old Cadillac hearse, then packed the remaining space with flower arrangements. When they were done, Lee looked down at himself. Dirty water from one of the arrangements had left one of his pant legs wet from thigh to knee.

"I'm going upstairs to change," he told Lester.

In clean clothes once again, Lee came back downstairs to find a young woman standing in the hallway. She had short and curly dark brown hair and was wearing a black, knee-length skirt and high heels that made her look awkward and uncomfortable. Appearing nervous, she craned her neck to peer into the parlor.

"Can I help you?" Lee asked in his most professional tone.

"I… don't know," she said hesitantly. "I was looking for the owner."

"I'm Lee Lamberton," he answered, putting out his hand.

"Oh…" She looked perplexed. "I thought… Didn't your father own the home?"

"My father passed away last year. Can I help you?"

"Lee?" She gave him an appraising look, then smiled just a little. "I think we might have been in school together."

He smiled back. "Alison? Alison Dobbs?" She didn't look anything like he'd remembered. Back in grade school, she'd been stick-thin with long hair hanging down her back and bangs cut straight across her forehead.

"That's right." She took his hand now and gave it a gentle shake. That's when he noticed the dark circles under her eyes that she'd tried to cover up with powder. "My father…" She broke off to stifle a quick sob.

"I know about the… death." Lee had almost said "murder," but thought that seemed a little harsh to say to the man's daughter, even if it was accurate.

"I remembered this funeral home. Your father buried my grandfather."

"I'm sorry that I don't remember it."

"I was only six or seven at the time. I remember that your father came over and talked to me. I'd been feeling lost, with all the adults crying and hugging. It wasn't like other family get-togethers, when I was the center of attention. I was starting to cry, more out of loneliness than over a death that I didn't understand, when your father put his hand on my shoulder. After I had calmed down a bit, he took me into his office where there were some toys that I could play with. Heh, they were probably some of *your* toys. Anyway, I remember thinking that he must be the nicest man who ever lived. Funny how the memory stuck with me."

"Even more funny if you'd grown up with my dad. He could be a harsh taskmaster when he wanted to be. On the other hand, I always thought of *your* dad as Santa Claus."

"And I hated that!" Alison said, allowing her smile to return. "Dad playing Santa ruined the illusion for me, even though he promised that he was just Santa's hired help. One time he even showed me an invoice he supposedly sent to Santa."

Lester came into the front hall, caught Lee's eye and pointed at his wristwatch. "We need to get to the church."

Lee nodded, then looked at Alison. "We have a funeral this morning. Would you like to ride to the church with me? We could talk in the hearse." He knew it was a ridiculous suggestion, but he didn't want to break off their reunion.

Alison looked at Lester and Lee for a moment, then said, "Sure. I need to get this settled."

"You can go with Kay," Lee said to Lester, who started to object until he realized what Lee was up to. He settled for giving Lee a grumpy look.

"I've never ridden in a hearse," Alison said when they were standing next to the new Cadillac.

Lee was glad that his father had bought it the year before his death, because he doubted that he could have convinced Kay to invest in a new vehicle, even though they would have needed it. The old Lincoln, nicknamed Bertha, was fine for picking up bodies from the morgue or transporting them to the airport, but it wasn't reliable or nice-looking enough for funerals.

"This must be very upsetting for you. I can just call you when the funeral is over," Lee said, rethinking his offer to let

Alison ride with him.

Alison shook her head. "No. It's fine."

Lee opened the door, and she gave the funereal interior a long look before climbing in.

"I don't want to be presumptuous, but I assume you stopped by because you want us to take care of your father's funeral," Lee said as he drove down the street toward the church. The First Baptist Church was ten blocks from the funeral home, on the other side of the town's oldest residential neighborhood.

"Yes, but I don't know how much I can afford right now. The police have everything locked up and don't want me going through Dad's things until they're done."

"Don't worry about anything. We'll work it out," Lee said, knowing that Kay wouldn't be happy with this approach. But he thought about his dad comforting a young Alison at her grandfather's funeral, and he was sure that he would want Lee to do whatever was necessary to ensure that Mr. Dobbs was well buried.

"I knew I could trust you all. His death was so sudden. On top of that, I haven't seen my father in years."

"I'm sorry. I didn't know you two were… estranged."

"Once Mom moved away, she didn't want me to have anything to do with Dad. Dad tried but… he just wasn't very good at communicating. I guess I didn't like the awkwardness, so I didn't do much to encourage him. When I graduated from high school, I moved to Pensacola and that's when we just sort of lost touch."

"When was the last time you talked to him?" Lee asked.

"February. He called me on my birthday."

"What has the sheriff's office told you about your father's death?"

"Not much, except not to bother them or any of Dad's stuff while they're conducting their investigation."

Lee involuntarily let out a huff of derision. "You shouldn't wait for them."

"You don't think they'll do a good job?" Alison asked with a raised eyebrow.

"I don't think they're *capable* of doing a good job." Lee took a deep breath and considered his next words. "They have some good officers working for them, but the problem is at the top. The sheriff is a bit of an ass."

"I didn't think much of the detective assigned to Dad's case."

"Wade Sutton is the sheriff's brother-in-law."

"That doesn't sound good," Alison said, sounding frustrated. "What can I do?"

"Do you have money to hire an attorney? Or a private investigator?" Lee asked, already suspecting the answer by the way she'd approached the topic of the funeral costs.

"No. My mother was diagnosed with breast cancer three years ago and we're still paying off medical bills."

"I hope she's all right."

"Fingers crossed they got all of it and it hasn't come back. We just don't have any money."

"Do you know if your father did?" Lee asked as he drove the hearse into the church parking lot.

"I don't have any idea. He paid Mom child support for years. I know she always thought he was hiding money from the judge, but he didn't seem to have a lavish lifestyle."

Lee parked near the side door of the church. Lester and Kay were already there with the additional flowers that they'd put in the trunk of the family car.

Before getting out of the hearse, Lee turned to Alison. "I don't know what I can tell you except that we'll help as much as we can to keep the funeral costs low."

"These aren't your problems." Alison looked down at her hands and tears formed rivulets on her cheeks.

Lee reached out and took her hand. "A friend of mine is a deputy. I can ask him to look into the investigation," he promised, knowing he was writing checks on Jerome's account... checks that were going to come back as insufficient influence. The problem was that Lee was captivated by Alison. Her vulnerability made him want to solve all of her problems.

"I feel so useless. I just want to do something for Dad."

"I'll help you all I can." Lee gave her hand a squeeze. Outside the hearse, he could see Lester and Kay staring at him. "But right now I have to get the church ready for Mrs. Ward's funeral. I can ask Lester to drive you back to the funeral home."

"Would you mind if I stayed?"

"Of course not," he said, seeing Kay walk toward the hearse. He let go of Alison's hand and opened his door. "You can ride to the cemetery with me if you want."

"I'd like that," she said and got out on her side of the hearse.

Kay gave Alison a nod as she came around to the back to help with the flowers.

"Who is that?" she asked Lee.

"The good news is we have the Dobbs funeral. The bad news is that I don't know if we'll get paid for it." Kay's face flushed and Lee quickly said, "You can dock my salary."

Kay just shook her head and started unloading the flowers.

The funeral featured several poignant eulogies for the well-liked Mrs. Ward that brought most of the attendees to tears. During the service, Lee kept looking to the back pew where Alison sat alone, wiping at her own tears. He had to fight the urge to go sit with her. *What is wrong with me?* he asked himself. *Is it just some leftover puppy love from school?*

Lee had to make himself focus on his responsibilities as the funeral drew to a close. Moving calmly, he assembled the pallbearers in the proper order to lift the coffin and carry it solemnly out to the hearse. Lee could remember a dozen times where he had seen this part of the ceremony almost end in disaster. He and Jerome always followed close behind the coffin so they were ready to step in if anyone looked like they were going to falter, trip or let the coffin slip from their grasp.

With the coffin installed in the back of the hearse and the largest of the flower arrangements positioned around it, Lee opened the door for Alison before getting in on the driver's side. Jerome mouthed: *Who is she?* Lee mouthed: *Later*, and saw Kay move over to whisper in Jerome's ear.

Lee wondered how he was going to get Jerome to dig into the Dobbs murder. *Can Jerome even get any information?* he thought.

"That was a nice service," Alison said as Lee started the motor and pulled out of the parking lot. Jerome and Lester followed in the two family cars.

"Your father's will be too. I know that he had a lot of friends in the community." As he said it, Lee wondered about the one person who clearly *wasn't* Dobbs's friend, the person who had stabbed him. "Did your father have any enemies that you know of?"

"It's been so long since we talked about anything beyond the weather that I just don't know. I don't even know who his friends were, let alone his enemies," Alison admitted.

Lee decided to focus on something other than the murder. He'd promised her a funeral and he needed to start figuring out how to deliver one. "Do you know if your father has a burial plot?"

"I hadn't even thought about it," Alison said, her voice a

mix of sadness and frustration.

"Did he go to church?"

"I think so… sometimes."

"If the sheriff's office won't let you look through his papers, then maybe one of his friends would know if he had any funeral plans."

"That makes sense, if I just knew who they were. I feel lost with all of this. Mom spent so many years talking Dad down that I kind of didn't want to get involved in his life. That sounds awful. In the back of my mind, I think I always saw us reconnecting at some point. Maybe when I got married or had kids, you know?"

Lee focused on entering the cemetery. The procession drove in past slightly crooked wrought-iron gates and down a narrow lane through the older part that always reminded Lee of the classic image of a haunted cemetery—full of sprawling live oak trees, crypts and crumbling tombstones that dated back before the Civil War. Eventually they approached the newer part of the cemetery where the green Lamberton Funeral Home tent could be seen over Mrs. Ward's freshly dug grave. The mounds of dirt left by the backhoe were covered with sheets of artificial turf, as though everyone couldn't see through the ruse.

The pallbearers met at the back of the hearse and, under Lee and Lester's guidance, took hold of the coffin as it was rolled out of the back and into their hands. After a slow walk to the gravesite, the coffin was carefully placed on the hydraulic lift that would lower it into the ground.

After the brief service, Jerome and Lester drove the family cars back to the funeral home while Lee waited at the grave for a few minutes. His father had always believed it was best for the family not to see the hearse return to the home without their loved one. Lee remembered his dad telling him that it was the small courtesies that separated the funeral homes that were in it for the money from the ones that existed to provide a service to those who were grieving.

"I'm glad that you're going to help me through all of this," Alison said after the last of the cars had driven away. "I didn't stay in touch with anyone in town and the only family I have is on my mother's side. All of them believed what my mother said about Dad."

"Why did they get a divorce?"

"Mom swears that he was cheating on her and that he had a gambling problem. I don't know Dad's side of the story. He never defended himself or talked about her."

"I think the first step will be to find some of your dad's friends. I can help you with that. I know most of the people in town."

"That would be great." She gave him a smile.

"I'll start as soon as we get back to the funeral home." Lee looked at his watch. "I guess we should…" He paused when a slight movement near one of the tombstones caught his eye.

A fat tabby cat was stalking around a plastic vase of faded flowers. The cat picked something up in its mouth before scooting off toward the street.

"That's odd. I'd swear that was my housekeeper's cat," Lee said. An odd shiver ran up his back and he shook himself. "We can go now."

When they got back to the funeral home, Alison left to return to her motel. Lee had been on the verge of asking her where she was staying before he reminded himself that she was mourning the death of her father.

Kay popped out of the office as soon as he came inside the home. "What are you doing?" she asked.

"I'm getting us a funeral. Didn't we want Dobbs?" Lee

asked, feigning innocence.

"What I saw didn't look like the beginnings of a business relationship."

Lee decided that the best defense was a strong offense. Pretending to take umbrage, he shot back, "I can't have a life? I knew Alison when we were kids. I can be... smitten with her if I want." He didn't like the word "smitten," but it was the first thing that had come to mind

"Just don't mix business with pleasure. You don't make the best financial decisions as it is." Seeing her words hit their mark, she said, "Is that what you meant about not knowing if we'll get paid for the funeral? What did you promise her?"

"I just said we'd help her out."

"Help her? How?"

"Listen, the sheriff is being an ass and not letting her get into her father's house to look through his papers. I'm sure that he has the money for the funeral, but it just might take her a while to get everything sorted out."

"So we're talking a loan. You know loans usually have a specified interest rate and a deadline for repaying the debt?"

"Ease up, will you?" Lee said and immediately realized it had been the wrong angle to take.

"If I ease up, then we're all out of a job. I quit my nursing position—which paid good money, by the way— to come down here and run the business. The only way I can do that is if you *let* me run the business." The last sentence was delivered with enough volume to be heard in every corner of the house.

Lee's irresponsibility was particularly galling to Kay since they'd had a similar conversation only days earlier. Knowing she'd let herself lose control, she wheeled away from him and headed upstairs to her bedroom. She slammed the door behind her for effect, then stripped out of her funeral clothes and threw herself on the bed.

What do I really want? she asked herself.

Rolling over onto her back, she looked around the room—the same room where she'd spent the first eighteen years of her life. Then she had escaped, first to nursing school, then into the Army and Vietnam. It had all added up to a life that was her own—not her father's or her brother's.

What was she really doing back here? Was she helping Lee or hiding from that other life that had not turned out the way she'd expected? No husband. No children. Just work and a few friends.

Did I come back to look for the family I had because I couldn't make one of my own? she wondered, feeling hot tears on her cheek and cursing herself for letting her emotions get the best of her.

I just need to get the business back on solid footing, then I can go where I want. Lee is my little brother and helping him is part of my responsibility as a big sister. The trouble is, he won't help himself, Kay argued with herself.

She rolled over and turned on the clock radio next to her bed. The soft sounds of Air Supply's "I'm All Out of Love" filled the room. She let the cool November breeze from the open window loll her into dreams.

CHAPTER THREE

Lee found Lester and Jerome in the kitchen eating a lunch of ham sandwiches and baked potato slices. Ruby was interrogating them. She loved to hear every detail of funerals and graveside services. As they filled her in, she'd interject seemingly unconnected thoughts and ideas. Only occasionally did Lee understand the relationship between what was being said and what she was talking about.

"Hurry up, we need to go back over to the cemetery and take down the tent," Lee told the two men. He received waves and nods as they ate.

"You need some lunch. Now sit down right here," Ruby said, taking a plate out of the cupboard.

"I want to get everything cleaned up," Lee's mouth said, even as his butt started to sink down into the chair at the end of the table. It was the smell of garlic-salted potato and honey-baked ham that he couldn't resist.

"It's worth the time," Jerome assured him.

"What have you heard about the Dobbs murder?" Lee

asked Jerome as casually as he could.

"Why?" Jerome gave him his best *Who-do-you-think-you're-kidding?* look.

"Just curious," Lee said innocently.

"Bullshit. Kay and I watched you dancing around that woman. What'd you tell her, that you'd help find her daddy's murderer?" Jerome asked.

"Don't be ridiculous. Why would I tell her something like that?"

"'Cause she made you all gooey-eyed." Lester snickered into his ham sandwich.

"If we can help, we should." Lee changed tack to run before the wind.

"But who's going to be doing all the heavy lifting? The black man." Jerome pointed at himself. "It's going to be my job on the line when I go snooping around a case that isn't mine."

"Did you get fired this spring when we solved the Bruhn murder?"

"No, but only by the skin of my teeth. You can bet I didn't get an award or a promotion."

"I only told her I'd look into it." As soon as he said "I," Lee knew he'd made a mistake.

"I? You mean *me*."

"Helping a woman in distress is a noble pursuit," Ruby said as she cut up some of the ham for Yin and Yang, her cats. Watching her, Lee was reminded of the tabby he'd seen earlier.

"I saw one of your cats in the cemetery today," he told her.

Ruby smiled at him and pulled out a weather-worn playing card, the six of clubs. She put it down in the center of the table.

"Yang brought this card back."

"I knew he had something in his mouth." Lee was puzzled. The cats had done some odd things, but dragging home an old playing card was near the top of the list. He reached out and picked up the card. The back side had the bicycle design, dirty but in better shape than the face of the card, which was barely legible.

"Another fifty-one and we can play poker," Jerome said. He tended to make a joke whenever one of the cats did something weird.

"Is Yang trying to tell us something?" Lester asked Ruby. He was the opposite of Jerome when it came to the two cats—completely fascinated by the weird vibe that Ruby and her animals put off. Once he had even told Lee that he thought Ruby was a gypsy.

"I believe he is," Ruby said, sounding like a parent reading a book to a child. "But his ways are mysterious and whatever the revelation will be, it will come in its own time. I'm going to wax all of the public room floors on Monday," she finished, as if the rest of the conversation had never happened.

Lee just shook his head.

After they helped Ruby clear the table, Lester jogged the two blocks to the cemetery to meet Buck Watson, the backhoe operator who dug the graves and put in most of the septic tanks in Melon County. Lee followed him in old Bertha with a reluctant Jerome riding shotgun.

"You aren't going to convince me to put my neck on the line just 'cause you got the hots for this girl," Jerome had said before Lee started the hearse.

"Sutton won't even let her go through her father's papers," Lee argued as he cranked the engine. Bertha always took a couple of attempts before she grudgingly agreed to go anywhere.

"He's an ass. I told you that."

"So wouldn't it be fun to undermine him?" Lee glanced over at Jerome, who seemed to think about that.

"I sure don't like him."

"A little help is all she's asking."

"Just her father's papers?"

Lee nodded. "Then she might be able to find out if he made any plans for his funeral. Or if he set any money aside for the burial."

"I might be able to help a little. Don't see why she can't get into her father's house, which isn't even the scene of the crime. Besides, it's going to be hers soon enough," Jerome said, talking himself into it.

At the cemetery, they broke down the tent with Lester's help and packed it in the back of the hearse. After picking up the last of the artificial turf from beside the grave, they watched Buck fill in the hole with dirt.

Jerome bailed out of the hearse at the funeral home and was halfway to his motorcycle before Lee caught up with him.

"I got to get going. I'm covering a shift for another deputy." Jerome had already straddled the motorcycle and was strapping on his helmet. He nodded his head before Lee could say anything. "I'll look into it. Does she have a key to her dad's house?"

"I don't know."

"Check. It'd be better if we don't have to break in." He kicked down on the starter and the Kawasaki roared to life. He wheeled it around and took off down the driveway and into the street.

Lee wished now that he *had* asked Alison where she was staying. She'd told him she would come by in the morning, but he wanted to go ahead and find out if she had a key to her dad's house or if this was going to get even trickier.

On a hunch, he called up the Howard Johnson's at the

interstate and asked to be connected to her room. After just a few seconds, he heard the phone click, a couple of rings and then Alison's voice on the other end.

"Hello?"

"Alison, it's Lee." He paused to give her a chance to realize who he was.

"Did I tell you where I was staying?" she asked, sounding a little confused.

"It's the only decent motel in the county, so I made an educated guess. I didn't mean to invade your privacy or anything." He was afraid he'd screwed up any chance he had with Alison by making her think he was stalking her.

"No, I'm glad you called. As soon as I left, I thought I should have told you to call me if you had any news."

"My friend has agreed to help and he asked me to find out if you have a key to your dad's house."

"Gee, I don't."

"Where did your dad live?"

"578 Roosevelt Street."

"Got it." Lee wrote the address down. Roosevelt was only a few blocks from the appliance store. "I'm going to go talk to the neighbors. Your dad might have left a key with one of them."

"That's a great idea. But I was told that I couldn't go into the house."

"We'll work that out once we have a way in."

"I can't believe you're going to all this trouble for me."

"This is our deluxe service," he joked. "I'll let you know if I find a key."

"Thank you," Alison said and Lee felt light-headed.

What is wrong with me? he chastised himself as he hung up the phone.

It was almost three o'clock when Lee headed over to Hubert Dobbs's house. He wondered what his odds of success were for finding a key. He hoped that Dobbs had taken advantage of his neighborhood's stable, mostly retired population to trust someone with his house key in case of an emergency.

Dobbs's house was nicely kept, but suffered in comparison to the houses on either side, which all looked like their owners were competing for the garden club's "yard of the year" award. All of the homes were in the Craftsman style, but varied widely in size. Dobbs's home was in the middle of the pack—lots of room for a man who lived alone.

There was no car in the driveway of the house to the right of Dobbs's, but the one on the left sported a fairly new, gold Oldsmobile Cutlass. Lee decided to start there.

The black mailbox by the door had *Martelli Family* stenciled on it red letters. After two knocks, the door was opened by a balding man wearing a white tank top and shorts. Lee thought he looked a little underdressed for the fall weather.

"What?" The man's New Jersey accent explained his clothing choices.

"I'm Lee Lamberton. I own the funeral home in town and was…"

"Yeah, not interested. Do I look like I'm dead?" The man started to swing the door shut.

"I'm not selling anything." Lee resisted the urge to stick his foot in the door. "I just wanted to ask you a few questions about your neighbor, Mr. Dobbs."

Mr. Martelli kept the door open, but he looked at Lee with suspicion. "Who are you to be asking questions about a dead man?"

"I'm a mortician who's helping out Mr. Dobbs's daughter. She's trying to find a key to his house. The sheriff's department is keeping everything Dobbs had on him when he was arrested as evidence."

"Those people. What're ya gonna do? Yeah, I saw where he was killed. Nice enough guy. First person in the neighborhood to come to the house when we moved in. Invited me to play cards with him. But I ain't got no key to his house. Try the house on the other side. I got the feeling that Dobbs and that guy got along pretty good."

"What's his name?"

"Arthur something." He turned and shouted into the house: "Pat, what's that guy Arthur's last name?"

"Bigelow!" a woman shouted back.

"Yeah, that's it. Arthur Bigelow."

Lee hesitated before asking another question. "I know this is going to sound strange, but did you notice anything odd going on next door before Dobbs was killed?"

"Nah. I mind my own business. What's funny is the cops ain't been by. Up in Jersey, guy gets offed in a neighborhood, the cops are swarming all over the place."

Lee nodded. "Thanks for your help."

"No problem."

Lee thought about the incompetent sheriff's investigation as he walked over to the Bigelow house. Why did the voters in the county put up with it? Sheriff Pratt had been reelected two years earlier after eight previous years of bumbling police work. Of course, he knew how to shake babies and kiss hands. Maybe that was all anyone wanted.

The Bigelow house was more imposing than Dobbs's or Martelli's. A porch stretched across the entire front of the house and was well decked out with wicker furniture, including a large porch swing. Lee rang the bell and waited. He could hear its Windsor chimes ding-donging inside. After waiting a bit, he rang the bell twice then gave up.

As he walked back down the steps, an older model Ford Pinto pulled into the driveway. The young man behind the wheel looked at him curiously. Lee waved and the blond-haired man pulled himself out of the car, revealing a lanky six-foot-tall frame. He was wearing a University of Florida sweatshirt and jeans.

"Can I help you?" he asked.

"Do you live here?"

"No, it's my parents' house."

"I'm Lee Lamberton," he said, walking toward him with an outstretched hand.

"The funeral home guy?"

"That's me."

"I'm Barry Bigelow." He shook Lee's hand reluctantly. "My folks have already made arrangements to be cremated."

"I'm not selling anything. I wanted to ask them about their neighbor."

"Santa Claus? What a bummer. Who in the world would want to kill him?"

Lee resisted the urge to say that he was trying to find out. Instead he said, "We're going to be conducting the funeral and need to get into the house to pick up a set of clothes. Unfortunately, the cops are keeping the keys he had on him as evidence, and Mr. Dobbs's daughter doesn't know where to find a spare set." Lee thought this sounded logical and it was all mostly true.

"Dad and Mom are on vacation. I'm just watching their house while they're gone. I know that Dad used to do the same for Mr. Dobbs from time to time, so he might have a key. Do you want to come in while I check the house and water the plants?"

Lee nodded and followed the man back to the house.

"You think you're safe living in a small town and then something like this happens," Barry said, taking a key out of his pocket and unlocking the door.

The inside of the house was as nice as the outside. Lee

followed Barry as he walked through the house and watered plants as he passed them. "Did you know Mr. Dobbs?"

"He was always nice to me. I mowed his lawn for extra money when I was in high school."

"Did he have many friends that you know of?"

"He had people at his house quite a bit. Never anything like a party, but for an old guy he seemed to have a few good-looking girlfriends."

Lee's ears perked up. "Did you ever meet any of the women?"

"Not really. They never lived at his house. I just saw them coming over sometimes."

"What did they look like?"

"Nice, I guess. Nothing special."

"We're both men of the world. Did they look like working girls?" Lee asked.

"No, nothing like that." Barry gave a little laugh as he refilled a jug with water.

"Your parents sure have a lot of houseplants."

"Sort of Mom's thing. That's why I got to make sure I do it."

"Can you remember anything else about Mr. Dobbs's visitors?"

Barry turned off the water and stared at Lee. "You sound like a cop."

Lee raised his hands. "Sorry. It's just that his daughter hadn't really stayed in touch with her father. She couldn't tell me much about his friends, and I want to make sure that we get the information about the funeral out to everyone who cares."

Barry nodded and went back to watering the plants.

"I remember there was a big fight one night. I guess I was about thirteen. My room is… well, was on that side of the house." He pointed in the direction of Dobbs's house. "I woke up to this big yelling match between some guy and Mr. Dobbs. There was a woman there too. I got out of bed to see what was going on and, about the time I looked out the window, I heard Dad cuss and go down the stairs. He had just retired from the Marines and wouldn't put up with shit. That was when I really got interested in what was going on outside."

"Your dad intervened?"

"Oh yeah. He came storming out of our house wearing just a T-shirt, boxers and a pair of shoes. The others stopped arguing for a minute when they saw him. He gave them his ol' drill sergeant routine. The other guy started to say something, but backed down when my dad bowed up on him. Got to admit, it was kinda cool seeing Dad play cop like that."

"What did Dobbs do?" Lee was trying to picture the Santa Claus from his youth involved in a yelling match.

"As soon as he saw Dad, he started trying to get the others to come back into the house."

"When are your parents coming home?"

"Another week. They're in North Carolina."

"Any chance you could call them? See if they have a key?"

Barry seemed to weigh this over in his mind. "I guess. The number of the hotel they're staying at is on the refrigerator. It's long distance," he added with a little hesitation.

"I'll be glad to pay for the call."

"Dad's just a bit of a freak about the phone bill. Of course, he'd probably want to know about Mr. Dobbs's death."

Lee followed him to the refrigerator where Barry took down a long note of instructions. With the number in hand, he called the hotel. After a bit of back and forth, he got ahold of his dad and told him what had happened to Dobbs. As he explained what Lee wanted, it was clear that his dad wasn't keen on handing over the key.

"I'll talk to him," Lee offered, holding out his hand.

"He wants to talk to you," Barry said into the receiver before handing it to Lee with a roll of his eyes.

"Who are you?" Arthur Bigelow demanded of Lee, who patiently explained who he was and why he was there.

"I didn't even know he had a daughter," Bigelow said.

"They haven't spoken much since her parents got divorced."

"And she doesn't have a key?" Bigelow insisted on going over the facts again. "How do I know you're who you say you are?"

"I'm giving your son one of my cards as we speak." Lee held the receiver between his cheek and shoulder while he dug through his wallet.

"Put Barry back on."

Lee handed the phone back, along with his card. After a few minutes, Barry hung up.

"He said the key is in the kitchen drawer. The one closest to the pantry. I'd say it's a toss up if it's in there or not. I would have asked to speak to Mom—she knows where everything is— but Dad was pretty worked up."

"Understandable."

Lee watched Barry dig through the drawer before triumphantly holding up a key with a plastic tag.

Walking out to the car, Lee was shocked by his own success. Now he had to figure out what to do next. Should he try to contact Jerome, who was in the middle of his shift at the sheriff's office, or should he call Alison and tell her the good news? And was it really good news? Now that he had the key, he was nervous about going in to Dobbs's house without the sheriff's permission. *You sure know how to talk a big game, but can you play the game?* he asked himself.

He decided he needed to find Jerome. Maybe he could get Deputy Sutton to give them permission to enter the house.

CHAPTER FOUR

Kay woke up feeling groggy. She never felt as good as she thought she should after a nap. She crawled out of bed and slipped into jeans and a flannel shirt, then turned off the radio in the middle of "Never Knew Love Like This Before" and headed downstairs.

She grabbed a glass of tea in the kitchen, where Ruby told her that Lester was washing the cars, Jerome had gone to work and Lee was off on a mysterious errand. Wondering vaguely what Ruby considered mysterious, Kay took her tea into the office to sort through recent orders.

As soon as she sat down at the desk, the phone rang.

"Is Lee there?" asked a woman's voice.

"No. May I take a message?"

"I guess not." The person hesitated. "Are you his sister?"

"I am. Can I help you?"

"It's just that I might have… I didn't mean to make it sound like I was some damsel in distress when I talked to him earlier. I don't want him doing anything that…

Anything he wouldn't do for anyone else. If that makes sense?"

"You're Alison Dobbs, right?"

"Yes. Sorry, I guess I've been babbling."

"I don't know exactly what you and Lee talked about, but I can assure you that we treat all of our clients with respect and try and help them in any way we can."

"I'm just weirded out by all of this. My dad's death was so sudden. And I can't even begin to wrap my head around the fact that someone killed him."

"Do you have any family or friends nearby?" Kay asked, already knowing the answer.

"No. Lee said he was going to try to find some of Dad's friends."

"Are you at your motel now?"

"Yes."

"Meet me here as soon as you can. I'll go with you to the sheriff's office and see if we can at least get them to let you into your dad's house."

"Lee said he was going—"

"Let's not worry about what Lee is or isn't going to do. Instead, let's see what we can get done. Get here as soon as you can. If we don't go in the next hour or so, we won't be able to meet with the detective until tomorrow."

"I'll be there in twenty minutes."

When Kay hung up the phone, she mentally kicked herself for getting suckered into helping Alison. The woman was vulnerable and that brought out her nurturing instincts. *That damn nursing gene*, she grumbled to herself.

Kay considered her clothes. They were what a friend of hers had once called "downhome kickass." She briefly wondered if she should change into something a little more distracting, but then decided that "kickass" fit her current mood. Her recent interactions with local law enforcement,

Jerome excluded, hadn't left her believing that "softly, softly" was the way to catch this monkey.

Alison beat her own time by five minutes. Kay had been watching for her through the window and got to the car before Alison could climb out.

"It's not far," Kay told her, pointing toward downtown and the sheriff's office near the town square.

"I talked to that Detective Sutton. He's the one who told me I couldn't go in Dad's house because they weren't done processing it. Whatever that means."

"We'll see about that."

As they walked into the building, Kay wasn't sure what she was going to say. She thought her best argument would be that it was absurd to make the victim of a crime, which Alison certainly was, suffer simply because they couldn't get their job done in a timely manner.

"We'd like to see Detective Sutton," Kay said to the duty sergeant at the front desk.

"Do you have an appointment?"

"No. This is Hubert Dobbs's daughter." Kay stopped herself from adding, "You know, the guy who was just murdered," but she didn't think it was time to go full-throttle on the smartass approach. *Kickass, not smartass*, she told herself. In the Army she'd become very familiar with the different levels of showing her butt.

"I'll see if he's at his desk." The sergeant punched numbers on his enormous switchboard phone. He listened for a minute before hanging up. "The detective isn't at his desk. I suggest you make an appointment with him." The sergeant looked at his watch, which showed it was almost four. "Probably too late today. He should be back in around nine tomorrow morning."

"Can you call him on the radio?" Kay asked.

"I can," the sergeant said, picking up a newspaper and

beginning to read.

Kay felt her blood simmering. She looked at the door that separated the lobby from the rest of the office. She caught Alison's attention and nodded toward the door. Alison's eyes got large. Kay moved fast, opening the door and rushing through with Alison scooting along behind her. Within seconds, the heavyset sergeant was out of his seat and coming after them.

"Hey, you can't just wander around back there!" he shouted.

Kay stopped and spun around to face him. Failing to anticipate the move, he almost ran into her. Now face to face, Kay moved toward him.

"You didn't give us a chance. All we asked was for you to try to contact Detective Sutton which, I'll point out, is your job as the duty officer."

Taken aback, the sergeant stuttered as he tried to defend himself. "I... can't just... radio... every investigator whenever."

"You have three choices. Do as we ask, arrest us or shoot us." Out of the corner of her eye, Kay say Alison's jaw drop.

"I *should* arrest you," he mumbled. "Get back in the lobby and I'll call him on the radio."

Kay wanted to make a smart-mouthed comment, but she held her tongue. *Don't turn victory into defeat,* she lectured herself as they returned to the lobby.

The sergeant went back and forth on the radio before finally turning to Kay. "I guess you got lucky. He should be pulling into the parking lot any minute."

Kay thanked him, lingering on his title of sergeant as though she were a general who was acknowledging a barely acceptable underling.

"If I ever see you come back through those doors," he muttered, just loud enough for them to hear as they went outside to meet Sutton.

"That was impressive!" Alison said.

"Army training," Kay explained with a smile.

"I'm such a nerd. I've spent my whole life with my nose in a book or with the science club kids."

"I've had many days when I wished I was sitting in a quiet library. The grass is always greener."

A dirty brown Ford Crown Victoria pulled into the lot, bumping its rear end on the pavement.

"That's him," Alison said.

Wade Sutton was blond with a mustache that drooped down on both sides of his mouth. Kay thought he looked like a giant walking catfish. With his ill-fitting brown suit and heavy-footed gait, he didn't inspire confidence in his investigative skills.

"You the girls looking for me?" he asked. Kay was surprised he didn't leer at them. Instead, his face maintained a hang-dog expression. "You're Dobbs's daughter."

"I want to get into my father's house." Alison tried to channel some of Kay's attitude, but she couldn't stop herself from adding, "Please."

"Not right now. We still got to go through the whole place. Now, I do have one piece of good news for you. We think we got the man who stabbed your father," he said without an ounce of compassion as he patted himself on the back.

"Really?" Kay didn't hide the surprise in her voice.

"Who are you?" Sutton asked, squinting at her.

"I'm Kay Lamberton. We're handling Mr. Dobbs's funeral."

"And you're here asking questions. I guess y'all really are a full-service funeral home."

"She's a friend," Alison shot back with more backbone than Kay had yet seen from her.

"I see."

"Who is this suspect?" Kay didn't want to let that subject go without getting some answers.

"Husband of the woman her father was fu… having an affair with," Sutton said, not bothering to hide the smirk on his face.

"I just want to see if there's a will, or even the name of a lawyer that Dad had who I could talk to," Alison pleaded.

"We'll be done processing the house in a week… maybe."

"One of your officers could go with Alison to make sure that she doesn't disturb any evidence," Kay pointed out.

"I guess we could if we had the time. Unfortunately, we're shorthanded. You two just need to be patient." Done answering questions, Sutton tried to brush past them. Kay wanted to punch him in the ample gut that was beginning to spill over his belt.

"Please… I…" Alison started to beg, but Kay took her arm and led her away gently.

"Screw that bastard," Kay whispered in Alison's ear. "When you run up against a roadblock that stupid and arrogant, the best thing to do is go around him."

Once they were in Alison's car, Kay told her to head back to the funeral home.

"What are we going to do?" Alison asked.

"Not let that son of a bitch win," Kay said through clenched teeth. "We need to talk with Lee and Jerome."

CHAPTER FIVE

As Lee drove toward the sheriff's office in search of Jerome, he saw a patrol car parked in the Supersave lot. Thinking the deputy inside might be able to locate Jerome, he pulled up beside the car. A quick glance in the window showed him that the car belonged to Henry Booker, one of the county's more congenial deputies and an old classmate of Lee's. *This is a spot of luck*, he thought.

"You always make me nervous creeping around in that big black car like a vulture," Henry said, rolling down his window and smiling at Lee.

"You know, there isn't that much crime in this parking lot," Lee joked.

Henry held up a clipboard. "I spend ninety percent of my time sitting in my car writing reports."

"I need to get up with Jerome."

"He just signed in a few hours ago. By the way, how much do you pay him to drive for you?"

"More than he makes an hour working as a deputy," Lee

said sardonically.

"That's what he says. I could use some of that off-duty cash."

"If business picks up, I'll give you a call. Speaking of calling, could you let Jerome know I want to talk to him?"

"He's working a traffic accident over on West Main and Cleburne. If you want to head that way, I'll radio and let him know you're coming."

"Don't tell him it's me."

"10-4. And keep me in mind if you need some help at the funeral home. Celeste is pregnant again."

Lee gave him a thumbs-up and started the car. He found Jerome about half a mile away, talking to an elderly lady with blue hair and nervous hands. A tow truck was pulling away from the intersection with a ten-year-old station wagon that looked like King Kong had kicked in the front end. Sitting in the road was a blue Chevy C10 pickup with its right fender pushed far enough into the wheel-well that it was pressing on the tire. A teenage boy stood in front of it, staring at the damage forlornly.

Lee found a spot to park his car and waited for Jerome to deal with the accident. Thirty minutes later, the deputy pounded on his window.

"What are you bugging me for? Don't I have enough aggravation with drivers who don't know what a stop sign means and then decide to argue with me about what they saw? Fool, you didn't stop. Doesn't matter what you think you saw."

"I got the key to Dobbs's house," Lee told him, grinning.

"Don't even go there. I got news for you, and I didn't even have to go snooping around to get it. Sutton was strutting around the station like a peacock, bragging about how he'd solved the Dobbs murder in record time."

"What?"

"That's what the idiot was saying. Unless the killer threw himself in front of Sutton's car, I don't see how that moron could have caught him."

"Who is it?"

"From what Sutton was saying, it's Fred Goody. Sutton says Dobbs was doing the dirty with Goody's wife."

Lee's eyes were wide. "Fred Goody who owns the produce stand on the way to Gainesville?"

Jerome nodded. "He owns about a thousand acres of land too. I got a bunch of family that's worked for him over the years."

"One of Dobbs's neighbors told me about a fight he witnessed several years ago between Dobbs and another couple."

"Apparently, ol' Dobbs had it goin' on." Jerome chuckled.

"You think Sutton will let Dobbs's daughter in his house now?"

"The man is as slow as a snail riding a tortoise. She'll be lucky if she gets in there by Christmas."

"I repeat: I've got the key."

"If I don't see anything or hear anything, then I can't be held accountable for anything." Jerome tapped the side of his head. "See, I'm thinking."

"Coward."

"But a coward who has a job."

Lee couldn't argue with that. "Fine. I won't tell you what we find then."

"The less I know, the better."

"What evidence does Sutton have against Goody?"

"Sutton didn't go into details. He was just doing his rooster strut."

"See what you can find out."

"Ha! You pay me to help out at funerals, not to be your

spy."

Lee shrugged. "If you want to be on Sutton's side, I guess that's fine with me."

"Jerk," Jerome said with a smile as his radio crackled and the dispatcher called for him. "Gotta go."

Lee headed back to the funeral home. Recognizing Alison's car in the driveway, his heart beat a little faster as he jogged into the house. He found Kay and Alison in the parlor and they all quickly caught up on each other's afternoon activities.

Lee handed Alison the key to her father's house.

"What should I do?" she asked.

"I say we go into the house tonight," Kay said with a certainty that caused Lee to look at her.

"What's set you on fire?" he asked.

"Wade Sutton. The man's an ass. I agree with Jerome. Having met him, I don't believe for a minute that he's solved this murder."

"Why are we even talking about the murder? Aren't we just helping Alison with her father's funeral?" Lee asked, his eyebrows raised.

"Don't lie to me. As soon as you met Alison, you were all fired up to solve the murder," Kay shot back.

Alison's eyes went back and forth between them, afraid to jump in the middle of the siblings' exchange.

"So now you're on a mission to prove that Sutton is wrong?" Lee asked.

"It wouldn't hurt my feelings any if I could shove that fact down his throat," Kay admitted.

"You know we'll be committing a crime by going into the house without permission?"

"Then why did you get the key if you didn't plan on going into the house?"

"Stop!" Alison shouted, causing Lee and Kay to stare at

her. Now that she had their attention, she went on in a softer voice, "I don't want anyone getting into trouble because of me. If anyone is going into Dad's house, it's going to be me and me alone."

"No way," Lee said. "I'm not going to let you do this by yourself."

"If the killer is still on the loose, it could be dangerous," Kay pointed out.

"Maybe if you just wait outside," Alison suggested.

"Legally, that wouldn't make a lot of difference. We'd still be accessories," Kay told her.

"If you go in, we're going in." Lee wanted to reach out and take Alison's hand, but he couldn't find the nerve.

"I don't know." Alison pursed her lips. "Maybe all of this is a bad idea. I can probably scrape up the money for the funeral."

"It's up to you, of course, but we could be in and out in no time. And it could answer some of your questions. At least we'll know if your father left any instructions about his funeral," Kay encouraged.

"What if we do get caught?" Lee asked. Seeing Alison's hesitancy, he was feeling guilty about pushing her too hard.

"I've thought about that too. I'm going to touch base with Madison," Kay said.

"Who's that?" Alison asked.

"Chester Madison. He owns an insurance company and helped run interference with the sheriff when we were helping him investigate the murder of one of his employees," Lee explained.

"Why were you all involved in investigating a murder?" Alison asked, shocked.

"The victim was an old boyfriend of mine," Kay explained. "And, as you can tell, you can't rely on our sheriff to solve a murder."

"And you think this guy could help you out now?"

"Maybe." Lee wasn't so sure.

"I don't think he'd let us sit in prison," Kay assured them both. "Lee, remember that we also helped Madison with that accident this summer."

Lee nodded. The victim had held a hefty insurance policy with Chester Madison's company, so he had asked Lee to talk to his morgue contacts and make sure that the injuries and cause of death were consistent with the police report.

"I guess it can't hurt to call him," Lee finally said.

"Hell, for all we know, Hubert Dobbs might have had a policy with Madison," Kay said as she got up and headed for the phone in the office.

"We better go listen in," Lee told Alison.

Kay had opened up the address book on her father's old roll-top desk and looked up the numbers Madison had given them. When she called his office, all she got was a recording telling her to leave a message. She hung up and paused. "I also have his home number." She sounded hesitant for the first time since the three of them had started talking.

"You've gone this far," Lee urged.

Kay dialed the number, but was still a little surprised when Chester Madison answered. She quickly explained why she were calling.

After promising to check on any policies held by Hubert Dobbs, Madison asked, "Are you sure you want me to get involved? I can only use my influence so many times before it's going to start having a negative effect. It's based on perceived carrots and sticks, not actual ones."

"I understand. Sort of," Kay said. "We'll try not to… have to ask you for any more help. I just wanted to let you know what we're getting involved in."

"Watch your backs. I don't want to lose my investment." Having reminded Kay about the loan he'd made them to help keep the funeral business afloat, Madison hung up.

"That didn't go so well," Lee said.

"Could have been worse." Kay knew that she was letting her emotions push her into acting a little rashly, but Sutton had pissed her off.

"So what are we going to do?" Alison asked.

"In my opinion, we have three choices." Kay held up her hand with three fingers extended. "First, we can go over to your dad's house and park in the driveway. If we see any neighbors, we can wave to them and pretend like we have the right to be there. The advantage there is that we won't have to sneak around. If people see us, they'll assume we're there legally. No one calls the cops. The downside is that someone who sees us could mention it to Sutton or some other deputy, which would mean we'd be screwed."

"What's the second choice?" Lee was pretty sure he knew what Kay had in mind.

"We wait until the dead of night and sneak in as stealthily as possible. The plus side with that is we might get away with it, in which case we don't have to worry about being locked up in the slammer. However, if we're seen sneaking around at that time, then the neighbors will certainly call the cops. Who wouldn't when they see creepy lights inside the house of a man who's just been murdered? Then the cops come and we don't pass Go or collect two-hundred dollars."

"So what's the third choice?" Alison looked worried.

"We chicken out and the bad guys win," Kay said flatly.

"Let me guess—you don't want to go with the last and sanest option," Lee said.

"Do you?" Kay threw back at him.

"Not really." He turned to Alison. "But I don't think we should be the ones to make the final decision."

Alison sighed. "I'd never be able to pull off the nonchalant act."

"After midnight then?" Kay pushed.

"I…"

"Or we don't have to do it at all," Lee intervened.

"I need to look through his papers. If he had any specific wishes about his funeral or… or… final resting place, I want to honor it."

"We haven't talked to any of his friends or found his lawyer yet," Lee reminded her.

"This will sound silly, but…" Alison looked down at her hands. "The truth is: I don't want to go around like a beggar asking his friends to tell me things about my father that I should know myself."

"I understand that." Kay nodded. "So early morning it is." Lee thought she sounded more like a commando than his sister.

"All for one and one for all," he muttered, not at all sure that he was happy with the decision.

"What time?" Alison asked.

"We'll leave here at three o'clock. That should give us plenty of time. What kind of flashlights do we have?" Kay asked Lee.

"I've got a couple of Maglites. They're big and heavy."

"I've got a small one in my car," Kay added.

"I know I should have one in my car, but… sorry," Alison said.

"We'll make do," Kay said, looking thoughtful.

"You act like this is a military operation." Lee frowned.

"Since failure will mean jail, yeah, I *am* looking at this like it's a military operation."

"She was in Vietnam," Lee explained to Alison.

"Really?" Alison sounded impressed.

"It wasn't an experience I would wish on anyone. The upside is that I can occasionally draw on some… unusual skills."

"Like breaking the law?" Lee said in snarky tone that irritated Kay.

"It was your… interest in helping Alison that got us into this," Kay said and saw Lee's face flush.

"I don't want to cause any trouble," Alison said.

"You're not," Kay and Lee said in unison, then stared at each other.

"If we're going to do this, we'll want to cover the flashlights with some red cellophane or a piece of red cloth," Alison said, causing Kay and Lee to break off their staring contest and look at her. "Red light won't mess up our night vision. I was in the astronomy club at college."

"I'll go get the flashlights and ask Ruby if she has some red fabric." Lee trotted out of the office and headed for the embalming room.

"What are you hunting for?" Lester had been washing the cars in the driveway and came in to find Lee looking through the cabinet where they kept various tools.

"Nothing." Lee knew that the last thing they needed was Lester tagging along or blabbing to someone with big ears.

"You're looking for something." Lester sounded offended that Lee wouldn't let him in on what he was doing.

"Sleep well last night?" Lee asked, stopping his search because he'd seen the flashlights and didn't want to pull them out with Lester standing there.

"Yeah. Why?"

"You know, if you're in our spare room for more than a couple of days, Kay's going to get mad."

"Yeah. I guess."

"Are you looking for somewhere else to go?"

"I've stayed up there before. Like for a month or so."

"Kay's not a fan of that."

"Your dad didn't mind so much."

"Kay isn't Dad."

"I'd better go finish the cars," Lester mumbled, falling back on his tendency to avoid uncomfortable conversations, as Lee had known he would.

"We should talk about this," Lee pressed, just to make sure Lester didn't come back in too soon.

"Later. I don't want the hearse to get water spots." Lester was already halfway out the door.

Ruby was finishing dinner when Lee came into the kitchen. He'd left the flashlights on a table in the hall so he wouldn't have to explain them to Ruby.

"Do you have any red cloth or know where I can get some?"

"What's it for?"

"A project."

"How much do you need?"

"Not much."

"What type of material?"

"Depends."

Ruby gave him a sharp look. "You're up to something," she said, pointing at him with the ladle in her hand.

"Maybe."

"Are you going to tell me what's going on?"

"No."

"I probably have something in my sewing basket. How soon do you need it?"

"The sooner, the better."

Ruby frowned. "You sure are playing it close to the vest. All right. Stir the stew and I'll go see what I've got."

She left him manning the stove while she went outside and up the stairs to her apartment above the carport.

Back in the office with the sixteen-inch flashlights and a piece of red cotton cloth, Lee told Kay, "We'll need to sneak out of the house so Lester doesn't hear us and want to join in."

"I told you not to let him move into the guest room," Kay grumbled, taking one of the flashlights. "You could knock someone out with one of these."

"That's one of the things people use them for," Lee admitted.

"Wow, that's heavy," Alison said, taking the other one.

Closing the office door, they cut the cloth and fitted it to one of the flashlights using rubber bands.

"I'll fix my light up later." Kay took the remaining cloth and a couple of rubber bands. "I guess that's it until this morning."

Lee walked Alison out to her car.

"What have I gotten you all into?" she asked.

"Nothing we didn't want to get involved in." Lee touched her arm, afraid to do more. He hadn't felt this nervous around a woman since high school.

"I just want this to be made right. I know I can't bring my father back or make up for the years we didn't have together, but I want to do this last thing the way he'd want it."

Lee locked eyes with her. "You know, you might find out that your father did… bad things."

"We all make mistakes."

"It might be worse than just mistakes."

Alison looked thoughtful. "I want to know who my father was. I'm not scared of the truth, only of failing to find it."

"Those are brave words." He smiled at her. For a moment, the possibility of a kiss hung in the air between them, but when neither of them moved forward, the moment passed.

"I better get back to my motel room and get some sleep." Alison gave Lee one last smile before getting into her car and driving away.

CHAPTER SIX

An hour later, Kay, Lee, Lester and Ruby sat down to dinner in the kitchen.

"What are y'all doing tonight?" Ruby asked, looking directly at Lee.

"I'm going into Gainesville to see *Time Bandits*. It's this weird movie with little people doing time-travel stuff. My buddy Sam said it's a trip. Of course, I'm sure he was tripping anyway," Lester said, not noticing the look that Ruby was giving Lee and Kay.

"Anyone else got plans?" Ruby ignored Lester, who was too involved in dipping homemade biscuits into his stew to notice or care.

"I'm going to pay some bills and then read for a while. I'm almost done with *Firestarter*." Kay smiled at Ruby.

"I almost bought *Cujo* the other day at the mall, but I'll wait 'til it's discounted." Lee was trying to avoid Ruby's scrutiny.

"I like mysteries better," Ruby said, giving the phrase a

double meaning. Then, in true Ruby fashion, she went off on a wild tangent. "I saw an eagle yesterday."

"Really?" Lester said, looking up from his dinner.

"Off the McIntosh Highway by the Goody Produce stand."

Maybe this isn't one of her crazy digressions after all, Lee thought. He wanted the conversation to stay on eagles, not fruit stands, so he said, "There's a big lake back there. I wouldn't be surprised if you saw an eagle, though are you sure it wasn't an osprey?"

"I know my birds. You never said what *you're* doing tonight."

"You know me. All work. I'm going to clean the embalming room and watch *Taxi*." Lee looked at Ruby, hoping she would let it go. She looked like she was considering her options when Lester asked if he could have more stew. Lester's appetite sidetracked her and, before she could get back to them, Lee and Kay both excused themselves from the table.

Lee only got an hour's rest that night. He was too nervous to sleep, and even if he hadn't been, he didn't want to set his clock radio for fear that it would wake Lester in the next room.

At three, Lee grabbed his flashlight and shoes, wanting to creep silently down the stairs. Easing the door open, he saw the light on in Kay's room. Halfway to the front hall, he heard Kay coming down behind him. They didn't talk until they were outside.

"We look like redneck burglars," Kay said as they both slipped on their shoes. She was wearing jeans, a dark sweater, black gloves and black boots. Lee was similarly dressed, with a flannel shirt and sneakers.

"If we do this on a regular basis, we might want to invest in clothes that are more professional burglar chic," he said.

"Let's go before someone notices we're gone."

"Who's going to notice?"

From the window of her apartment, Ruby watched as the Lamberton siblings walked down the sidewalk.

"I hope they don't get themselves into any trouble tonight," she said to her two cats. Yin and Yang were sitting on the back of the couch, looking out the window beside her and purring softly as Ruby petted them.

Kay and Lee had arranged for Alison to pick them up around the corner from the funeral home. She was parked with the engine running as they jogged up to her car.

"Feels good in here," Kay said as she folded herself into the back seat. The temperature outside had dropped into the forties. Damp air and a north breeze made it feel even colder. A light drizzle began to fall as they drove.

Lee directed Alison to a dark alley near her father's house where they could park.

"The rain is going to give us some cover, but we'll need to try to hide any signs we've been in the house," Kay said as they traveled single-file, tucked up in the shadows. Once at the house, they approached the back door.

"Cross your fingers. I didn't think to ask if the key fits the back door or not," Lee said, trying to fit the key into the lock in the dark. With a little jiggling, it slipped in and the lock turned. He pushed the door open and they walked into the kitchen.

"I'm going to turn on my flashlight." Kay clicked the button and a red glow illuminated their surroundings. "Did you ever live in this house?"

"No. He moved here after the divorce."

"We should probably take off our shoes," Lee suggested. There was a muddy puddle already forming around their feet from the rain.

"Good idea, but let's hope we don't have to make a run

for it," Kay said, pulling off her boots. "We'll use my flashlight and have a quick look around to get the lay of the land before we do anything else."

They followed her from room to room. The house was neat, if somewhat spartanly furnished.

"That's a little odd," Lee said, tapping a poker table in the living room that was large enough to seat eight people.

"Mom said Dad liked to gamble. That was item number three-hundred and fifty-eight that she cursed him for," Alison said lightly.

Lee thought about the possibility that Dobbs had been a womanizer and a gambler. Santa was quickly becoming more and more interesting and much less G-rated.

Kay let the dull light from her flashlight play over a wall of photographs. Most appeared to be family pictures dating from recent decades back to faded sepia-toned images of men and women in Edwardian fashions.

Alison walked over to the photos. She put her hand out and lightly touched a picture of herself as a child with her father dressed up as Santa.

"Jordan?" Lee asked, pointing to another photo where a very young Alison was standing next to an old man and woman in front of a farmhouse. The caption read: *Alison with Ma and Pa Jordan.*

"Those are my father's maternal grandparents. They were like ninety when that was taken and both of them died less than a year later. They came over here from France in the 1890s."

"Jordan doesn't sound very French," Kay commented.

"I can't remember if they changed it or if it was one of those Ellis Island things where the official filling out the paperwork decided that he couldn't pronounce their French name."

"Your father probably didn't keep any private documents

in the front rooms. I think the office and his bedroom upstairs are the best bets," Kay said. "If we stay away from the front of the house, we can probably take a chance on all of us using our flashlights while we search the two rooms. I'll take the bedroom."

"And we'll take the office," Lee said. He didn't see Kay raise her eyebrows at his use of "we."

After Kay left them to go upstairs, Alison put her hand on Lee's arm.

"Thanks for staying with me," she told him before they began searching the office.

The room was more nicely furnished than the rest of the house, with a desk larger than the poker table in the dining room, a wall of bookcases and several shoulder-height filing cabinets. Lee wondered how long it would take to search through all of them.

Longer if I don't get started, he thought. As he opened the first drawer, Alison sat down at her father's desk and began sorting through the papers on the desktop.

Everything in the first file cabinet was related to Dobbs's appliance business. Lee flipped quickly through those. It was the second cabinet where things became interesting. The files alternated between ones labeled with names and others labeled with months and years. Inside each were long and complex accounting sheets that Lee couldn't make heads or tails of. Some of the names were very interesting. Lee recognized five prominent people from Melon County: Alton Singleton, a Lang city commissioner; Milton Campbell, the deputy fire chief; Courtney Webber, the school superintendent; Walt Lawson, the owner of the local Fast Marts; and, most interestingly, Victor Pratt, the sheriff's brother.

"I've found some odd files," he told Alison, who looked up from her search of the desk drawers as Lee brought one of the files over to her. "They're full of accounting sheets that don't make any sense to me. Kay might have an idea what they mean."

"I haven't found anything yet. Just papers related to his appliance business, nothing personal."

Upstairs, Kay scanned the bedroom while being careful not to let her light sweep the windows. The room was located at the front of the house, so she knew she needed to be extra cautious about alerting anyone outside that there were people sneaking around inside.

The room was dominated by a king-size bed with silk sheets. Through the red glow of the flashlight, she couldn't tell what color the sheets were, but they looked clean and expensive. There was also a chest of drawers, a dresser, a wardrobe and another door leading to a closet.

She decided to start there, opening the door to reveal the largest closet she'd ever seen. It was at least ten-by-ten and filled with racks of clothes and shoes. *What use did a single man have for all these clothes?* she thought. Looking closer, she was surprised to find that at least half of the clothes were women's. There were dresses, cloaks, fur coats, high-heeled shoes, blouses and nightgowns.

Then a thought crossed her mind. As a nurse in the Army, she'd met a young man who had liked to wear women's clothes. Could Dobbs have been a cross-dresser? She checked the sizes and saw that they varied too much to belong to one person's wardrobe.

Digging deeper, Kay found a costume section that included several Santa Claus suits, as well as several fantasy outfits that varied from the tame to the risqué. The smallest section of the closet held everyday men's clothes that she assumed had been Dobbs's wear-to-work attire. All of it was very conservative and similarly sized.

Reluctantly, Kay pulled herself away from the closet.

There was too much stuff in there to go through it thoroughly while still leaving it like she'd found it.

The chest of drawers was her next target. The top drawers were filled with the usual—underwear, socks, handkerchiefs, old billfolds, keys and undershirts. The bottom drawer was different, but after seeing the closet, it wasn't a big surprise. It held a collection of mild sex toys, some that she recognized from browsing the aisles at Spencer's Gifts at the Oaks Mall in Gainesville. Dobbs had apparently enjoyed padded handcuffs, feathers, a few battery-operated toys and a whip that was more of a prop than a real whip.

Chuckling a little to herself, Kay moved to the antique wardrobe that was a good foot taller than she was. There were half a dozen hats piled on the top of it, while inside were a variety of suits, ranging from a tuxedo to a black suit that would have looked at home at every funeral she'd ever attended. Otherwise, the wardrobe was empty.

All that was left was the bed and two nightstands. First she chose the nightstand on the right, with only a phone on top. Inside the drawer were some notepads, pens and some random change. As she slid the drawer closed, she felt a slight hitch. Kay opened and closed the drawer again, still feeling resistance, so she pulled the drawer all the way out of the nightstand. On the bottom of the compartment that held the drawer was a small, leather-bound booklet.

Inside the booklet were the names, phone numbers and addresses of hundreds of women. Many of the names had detailed notes beside them and Kay was grateful that they referenced only the women's preferences in restaurants, alcohol, flowers and other romantic aspects.

It took twenty seconds of vacillating before Kay decided to take the book. She stuck it into her pocket and slid the drawer back into place. It took her only five more minutes to look in the other nightstand and under the bed, then she headed back downstairs.

She found Lee and Alison checking the office to be sure that they were leaving everything just as they'd found it.

"It's four-thirty. We should probably get going before people start waking up," Kay told them.

"Did you find anything?" Lee asked.

"We can talk after we get somewhere far away from here."

"Alison got the name of his lawyer, at least. Before we leave, I want you to look at some files."

Kay glanced nervously at her watch before following Lee over to the file cabinets. In spite of herself, she became engrossed in the columns and numbers on the different accounting sheets.

"We probably need to go." Lee touched her arm.

Kay looked at her watch to see that half an hour had gone by while she was looking through the files.

"I wish we could take them with us or take pictures," Kay fretted, but she put all the files back in their place.

By the time they'd cleaned the muddy water from the floor of the kitchen and put their shoes back on, lights were coming on in some of the neighboring houses. They turned off their flashlights and hurried back to Alison's car.

"I found his little black book," Kay said, pulling it out and handing it to Lee as Alison drove.

"Was it a good idea to take it?" Alison asked. Lee could see that her hands were shaking slightly as she steered the car over the damp city streets.

"It wasn't like I had time to make a lot of notes," Kay said. "I wish I could have taken some of those files. Those were accounting sheets of some sort. I don't know what they were accounts of, but I think there was a lot of money represented by those numbers."

"Your father was a complicated man," Lee said as he looked through Dobbs's little black book. "At least he was a romantic."

"All of that romance didn't come cheap," Kay reflected.

"You think he might have been into something illegal?" Alison asked.

"I don't think he financed his lifestyle off the appliance store," Kay said.

"Those names we saw in the files are bigwigs in the county," Lee said.

"Blackmail?" Kay wondered.

"Maybe. I think it explains why the sheriff's office is playing this one so close to the vest, and maybe why a suspect has emerged so quickly." Lee was thinking out loud now.

"Stop and let us out here," Kay said as they neared the funeral home. "We'll walk the rest of the way."

"Call me later," Lee told Alison.

"When we've had a chance to think about all this, we need to sit down and talk," Kay added.

"I'll call before noon. I'm going to get ahold of Dad's lawyer too," Alison said, sounding determined.

As they walked the last block to the funeral home, Kay told Lee, "We're going to need Jerome's help. That idiot Sutton will just foul this all up."

"Jerome doesn't want to be involved." Lee was keeping his head down and watching his footing as they moved through the shadows.

"It's that or go back to Madison, and I don't think that's a good idea right now."

"I'll talk to Jerome."

They would have made it into the house without making any noise except that one of Ruby's cats—Lee couldn't tell if it was Yin or Yang—walked right in front of him and tripped him. He cursed, barely managing to catch himself on Bertha's fender.

"Stupid cat, you could have killed us both," he groused at the animal, who rubbed up against the hearse's tires and arched its back contentedly while giving Lee a yellow-eyed glare.

"I still can't tell them apart," Kay said, looking up at the windows in Ruby's apartment to see if Lee's cursing had woken her. All of the lights remained off. "Come on. Let's get out of these wet clothes," she said and pulled Lee into the house.

CHAPTER SEVEN

At nine o'clock Friday morning, there was a knock on Lee's bedroom door.

"Whatever you were doing all night, you need to get up now. There's a guy downstairs whose uncle is in hospice and he wants to make arrangements. I've talked him all the way up to the point where money's involved," Lester said through the door.

The thought of Lester talking money with a potential client brought Lee wide awake. "Tell him I'll be down in a minute," he said, hopping around the floor as he tried to slip on a nice pair of slacks.

Lee spent half an hour with Dennis Hartfield, going over all the price options, but saying that he wanted to discuss the details with other relatives, the man left before signing a contract. Lee could only shrug when Lester asked if he thought the man would be back. Lee had learned long ago that he could only push a sale so much. He knew of a few funeral directors with reputations that rivaled the pushiest of used-car salesmen, but he refused to be one of them.

Ruby was waiting in ambush when he walked past the kitchen.

"Sleep well last night?" she asked in a way that left no doubt that she knew they'd been up to something other than sleep.

"Fine," Lee said, not taking the bait. He wondered if she'd heard him trip over her cat.

"There is a gathering storm," Ruby said ominously. Lee was about to ask what she meant when she added, "Should be cooler tomorrow. We'll have chili tomorrow night." With that, she retreated back into the kitchen, leaving Lee feeling spooked. The jangle of the ringing phone in the hallway made him jump. He took a deep breath and grabbed the phone before it could ring a third time.

Alison's voice made him feel better. "How are you this morning?"

"I got some sleep. What about you?" he said.

"A couple of hours. Honestly, that's been the norm ever since I heard about Dad's murder."

"I know it's been hard for you," Lee said, looking over though the kitchen door and seeing Ruby eyeballing him from the stove. Pulling on the phone cord, he shifted around the corner to make it harder for her to eavesdrop. "Why don't you come over so we can talk about last night?" He was whispering in the hopes that Ruby's sharp ears wouldn't pick up his words.

"Will your sister be there?"

"I don't know what her plans are."

"I want to look at the black book." Alison was quiet for a moment. "Can I tell you something?"

"Sure, anything."

"Your sister intimidates me."

Lee chuckled. "She intimidates me too. Don't let her

bother you. I'd say it was her time in the Army, but she wasn't much different before she enlisted. Over the last six months she's done a lot for me. Don't tell her I said that."

"I'll come over now."

Lee reached around the corner and hung up the phone without looking at Ruby, who was tapping a spatula on a skillet and humming to herself.

He went looking for Kay to let her know that Alison was on her way. He wasn't surprised to find her in the office. What did surprise him was that she was drawing on a sheet of paper instead of looking through Dobbs's little black book or going over the funeral home's accounts.

"Whatcha doin'?"

"I'm trying to duplicate one of the accounting sheets from those files. I should have taken one. What difference would one make?" She frowned at what she'd drawn on the paper. "I remember there were four columns, but they didn't look like regular columns in a budget ledger. More like a bank ledger with individuals making withdrawals and deposits." She pushed the sheet away in frustration and picked up the black book.

"I recognized some of the names in that book," Lee told her, walking around the desk so that he could look over her shoulder. "There's one right there." He pointed to one of them. "Candace Powers worked at the Forty-eight Bar when I was in high school."

"You went to the Forty-eight back then?"

"We'd hang out in the parking lot and chat up the girls. Looking back, I'd say we just made fools of ourselves, but we thought we were acting like the big boys."

"Sorry, but you strike me as more of an AV club kind of guy."

"Don't pigeonhole me. I was AV boy during the day and burgeoning small-town drunk at night," Lee said with a grin.

"Seriously, she was a nice woman. She didn't treat us like we were the before ads for acne products, even if we looked like it. Haven't seen her in years."

"Who else?" Kay held the book out to him.

"There are dozens of married women on the list. Also a bunch of names I don't know." He flipped to the back of the book. "The oldest entry is from twenty years ago. March 30, 1961. That would have been a couple of months after Kennedy was inaugurated. The last entry was in August of this year." He turned a few more pages before he squealed and tossed the book down on the desk.

Kay stared at him, half expecting to see blood gushing from a cut on his hand or something. Instead, Lee was backing away and staring at the book as though it was a rattlesnake.

"What's wrong?"

"Mrs. Goody! Her name is in there." He pointed at the book. "That thing is material evidence in a murder. We've tampered with evidence. We're going to end up in jail. No doubt about it." Lee's eyes were wide as his mind raced to find a solution that didn't end up with him bunking with a sexually active criminal. "Unless we destroy it," he suggested hopefully.

"Calm down and quit acting like you're in an Abbott and Costello movie. If Sutton says Goody killed Dobbs, then I'll lay you odds that Goody is an innocent man."

Lee snapped his fingers. "I forgot. We also know the sheriff's brother may be involved somehow. Victor Pratt's name was in Dobbs's files, big as life. You're probably right about Goody." He paused. "Still, I think that book represents as big a risk to us as it does to the killer."

As they pondered the book, the doorbell rang.

"That could be Alison," Lee said, temporarily forgetting his worries about a future prison buddy.

"You need to get a handle on your emotions," Kay said as he hurried for the front door.

Lee surprised her by tossing "You're right" over his shoulder without slowing down.

Alison gave him a big smile when he opened the door.

"Come in," he said, fighting against the wind to hold the door open. The trees in front of the home were swaying as an approaching storm lit up the sky with streaks of lightning. In the distance, Lee heard sirens and wondered where they were going. *Fire engines by the sound of it*, he thought. *Maybe the lightning struck someone's house.*

"Have you talked to your friend the deputy yet?" Alison asked as he walked her to the office.

"Not yet. And now I don't know if I can," he said, closing the door behind them.

"Why not?" Alison asked as she smiled at Kay in greeting.

"That book we found. The man they arrested for the killing—his wife's name is in it. According to your dad, she likes Coors and carnations. That book would be front and center in any trial of Mr. Goody for the murder of your father. Unfortunately, we took it out of the house and, if Jerome finds out about that, he won't have any choice but to arrest us."

"He's not going to arrest us," Kay said with more confidence than she felt.

"Let's sit down and try to come up with a reasonable plan to get ourselves out of our predicament," Lee suggested.

"I never meant for anything like this to happen," Alison said.

"We dug our own hole," Kay assured her. "Those names on the files may be our ticket out of this. Lee, you said the names are important people in town, right?"

"School superintendent, the sheriff's brother, a city

commissioner. But what are we supposed to do, blackmail them?" Lee asked.

"You said it yourself. The reason Sutton came up with a suspect so quick and pounced on him was to direct attention away from whatever other shady business Dobbs was doing that involved all those big names."

"I'm following…" Lee acknowledged, not entirely sure where she was headed.

"We just have to let them know that we know and they will treat us with care. We'll explain about the book and insist that they encourage the sheriff to consider other suspects, not just Mr. Goody." Kay made it sound easy.

"Won't they be mad?" Alison asked.

"But what can they do?"

"What if they destroy the files?" Lee asked.

"If they were going to do that, they would have done it already," Kay said, and Lee felt his stomach sink.

"I need to make a call," he said, his face losing all color. He went to the desk and called a friend who worked for the fire department.

"Don, I heard the sirens. What's going on?" Lee listened for a minute before thanking Don in a strangely dead tone and hanging up the phone. "Your father's house is on fire," he told Alison, whose mouth dropped open.

"Son of a bitch!" Kay leaned back in the swivel chair and looked up at the ceiling.

Lost in their own thoughts, none of them said a word for several minutes.

"If all of those files are gone, then what can we do?" Alison finally asked.

"That's what I've been sitting here trying to figure out," Lee said. He looked at Kay, who shook her head.

"I shouldn't have taken Dobbs's little black book, but if I hadn't, it would have been destroyed with everything else."

Kay was trying to justify her actions while admitting to herself that they'd been wrong-headed.

"We'd have done better to steal the files than the book," Lee said.

Kay glared at him. "I know that now. If we'd known the place was going to burn down, we could have grabbed everything."

"You don't think we caused the fire by going there, do you?" Alison looked even more lost than she had when she'd first come to the funeral home.

"I didn't do anything other than open and close drawers and look at files," Lee said.

Kay raised her hands. "Don't look at me. I just searched his bedroom." Her eyes grew wide. "We might not have directly caused it, but what if someone saw us in the house and decided it was time to get rid of all the evidence?"

"I was thinking that," Lee said, feeling even more depressed about the hole they had dug for themselves.

"My science teacher used to say that what you do next is more important than what you've already done," Alison told them.

"A plan. We need a plan." Kay drummed her fingers on the desk.

"I can't talk to Jerome about this," Lee said.

"I agree with you." Kay nodded. "I don't think Chester Madison can dig us out of this either."

"We could just turn the book over to the sheriff. Like you said, you did them a favor by saving it from the fire." Alison was sounding a little desperate.

"Two problems with that," Kay said. "One—it would just cement the case against Mr. Goody, who we now know is just one of a *number* of suspects. Two—we'd not only be in trouble for obstruction of justice, no matter how well intentioned, but we'd become suspects in the fire, assuming it turns out to be arson.”

“There’s a third problem,” Lee said, hating to voice what he was thinking. “We could be witnesses against the people named in those file folders. Big fish in this small pond. One of them could be a murderer who would find it convenient if we were… silenced.”

“Wow,” Alison whispered, overwhelmed by the size of their problem.

“We have the black book. That’s our ace in the hole. Admittedly, it’s also an albatross around our necks or maybe the Sword of Damocles hanging over our heads.” Lee shook his head. “Anyway, we know who your dad’s girlfriends were, going back twenty years. We can use that information to dig a little deeper. Maybe we can come up with a way out of this if we know a little more.”

“I like it,” Kay said. “Of course, I can’t think of anything else, so what’s not to like?” She looked down at the paper where she’d been trying to recreate one of the accounting sheets. “I just wish I could remember exactly what one of those ledger sheets looked like.”

“I might be able to,” Alison said. When Kay and Lee looked at her, she added, “I almost have a photographic memory. I looked pretty closely at the one with Alton Singleton’s name on it.”

“Please,” Kay said, holding out a pencil and a sheet of paper.

Alison came over and stood at the desk. First she drew several columns. Then she filled in the first column with letters that looked like acronyms. There were several different series of letters. After that, she filled in the other columns with numbers. There were only thirty-five blank spaces when she was done.

“I’m sorry, but that’s the best I can do.” She sounded disappointed in herself, but Lee and Kay were staring at her with their mouths hanging open. "What?"

"You have to know that not everyone can do that," Kay said.

"I might have made a few mistakes." Alison blushed.

"Shazam!" Lee said in admiration. He wanted to reach out and give Alison a hug, but he settled for putting his hand on her shoulder. "That's amazing."

Her blush deepened.

"Do you have any idea what it means?" Kay asked.

Alison shrugged. "It's just numbers and letters to me. If I'd understood what the numbers and letters stood for, then I would have remembered all of it. It's harder if they seem random."

"I wouldn't know," Kay said. "Now that you've given me something to work with, I'll try to figure it out."

"When it comes to the black book, I've got a suggestion about where we should start," Lee said. "Mrs. Goody. She'll probably be glad to talk to someone who believes that her husband is innocent."

"I imagine that she's feeling pretty isolated right now," Kay agreed. "Especially with word going around about her affair with Dobbs."

"Alison and I can go out to the farm and talk to her," Lee offered.

"While you're gone, I'll try and make sense of this." Kay tapped the paper.

"We'll take your car. It's a little less conspicuous than mine," Lee told Alison as they left the office.

"Y'all aren't going to miss lunch?" Ruby said when she saw them heading for the door.

"Save us some," Lee said, not taking his eyes off of Alison.

"I see how it is." Ruby shook her head and chuckled.

"You know where you're going." Alison held out her

keys to Lee, who nodded and opened the passenger door for her. Since Alison was eight inches shorter than Lee, he had to make quite a few adjustments to the seats and mirrors before he could safely back out of the driveway.

"I don't even know what you do for a living," Lee said, pulling into the street and flicking on the windshield wipers. The storm had finally arrived.

"Four months ago I had a great job working at a plant that made turbines and other parts for jet aircraft in Pensacola. I'd left school for a while and was saving up money to go back. Then the company got sold and the new owners came in, laid a bunch of people off and moved everyone else to Arizona. So now I'm working as a projectionist at the AMC theatre until I can figure things out."

"What do you want to do?"

"I thought I wanted to be an engineer. I've done a lot of my undergraduate work, but the whole corporate world thing has sort of soured me on that." Alison grinned. "I'll tell you a secret. I actually *love* working at the theatre. The manager is pretty cool too. He's given me a couple of bonuses when I've managed to fix a projector without having to call anyone."

"You like movies?"

"I'm a total movie geek. I've watched *The Empire Strikes Back* twenty-two times so far."

"I'm a *Star Trek* fan," Lee admitted.

"It's all cool." Alison seemed to blossom as she talked about movies and her life. "You haven't even broken the surface of my geekdom."

"What? Do you play *Dungeons & Dragons* or something?"

"*Traveller*. It's a role-playing game in space. Takes nerd to the next level."

"Multi-sided die?"

"I've got a wooden box with maybe fifty."

"You'll have to teach me how to play sometime." Lee turned and gave her a smile. Then he remembered what they were doing and his smile faded. "Could help while away the hours in prison."

Alison looked down at her hands. "You and Kay are a little crazy to have gotten yourselves involved in my problems."

"I want to help you," Lee said, feeling his cheeks flush.

"Thanks." She reached over and put her hand on his arm.

"There's the produce stand." Lee pointed to a fifty-foot-long pole barn decorated with dozens of signs advertising the different fruits, vegetables and nuts for sale.

"Not surprised to see that it's closed," he said as they drove by. "If I remember right, the entrance to the farm should be about half a mile up here on the right."

The simple farm tube-gate was open, but a sign had been attached that told reporters they would be trespassing if they entered the property.

"The sign doesn't say anything about would-be detectives," Lee said and drove on through the gate.

The dirt road wound through pine woods before opening up to hay fields lying dormant as they waited to be to be fertilized in the spring. In the distance was a pristine two-story white farmhouse. As they approached the house, a large round bale of hay that had been painted to look like a turkey greeted them with a "Happy Thanksgiving" sign. A few raindrops fell from the sign, but the storm had blown itself out as quickly as it had started.

Lee couldn't see anyone in the yard or the house as he parked in the gravel driveway and they got out of the car. He half expected a dog to come running over to bark at them, but the yard was silent. The sky was overcast and gloomy as the cold front continued south. Lee shivered.

"Reminds me of *Night of the Living Dead*," Alison said as they walked toward the house. She was so close to him that they occasionally bumped hands, but Lee didn't mind at all.

The creak of the wooden steps leading up to the front porch seemed very loud in the absence of other noises. The screen door screamed as they pulled it open.

"Don't these people know you can buy a can of WD-40 for sixty cents?" Lee was surprised to find himself so unnerved.

"Shouldn't being a mortician make you braver?" Alison asked, taking his hand.

"There's been a murder and probably an arson. I don't have to be brave." Lee pressed the doorbell.

"I don't hear anything."

He pressed the white button again. He hated to admit it, but he didn't hear anything either.

"Nope. You'd better knock," Alison said, half hiding behind him.

"*You* could knock." Lee almost felt that the house did not want to be disturbed.

"Coward," Alison said, but she didn't knock either.

Finally, Lee reached out and gave the door a couple of solid raps. He waited and knocked again, but the house stayed silent.

"I guess no one's home."

"Maybe we should walk around back," Alison suggested tentatively.

"Or maybe we shouldn't." But Lee was already thinking of the questions that Kay would ask when they got back. One of them would certainly be: "Did you look around the house?" Trying to convey the eeriness of the house and grounds wouldn't do any good. Kay would just scoff.

"Okay," Lee said. "Let's make it quick. I don't want someone to come up the driveway and catch us snooping around the back of the house."

"We'll be quick," Alison affirmed.

They moved around to the back of the house where they found chickens, a few sheep in a pen and two barn cats hanging out by a food bowl, but no people. A few more minutes spent shouting into the outbuildings convinced them that they were truly alone.

"See, no zombies." Lee had his head on a swivel, half expecting someone to pop out from behind one of the old pieces of farm machinery. "Mrs. Goody might have gone to stay with friends or family to avoid any unpleasantness."

"You're probably right. Let's get out of here." Alison was half pushing him toward the front of the house.

As they reached her car, they heard vehicles coming up the road. Lee turned to look and, as soon as he saw them, he knew they were in trouble.

"Damn it! Those are deputies." He looked around like he expected to discover an escape route, but of course there was none.

A green-and-white patrol car was followed closely by a brown unmarked Crown Victoria. There was nothing for Lee and Alison to do but stand there and wait for the two cars to pull in and block Alison's car. Lee knew they would soon be asked a whole bunch of questions that he didn't want to answer. When he realized that the patrol car was being driving by Jerome, it only made him feel worse.

He took Alison's hand and squeezed it. "We came up here to talk to Mrs. Goody because we'd heard that she'd had a relationship with your father and you wanted to talk to someone who knew him," Lee said, not taking his eyes off of the approaching cars.

Alison squeezed his hand to let him know that she understood.

Lee could tell when Jerome recognized them, because the

patrol car suddenly speeded up. It reached them a good minute before the unmarked. Jerome jumped out and ran over to them.

"What the hell are you doing here?"

Alison repeated what Lee had told her to say.

"Well, you picked a hell of a time to pay a social call," Jerome said, looking hard at both of them.

"Mrs. Goody isn't here," Lee told him.

"We know that, fool. She's half burned up inside Hubert Dobbs's house."

CHAPTER EIGHT

For a moment, Lee thought he might pass out. It was Alison's hand in his that made him buck up and prepare himself for the unpleasantness to come. It started as soon as Wade Sutton pulled himself out of the Crown Vic.

"What are you doing here?" Sutton said when he saw Alison. Before she could answer, he pointed his finger at Lee. "Who are you?"

"I'm Lee Lamberton. Alison's friend."

"Friend, ha! Lamberton. You related to the funeral people?"

"My sister and I own the Lamberton Funeral Home."

"Your sister." Sutton snapped his fingers. "That's the smartass who was with you yesterday," he said, looking at Alison. "Y'all stick your noses into everything. I don't buy the 'I just wanted to talk to Mrs. Goody' stuff. I don't know what you're up to, but I'm going to find out.

"You." He pointed to Lee. "Go sit in that patrol car. I'm going to talk to Ms. Dobbs for a minute."

Reluctantly, Lee went over and sat in the patrol car. The only good part was that he was able to watch as Sutton attempted to get information out of Alison. Jerome stood to one side as Sutton barked one question after another. Lee was impressed with the way Alison just stood there, calmly shaking her head at most of his questions. The more Alison stonewalled, the more Sutton stomped around her. She was like a rock at the edge of an angry sea.

Eventually, Sutton stopped and looked over at the patrol car. Lee could almost feel the man's burning eyes trying to penetrate his skull. He gestured to Lee to come back while saying a few curt words to Alison.

Lee and Alison switched places. He gave her a wink as they passed each other and received a quick smile in return.

"Your friend told me everything," Sutton said in the most laughable attempt to deceive an interview subject in the history of the world.

"You might have fooled me if I hadn't just watched you interview her," Lee said, biting back some of the snarkier answers he'd wanted to give.

"Yeah, well, you're going to talk."

"We told you why we were here. Both of us were shocked to hear that Mrs. Goody is dead. We certainly wouldn't be here if we'd known."

"Maybe you wanted to break in and get something out of the house."

The comment almost tripped Lee up. He hoped that his face didn't reveal his momentary brain freeze when Sutton mentioned breaking into a house.

"We aren't lying to you. What caused the fire at Alison's father's house?" Lee asked, putting a slight emphasis on Alison's name.

"I think Mrs. Goody started it to destroy any evidence against her husband. While she was burning the place down, she got trapped and died of smoke inhalation," Sutton said.

Doesn't this guy know that you don't answer questions from the people you're interrogating? Lee wondered. Aloud he said, "I wish we could help. I understand that Mrs. Goody was having an affair with Dobbs."

He half expected Sutton to tell him to shut up, but instead the man continued to talk about the details of his investigation.

"I got on that real quick. A friend of mine had all the gossip and told me that he'd seen Dobbs and Mrs. Goody at the Forty-eight Bar twice in the past month. Married woman, jealous husband and a dead Casanova. Doesn't take a genius to figure it out," Sutton boasted.

Lee could see Jerome rolling his eyes behind Sutton's back as he explained how smart he was.

"Once I knew who killed Dobbs, I just needed to capture him. That was really easy. I just staked out the produce stand until he came by to check on the woman he had working it. Then, *swoop*, I pulled up and handcuffed the son of a bitch. Right there in his own store."

Lee worried that the man's shirt buttons might fly off his chest as he puffed himself up.

"Impressive," he said, working hard to keep the sarcasm out of his voice.

Sutton managed to bring himself back to the matter at hand.

"I don't know what you two were really doing up here. Whatever it was, I don't like it. When I started this investigation, I looked hard at your little girlfriend. Follow the money. She's the closest relative, so she'll inherit his store and house... or what's left of his house. Lucky for her, she was three hundred miles away when he was killed and could prove it."

"We really did just come out to talk to Mrs. Goody. I

guess I can see why it might look suspicious to you. Can we go now?" Lee was doing his best to sound contrite.

Behind Sutton, Jerome rolled his eyes and mouthed: *I want to talk with you.*

Sutton gave an exasperated sigh. "I guess. Can't see why she'd burn her father's house down when she was going to inherit it. But from now on, stay away from this investigation."

Lee nodded. He wanted to protest that Alison had every right to be interested in the investigation into her father's murder, but right now he just wanted to get as far away from Sutton as possible.

"Let's look around the house," Sutton said to Jerome, effectively dismissing Lee, who wasted no time hurrying over to Alison.

"We can go," he said. Alison hopped up out of the patrol car and followed him to her own car.

Lee was just able to maneuver around the two other cars and turn around. He made a note to himself to always back into a driveway when he was trespassing. It took all of his self-control to drive slowly away from the house.

"We're lucky he's a boob," Lee said when they were back on the main highway.

"I can't believe that someone was in the house when it burned." Some of the self-confidence Alison had seemed to gain in the last day was gone.

"The very person we needed to talk to." Lee doubted it was a coincidence.

"What do you think happened?"

"I don't believe for a minute that cock-and-bull story that she accidentally burned herself up. She was murdered so she wouldn't talk. I wonder if she could have provided her husband with an alibi. If that's the case, then her death would kick a leg out from under his defense. Very convenient for that oaf and his investigation."

"It's such a mess. All I wanted to do was bury my father," Alison said softly.

Hesitating only a moment, Lee put his hand on her knee in comfort and they drove the rest of the way back to the funeral home in silence.

"Did you hear?" Kay asked, meeting them in the driveway.

Lee nodded as he got out of the car. "Let's go inside."

"We better go through the front door," Kay advised. "If you go in the back way, you'll have to have lunch before we can talk."

Despite the warning, Ruby still tried to intercept them as they walked to the office.

"I promise we'll have lunch as soon as Alison and I have had a chance to talk to Kay." Lee made the Boy Scout honor sign to Ruby just before closing the office door in her face.

"So who killed her?" Kay asked as soon as the door was closed.

"The same person who killed Alison's father," Lee said. Then, just to cover his bases, he added, "Maybe."

"That jerk of a detective was at Goody's house," Alison blurted.

They filled Kay in on their encounter with Sutton.

"What do you think Jerome knows?" Kay asked.

Lee shrugged. "He certainly didn't like the fact that we were there. We've got to either tell him the truth or come up with a lie that he can accept, even if he doesn't believe it."

"Great." Kay dropped into the chair in front of the desk.

"What are you going to do now?" Alison asked, looking at Kay.

"All we have is that black book and this piece of paper with a bunch of figures on it."

"Have you had any luck figuring out what it means?" Lee

asked.

"I'd barely had a chance to look at it when Lester came in and told me that someone died in the fire. I found out who it was from Ruby. She heard it from some friend of hers that works dispatch for the fire department."

"Let's go back to the black book. There are lots of women in there." Lee picked up the book from the desk. "Let me look through it for a minute."

Mrs. Goody's name was the most recent entry. He didn't recognize the next two names, but the fourth was a different story.

"I know her," he said, pointing to an entry. "Lilly Osbourne is the head librarian. She's married to a math teacher at the high school. I can't believe that Mrs. Osbourne would… I mean, she wears her hair up in a bun and the frumpiest dresses you can imagine." He shook his head in disbelief.

"Apparently she lets her hair down on occasion," Kay said. "According to the entry, she likes strawberries and going nude."

"From the dates in the book, the affair lasted eight months starting two years ago. I'll go talk to her… but without any strawberries and trying very hard not to think of her in the nude," Lee said.

"What do you think she can tell you?" Alison asked.

"Tell *us*. You're going with me. We're going to go ask her what she knows about your father's habits and friends."

"While you all do that, I'm going to give this another go." Kay held up Alison's reproduction of the accounting sheet. "Fingers crossed that no one else dies before I have a chance to figure it out."

"At least we have a plan," Lee said.

"*Another* plan," Alison said, with just the hint of humor in her voice. The other two looked at her, unsure whether she meant to be funny or not.

"If at first you don't succeed…" Lee said. "Come on. We have a date with lunch."

Lee was feeling better when they left the office, but that lasted only until they entered the kitchen and Lee saw Jerome, in uniform and standing by the stove. Lee thought about sneaking back out, but it was too late. Jerome heard him and turned from the pot of yellow rice. He was holding a plate piled high with rice and chicken, but he wasn't smiling.

"Sit," he ordered when he saw them.

"Can we get some food first?" Lee was surprised to find that he was hungry.

"Be quick. I want to talk to you before I get called away."

Lee and Alison helped themselves to rice, chicken and biscuits, then joined Jerome at the table, looking like kids called before the principal.

"Where's Ruby?" Lee asked.

"I asked her to leave the kitchen so I could talk to you alone. I had to promise her you'd be a good boy and eat your lunch. So eat up." Jerome's tone was low and menacing.

"I know you're wondering what we were doing out at the Goody place." Lee thought he'd better start out strong.

"I ain't wonderin' nothin'. I know what you were doing. You were sticking your nose into a hornet's nest." Jerome punctuated his words with menacing stabs of his fork.

"There's a lot more to this than you know. And most of it you're better off *not* knowing," Lee said.

"Do you think for one minute I'm going to get away with the 'they never told me what they were doing' defense? Once y'all fall in the crapper, I'll get pushed in right after you."

"What do you expect us to do? You're the one who talks

about how bad your department is at solving crimes."

"That's not what I said. What I said was: they're bad at solving crimes they don't *want* to solve. And I'm telling you this in confidence—they don't want to solve these crimes. At least not really. Someone's going to jail, though, and it's just a question of who. If you aren't careful, it'll be you," Jerome said, pointing his fork in Lee's direction.

"So I should tell you everything that's happened? Is that what you want?" Lee was getting hot under the collar now. "You want to gripe about the bad detectives at the sheriff's office, but you don't want to do anything about them. You know what that makes you?"

"Employed," Jerome shot back. "An employed black man who's not in jail. But if you keep going down the road you're on, you're going to be an unemployed convict."

"Okay, I'll tell you what we did, if that will make you happy." Lee restrained from adding "you big baby" at the end of the sentence. "Then we'll see what side of the bread your butter's… knifed on. Whatever. You know what I mean. But I'm going to keep eating, 'cause you're probably going to have to arrest us when I'm done."

"Eat then." Jerome turned to Alison. "I'm not blaming you for anything. This one and his sister can get anyone into trouble."

"They're only trying to help me," Alison said.

Lee ate most of what was on his plate before leaning back and giving Jerome a hard look.

"I'll start off by saying that you're right. We dragged Alison into all of this, but only because we were trying to help her. What we did was: we took the key I got from the neighbor and sneaked into Hubert Dobbs's house at three in the morning."

"*This* morning? The morning right before the house burned down?"

"We'd been gone awhile before it burned," Lee said defensively.

"Did you happen to notice Mrs. Goody's dead body?" Jerome asked with a heavy dose of sarcasm.

"Noooo. Honestly, we were just looking for information to help Alison take care of her father's funeral."

"You had to break into the house to do it? You know, she could have gotten a lawyer. Maybe have *him* call up the sheriff. That's probably all it would have taken to get permission for her to go into the house. The only roadblock was that big ox Sutton."

"I don't think she'd have been allowed into that house until the files full of evidence against a city commissioner, the sheriff's brother and some other local bigwigs were destroyed."

Jerome's face turned deadly serious. "What evidence?"

"Files. A whole cabinet full of files."

"What was it evidence of?"

"I don't know," Lee said, hating to admit it. "It was a bunch of accounting sheets with weird acronyms."

Jerome sat back in his chair and stared at Lee. "Did you take any of them?"

"I wish we had."

"We only have you all's word that they existed, and you don't even know what they mean."

"They had a lot of numbers. Money. I don't know."

"You know that Dobbs offered credit to customers. Maybe they were just his accounting of what people still owed him. Did you ever think of that?"

"I don't think so," Alison said. Lee and Jerome stared at her as though they'd forgotten she was there. "I saw them, and they didn't look like regular accounting ledgers."

"You have bookkeeping experience?" Jerome asked.

"No, but I took some business classes in college."

"Great."

"She's got an almost photographic memory. In fact, she was able to reproduce most of one of the sheets," Lee said in Alison's defense.

"You were right. I *should* arrest you." Jerome had gone from angry to despondent.

"Then you're going to love this next part." Lee paused, hoping some *Deus ex machina* would save him from having to tell Jerome about the book. Nothing happened. "Kay found Dobbs's little black book and we took it."

"Little black book?"

"With names and notes on all the women he's been with over the last twenty years."

"And?" Jerome could tell that Lee was holding something back.

"Mrs. Goody was the most recent entry."

"Lord, why have you given me the burden of such friends?" Jerome looked up and held his hands stretched out to the heavens. He looked back at Lee. "I don't have to tell you that you've officially tampered with evidence. By not turning it in immediately, you're obstructing justice. And as far as anyone else knows, you killed Mrs. Goody while you were committing all these other crimes."

"It's those files. The killer murdered Mrs. Goody and burned the house down in order to destroy evidence," Lee argued.

"Evidence that no one but you, your sister and the daughter of a murdered man saw. You can't even tell me what it's evidence of. If anything. What we do know is the book that you stole is evidence."

"You're putting all of this in the worst possible light," Lee argued.

"Do you think Wade Sutton and the State Attorney are going to assume all of your intentions were pure? Not likely.

Sutton is already suspicious of you. As soon as he heard that Dobbs had an estranged daughter, he wanted to peg her for the murder. Now he sees you two working together… How long do you think it's going to take him to decide that you knew each other before Dobbs's death? Which will let him come to the obvious conclusion that you murdered Dobbs for Alison."

"That's crazy."

"You've met Sutton," Jerome said flatly.

"I see your point," Lee admitted.

"There's the problem. So how are you going to get out of it?" Jerome sounded like a professor asking a class to solve a difficult equation.

"We could destroy the black book. With or without it, Goody is probably headed to jail for the rest of his life."

"Don't be a smartass."

"Then we've got to solve the murders. Find out who murdered Alison's father and killed Mrs. Goody."

"You better solve it good. 'Cause you're going to have to drag Sutton and the sheriff along if the answer doesn't include Fred Goody killing Hubert Dobbs in a fit of jealousy."

"Y'all done talking?" Ruby stuck her head in the back door of the kitchen.

"I think I've heard all I can stand for one day. Walk me out to my car," Jerome told Lee.

A teeny, tiny paranoid voice in the back of Lee's mind wondered if Jerome was tricking him out to the patrol car so he could arrest him. Telling himself he was being stupid, he stood up and followed Jerome outside.

Jerome stopped by the side of his patrol car and looked at Lee.

"I'll give you forty-eight hours to fix this."

"That's not possible," Lee said.

"I want to at least see some light at the end of the tunnel."

"Can we count on your help?"

"You've managed to get me in it up to my neck. So, yeah, you haven't left me with any other option." He pulled the radio microphone strapped to his shoulder over to his mouth and keyed it. "Dispatch, I'm back in service."

Lee watched Jerome pull out of the driveway and felt guilty that he'd gotten him involved in this. As he walked back to the house, he thought about Alison. *Am I doing dumb stuff to impress a woman? Is that what this is all about?*

In the kitchen, Alison was helping Ruby clean up the dishes from lunch.

"She's better than Lester." Ruby smiled and handed her a plate to dry.

"Where *is* Lester?" Lee asked.

"A friend has an apartment he wants Lester to share."

"Cheers. Maybe one thing will go right today," Lee said, pitching in to help with the last of the clean-up.

"I need to go fill Kay in on what Jerome had to say, then we can head over to the library. If we're lucky, Lilly will be working today," Lee told Alison as they headed back to the office.

Kay was frustrated that Jerome had given them a deadline.

"I think we're lucky he's not putting the cuffs on us," Lee told her.

"That's a point," Kay said unhappily, picking up the accounting sheet again and hoping to see something different in the confusing mess of letters and numbers.

CHAPTER NINE

The new library had been built two years earlier. A single-story structure with tall, thin windows for light, it was clean and fresh, but Lee didn't think that it had the same ambiance as the old library on the town square. The old library had been a bank before the Great Depression, but it hadn't survived the stock market crash. With help from FDR's Civilian Conservation Corps, the local garden club had spearheaded the effort to convert the building into the Melon County Public Library. Lee had liked the dark, cool corners of the history section upstairs where he could lose himself for hours reading about World War II and the Civil War. Now the building was empty again, waiting for another group to save it. On the upside, Lee mused, the new library had a parking lot.

"Are you sure she'll talk to us?" Alison asked as Lee parked the car.

"Nope. She might kick us out on our ears. I don't even know if she's here today."

Alison sighed and opened her door.

They walked through the fallen leaves to the glass and steel front doors.

"We could always join the *Dungeons & Dragons* game." Lee noted the paper notice taped to the door, telling everyone that the D&D club was meeting in the media room.

"Don't tempt me," Alison said. "It'd be more fun than what we're about to do."

Lee looked at the three people behind the counter. None of them were Lilly Osbourne. After waiting in line behind an old man who looked like he couldn't have lifted a pencil, but who was carrying twenty pounds of thrillers by assorted authors, Lee stepped up to the counter to speak with a mocha-skinned woman whose fingernails defied reality.

"I'm looking for Mrs. Osbourne," he said when the woman reached out to take books he didn't have.

"She's in her office. What's this about?"

"It's personal." Lee smiled, trying to make it sound casual.

"You're the undertaker," the clerk said without inflection, leaving Lee unsure if it was a good thing or a bad thing that she'd recognized him.

"That's right. Lee Lamberton."

"You did a fine job with Helen Foster's funeral. It was real nice."

"We do our best."

"I'll let Mrs. Osbourne know you're out here." She got up and walked through a door behind the counter. "She'll be out in a minute," the clerk said when she returned.

Alison had hung back while Lee questioned the clerk. He went to stand beside her as they waited and Alison took his hand. He liked the feel of her soft palm pressing against his. Even if she *was* sweating a bit.

The head librarian didn't make them wait long. As Lee had remembered, she looked the part. Tall and dressed in a conservative skirt, her posture was aristocratic. She could have also served well as a principal.

Lee gave her a brief wave. Her face was open and interested as she approached them.

"Lee! I haven't seen you here in ages. What can I do for you?" Lilly Osbourne was relaxed and smiling now.

"I've been busy with the funeral home and all," Lee said, feeling like he was in middle school again. *Remember why you're here*, he told himself. "We'd like to talk with you in private."

"I don't see—"

"This is Alison, Hubert Dobbs's daughter," Lee said, and the expression on her face changed instantly from curiosity to caution.

"We can talk in my office."

They followed her around the front counter and into a small office. Lilly indicated the two stiff-backed chairs facing her desk as she took her place behind it.

"What's this all about?" There was a slight nervous tic at the corner of her mouth.

"We know that you were having an affair with Dobbs two years ago," Lee said, seeing no reason to beat around the bush.

"Oh, hell. This has to come up now." She closed her eyes and sighed. "Bertie and I saw each other for about seven or eight months. There's really nothing more I can say. What do you want? If this is an attempt at blackmail, you can forget it. First, I don't have any money. Second, you'd be doing me a favor by screwing up my life. I need a good kick in the ass to throw me out of the rut I'm in." She stared at them with frustration and pain in her eyes. Lee didn't doubt for a minute that she was serious.

"We aren't here to blackmail you," he assured her.

Alison nodded. "I don't want to cause you any trouble. I just want to know more about my father… and try to find out who killed him."

Lilly looked down at her hands. "I was sorry to hear about his murder. He was a nice man and treated me like a princess, which hasn't happened to me in decades."

"I notice that you didn't say you were shocked or surprised that he was murdered," Lee said.

"I wasn't. Bertie never pretended with me. I know he courted half the women in the county. You live that kind of lifestyle, it's going to catch up with you sooner or later. No matter how nice of a guy you are." She paused, but before Lee or Alison could say anything else, her mouth dropped open. "Oh, I heard about the fire too. I'm so sorry."

Lee didn't know if she knew that a body had been found in the house, but for now he wanted to focus on her relationship with Dobbs.

"How did the affair start?"

Lilly looked wistful. "I'd known Bertie for years. Then, about two years ago, he got an urge to read all of John D. McDonald's Travis McGee mysteries. *The Green Ripper* had just come out, and Bertie wanted to start at the beginning. So once a week he'd come in and check out two of them. At some point we started talking, then things just sort of evolved from there."

"Did you know about his reputation?" Lee asked.

"I'd heard rumors, but I only half believed them. I mean, Santa Claus? That's how I thought of him then. But there was something comforting, or maybe a little disarming about his appearance. He wasn't anything like other men. Admittedly it's been a while, but when I started working at the library, men would hit on me a lot. I guess there's an allure to the librarian persona. Or something." She waved her hand. "I always brushed them off because they came across as… creepy or overbearing. Not like your dad. He just seemed sweet. In fact, he *was* sweet." Lilly smiled at Alison.

"Why did you break up?" Alison asked.

"Bertie and I had agreed from the start that it was just a fling. I'm married and Bertie was… Bertie. He was always looking for the next conquest."

"Is that how he thought of women?" Lee interjected.

"You're seeing it from the wrong angle. Maybe it's my fault for using that word. Bertie hated to see women who were unhappy, so he took it upon himself to cheer them up. He was very good at it." She blushed and shifted in her chair.

"Did he ever mention me?" Alison asked, reminding Lee how personal this was for her.

"He did. You were a source of pride and… frustration for him. He talked about how he didn't know how to reconnect with you. He thought you must be angry at him for not doing enough to be in your life."

"My mother is a hard woman to live with. Unlike her, I never blamed him for the divorce."

"When he talked about you and your mother, he always took responsibility for the break-up."

"You said you weren't surprised that Bertie was killed. Considering what a Lothario he was, that's understandable. But was there anyone in particular that had threatened him or that he was scared of?" Lee pushed to get the conversation back on track.

"I can't think of anyone in particular, but there was always a little… secretiveness—or maybe a sense of adventure is a better term—around Bertie. He liked to keep secrets. I chalked it up to juggling all those affairs. After a while, I think it becomes second nature to lie and cover up your affairs. And, if I'm being honest, the *Spy vs. Spy* part was part of the fun and spiced up the…" Embarrassed, she looked down at the desk. "…affair."

"Was there anything in particular you thought was suspicious?" Lee asked.

"Never on a Wednesday night," she said.

"What?"

"He said we couldn't meet on Wednesday nights. I asked him why a couple of times, just out of curiosity, but he'd never give me a straight answer. I even thought of following him some week to see what he was up to."

"But you didn't?"

"No. He stayed out of my private life, so I respected his."

"Did you know that he was having an affair with Mrs. Goody?" Lee asked.

Lilly sat up and leaned forward in her chair. "I thought this was about Alison finding out more about her father? Why are you asking questions like you're some sort of detective?"

"Deputy Sutton is the investigator on the case," Lee said bluntly.

"Wade Sutton?" Lilly asked, and Lee nodded. "That man's a dullard."

"Exactly. What are the odds that he's going to arrest the right man?" Lee asked.

"I'd heard that he'd arrested Fred Goody, which didn't fit with what I know about the Goodys. I get it. Ask your questions."

"Did you know about Mrs. Goody?" Lee repeated.

"There was some talk. I even saw them out in the parking lot once. From a distance. It looked innocent enough. However, knowing Bertie... So, yeah, I knew."

"What'd you think?"

"Good for Ellie."

"You approved?" Lee asked with raised eyebrows.

"Ellen Goody is a nice woman. Her husband is a workaholic. I guess that comes with being a successful farmer. Before Bertie took up with her, Ellie always had this hangdog look about her. I'm actually more surprised that it took Bertie so long to get around to her."

Lee realized that Lilly Osbourne hadn't heard about Ellen Goody's death.

"Her body was discovered in the ruins of Dobbs's house," he said as gently as he could.

Lilly's face turned white and Lee detected a tremble in her hands.

"Oh no. No, you can't be serious," she stammered. "I saw her a week ago. She looked so happy."

"Hubert Dobbs and Ellen Goody. Can you think of anyone who would want to hurt both of them?" Lee asked.

"I guess you always have to look at the husband, but that's crazy. Fred and his family are good people. I can imagine him being upset, but enough to commit murder?"

"I think the murders might not have had anything to do with the affairs Dobbs was having." Lee hesitated before crossing the next line. He'd be exposing the fact that he knew more than he should, but the clock was ticking. "Do you know of any connection between Dobbs and Commissioner Alton Singleton?"

"Not that I remember."

"What about Milton Campbell?" Lee was trying to remember all of the names on the various files in Dobbs's office.

"I think I've seen Milton in Bertie's shop. But then almost everyone in town shops there."

"Courtney Webber?"

"There's a name for you." It was clear that there wasn't any love lost between Lilly and the school superintendent.

"What about her?"

"She's a jackass. Lyle's had a couple of run-ins with her. She has certain *opinions* about how math should be taught, but her background is in elementary education." Her disdain was clear.

"Is there any connection between her and Dobbs that you know of?"

"None. Ha! That would be a laugh if Bertie had ever had an affair with that harridan. I can't see it. Bertie always went for the sweet ladies who were being ignored. Trust me, no one ignores Courtney Webber."

Doubting that Lilly had anything else to add to their investigation, Lee turned to Alison. "Did you have anything else?"

"No… I don't think so. Not right now. But I'd like to talk more about my father sometime," she said, giving Lilly a nervous smile.

"I'd love to. I've got a lot of fond memories of my eight months with him that I've never been able to talk about."

"I do have one more question," Lee said. "Did your husband know about your affair with Dobbs?"

"I don't think my husband has noticed anything I've done for the last decade." She paused. "That sounds awful, and in some ways it is. That's just the type of person he is. He's a very good math teacher. That's what he loves, not me. When he comes home after school, he spends hours working on obscure equations that an international group of mathematicians send to each other. So, no, I'm sure he never noticed."

On the way back to the funeral home, Lee asked, "What do you think?"

Alison was quiet for a minute. "I don't know what to think about my father. I'm not even sure whether I would have liked him if I'd had the chance to get to know him. He sounds like he was nice, but also kind of a cad."

"People are complex. I believe Mrs. Osbourne was right about one thing. I think your father liked to make people happy, and he went about it in different ways. That's what playing Santa was all about. I remember thinking he was a great guy. I wanted to believe that he *was* Santa. Kids are pretty perceptive. If he'd been a creep, I would have heard about it."

"We didn't learn much to help us figure out who killed him."

"The more information we have, the better. In that vein, I think we need to go after some of the bigger fish. The trouble is, we need to have a hook. Otherwise, we'll be the ones in the frying pan," Lee told her with a wry grin.

Kay had been staring at the piece of paper for an hour, concentrating on the acronyms without any success. Some of the numbers in the columns were clearly dollar amounts, though there were no dollar symbols and the columns hadn't been marked in any way. Kay suspected that Dobbs hadn't wanted the files to be easily understood. *Is it actually code? Or did he just leave off some information to make the meaning more obscure?* Kay was pretty sure it was the latter, though the acronyms might have been in code.

One column held numbers running all the way down the sheet that read: *10/11, 9/4, 7/1* and so on; while another column held numbers such as: *+1.5, +2* and *+7.*

Kay heard a soft knock on the closed office door. Without looking up, she asked, "What is it, Ruby?"

"I wanted to talk to you about dinner."

"What about it?" Kay yelled back.

"We wouldn't have to yell if I open the door," Ruby reasoned.

Kay sighed. "Come in."

Ruby was all smiles as she walked straight to the desk. "I just want to make sure that spaghetti will be fine for dinner.

I've got some of that mushroom and sausage sauce that I made two weeks ago up in the freezer."

Kay almost started drooling at the mention of the sauce. All of Ruby's eccentricities were worth putting up with whenever Kay thought of her cooking. "That does sound good."

"Spaghetti is always good when the weather is cool. I'll make some garlic bread. What are you betting on?"

"What?" Kay was used to Ruby's frequent changes in topics, but she didn't even understand this one.

Ruby was looking at the sheet of paper that Alison had drawn from memory. "Those are odds and betting spreads. Are you going to start gambling?" Ruby turned to go, as though it was of no concern to her.

"Wait! Come back," Kay blurted.

"Yes, dear?" Ruby turned back, her mouth curved up in a smile.

"Tell me what you see on this piece of paper." Kay tapped the sheet while Ruby came back over to the desk.

"There, see those numbers? That's seven-to-one odds. That one is nine-to-four. Those must be racing odds. This row is probably a game. See, they put the spread." She tapped the number +7. "That team or person is being given a seven-point spread at five-to-three odds."

Kay pulled out her calculator and, following the rows and the odds, she was able to figure out who had won and who had lost. One column held the amount of the bets, while the second-to-last column indicated the payout. The final column must have been a running tally of the amount that person had won or lost. Now she could make an educated guess about the acronyms, figuring they stood for different sports teams.

When Kay looked up to thank Ruby, the funny woman was already gone.

CHAPTER TEN

It was late afternoon when Lee and Alison got back from the library. Kay was eager to tell them what she'd learned.

"Gambling. That could explain a few things. How'd you figure it out?" asked Lee, impressed.

"Not me. Ruby knew as soon as she saw them that the numbers were odds and point spreads. That woman is… strange," Kay said.

"I seem to remember her saying something once about working at a casino," Lee said, then he and Alison filled his sister in on what they'd learned from Lilly Osbourne.

"Your father certainly had his quirks," Kay told Alison.

Lee picked up the little black book from the desk and flipped through it page by page.

"Courtney Webber isn't in here, and we didn't see files for any of the women that *are* in here," he said. "Does that mean that her connection to Dobbs was gambling?"

"Maybe he was a bookie on the side," Kay suggested.

"That seems like the most reasonable possibility, and it

would explain where he got most of his money. It also provides a different motive for his murder other than a cuckolded husband."

"So what's the plan now that the killer has managed to destroy the evidence?" Kay asked.

"We can't be sure of that," Lee pointed out. "Whoever started the fire may have taken the files before they burned the place down."

"I hadn't thought of that. Maybe they destroyed their own files and kept everyone else's as potential blackmail," Kay mused.

"No one else knows that *we* know about the files," Alison said.

Lee nodded. "We need to find a way to talk to those people whose names were on the files. Our knowledge could be used as leverage when we talk with them."

"Which means the killer might give himself away," Kay said hopefully.

"Or herself," Lee pointed out.

"Or herself. Of course, they might just decide that they need to kill us too." Kay frowned.

"We could stop," Alison suggested hesitantly. "Just let the sheriff do whatever he's going to do. I don't want anyone else to get hurt because of me."

Lee put his hand on her shoulder. "This isn't because of you. The person who murdered your father started this."

"Lee's right," his sister said, surprising him. "The murderer is to blame for everything that's happened, and I can't let it go. I don't want to see the killer escape and I'm not going to let Sutton put an innocent man in jail."

"If you don't want to be involved, you can go back to Pensacola. We'll take care of your father until it's safe for you to return," Lee said.

"No way. If you're going to fight this, then so am I."

There was grit in Alison's voice.

"That's settled. Let's figure out our next move," Kay said.

"Dinner!" they heard Ruby yell.

"We'd better not keep her waiting," Lee said.

Lester was already sitting at the table, grinning at the large plate of pasta that Ruby had set in front of him.

"I know I'm not getting paid for today," he told them. "But I've found a place to stay."

"If you found a new place then I'll authorize a full day's pay," Kay said generously.

"Cool! Yeah, a friend of mine's got an apartment over on Sycamore Street. It's a converted garage. My share is a hundred a month, and that includes utilities." He looked at Alison as she sat down beside him. "I heard about the fire. That's a bummer."

"Thanks."

"You're having my kind of luck," Lester said, helping himself from a platter of garlic bread. "What've you all been doing today?"

"This and that," Lee said.

"Nothing much," Kay echoed.

"Now don't be modest. Kay solved a puzzle." Ruby had a smile on her face and gave Kay a wink.

"Actually, it was Ruby who solved it. I was trying to figure out the meaning of an accounting sheet with a bunch of figures and letters on it. She recognized it as a betting ledger."

"I saw all kinds of betting when I worked out in Las Vegas," Ruby said.

"You worked in Vegas?" Lester was in awe.

Ruby nodded. "I dealt cards. Worked the cage. Even did some security work watching the floor. I met Elvis."

This took the conversation down a path far away from accounting sheets and burning houses and what Lee and Kay had done that day, which suited them both just fine.

After dinner, Kay, Lee and Alison went back to the office while Lester gathered up his stuff and headed over to his new apartment.

As soon as the office door was closed behind them, Kay said, "Based on what we know, I think it's safe to assume that Alton Singleton, Milton Campbell, Courtney Webber, Walt Lawson and Victor Pratt were gambling and that Hubert Dobbs was keeping records of it all. I vote we confront one of them."

"Wade Sutton is a jerk and not for one minute do I believe he's right about Fred Goody. Still, jealousy is a strong motive, which means we've got a book full of possible suspects without tackling the gamblers," Lee said, vacillating.

"You're scared of them," Kay said, surprised.

"They're all very important people in this community. Running our business means getting along with the powers that be. I'm afraid that once we kick this hornet's nest we won't be able to un-kick it."

"I hate it when you're the one thinking like a businessman," Kay said. "I'd argue that we don't have to worry. I doubt any of them want this information made public. It's actually to our advantage that they're VIPs. If they were peasants like us, they might not care if people know they gambled."

"You have a point," Lee said. He noticed that Alison looked like she wanted to say something, so he added, "Don't say we should quit."

"I wasn't. I was going to say that I agree with Kay. Jerome told you that we need answers as quickly as possible. Seems the best way to do that is to stir the suspects up."

"There's a chance the killer might attack again," Lee

reminded them.

"That could happen even if we don't do anything," Kay said.

While Lee had been playing devil's advocate, in his heart he also wanted to take action. Sighing heavily, he said, "Okay, then who do we start with? Singleton, the commissioner; Campbell, the deputy fire chief; Webber, the school superintendent; Lawson, the store owner; or Pratt, the sheriff's brother? Actually, can we all agree that he's the *last* one on our list?"

Kay and Alison nodded.

"Tell me what you know about them," Kay said. She'd left the county after high school, bound for nursing school and the Army, and she hadn't had much time to become reacquainted with the locals since her return.

"Singleton is a wuss weasel," Lee said, earning a snicker from Alison. "Whenever Dad had to deal with him, he'd go back on his word in a heartbeat. Dad hated him. Milton Campbell, on the other hand, is a stand-up guy from all I've heard. If he gives you his word, he doesn't go back on it. He also has a strong sense of duty. I don't know Courtney Webber."

"The librarian hated her," Alison interjected. "She made her sound like a real iron-pants."

"I've met Walt Lawson a couple of times," Lee continued. "We buried his aunt. I got the impression he's a hard businessman. I remember thinking that I wouldn't want to try to negotiate the price of a funeral with him. As for Victor Pratt, all I know is that he isn't much like his brother. He comes across as the nice guy who never finishes first."

"Based on all that, I vote we start with Singleton," Kay said.

"Why wouldn't you start with the deputy fire chief?" Alison asked. "He sounds the most trustworthy."

"Exactly. Everyone else involved in the gambling ring, or whatever it is, can trust him too. He's not going to give anything up and he's not likely to lose his nerve."

"Ahhh, yeah, I get it." Alison smiled.

"I vote for Singleton too," Lee agreed. "Question is: Who goes to talk to him?"

"All of us would be too much." Kay frowned. "You at least know him."

"That might be a negative. I know him, but he also knows me. You, on the other hand, are an unknown quantity to him. And he might be caught off guard by being confronted by a woman."

"What about me?" Alison asked.

"Singleton isn't the type to be moved by the daughter of a murdered man. He's cold and calculating. I think Kay alone is the best move."

The women nodded.

"Hurray! We have another plan," Kay said. "I hope it goes better than the others."

Lee looked nervously at his watch. "Now's as good a time as any."

"Where's he live?" Kay asked.

"Two blocks off the courthouse square. You could walk there from here. He's actually *our* city commissioner."

They spent another half hour strategizing and coming up with a list of questions for Kay to ask. Then Lee thought they spent a bit too much time discussing what Kay should wear for the interview, but he had to admit that the final selection of black jeans, a blouse, leather vest and ankle boots made her look decidedly kickass.

"I'm going to come on strong," Kay said.

"That's your default," Lee said, "but keep your options open. Singleton is such a sleazy character, I don't think we can predict what he's going to do."

Kay nodded. Lee noticed that she was tense and shifting her weight from foot to foot. It made him realize how seldom he'd seen her look nervous.

"We'll drive you there and keep the car warmed up in case you have to get away fast," Lee offered.

"I'm not robbing a bank," Kay chided him, then added, "but I appreciate it."

The three of them were in the front hall getting ready to leave when Ruby popped her head out of the kitchen and asked Kay to join her.

Lee and Alison exchanged looks as Kay went into the kitchen. She came back ten minutes later looking puzzled.

"What was that all about?" Lee asked.

"I'll tell you when I know for sure." Kay shook her head.

Lee had chosen the black Lincoln Town Car for this mission.

"I feel like a gangster," Alison said from the back seat.

"We're doing gangster stuff," Lee said, parking across the street from the three-story Victorian house where Alton Singleton lived.

"Wish me luck," Kay said. She reminded herself that it was just a city commissioner and not the head of the CIA that she would be trying to buffalo.

The walk up the path to the front porch seemed to take forever. It was dark, but the moon was bright and there were plenty of streetlights illuminating the neighborhood.

Singleton's house looked well-kept, with the air of a dowager queen. Kay stood in front of the large mahogany door for a count of ten, composing herself before she pressed the doorbell. The chime was loud and clear.

Prepared to face the city commissioner, Kay was surprised when the door was opened by a fourteen-year-old boy who stared at her, first with disdain and then with a look that made her want to slap his face.

His eyes traveled up and down her body. "Who are you?"

"I want to speak to Alton Singleton."

"Dad doesn't like to be bothered at night," he said, his voice a mix of contempt and lust. Kay hoped the father wasn't as creepy as the son.

"Just tell him that Kay Lamberton is here to talk about the murder of Bertie Dobbs."

"You a cop or something?"

"Just tell your father I'm here." She liked the fact that the boy had jumped to the possibility that she was a cop. *That military bearing still comes in handy*, she thought.

"Sure. If you want to talk to me later, I'd like that." The boy walked away from the open door, not knowing how close he'd come to getting knocked clear through the house and out the back door.

As the little snot hadn't bothered to invite Kay inside, she took it upon herself to step in and close the door behind her. *Harder to brush me off if I'm already in the house.*

Alton Singleton was wearing a noncommittal expression on his face as he walked down the hall toward her. Kay figured he was about 5'7" and carried a good thirty pounds more than he should. His hair looked too dark for his age.

"Can I help you?" he asked, sounding like a jeweler who didn't think she had enough money to buy what he was selling.

"I want to talk to you about Hubert Dobbs's murder," Kay said, trying to sound tough.

"Why would you think I'd know anything about that?" While the words and his tone denied it, Kay thought she saw some hesitation in his eyes.

"Because I know that you and Dobbs were involved in gambling." Since they couldn't be sure if Dobbs had been acting as a bookie or if he'd gambled himself, they'd all agreed that Kay should be as vague as possible with her accusations.

"You don't know any such thing. Where did you get such a ridiculous idea?"

The question told Kay that they were on the right track. If he'd been completely innocent, he would have just kicked her out of his house. Instead he obviously wanted to know what she knew and where she'd learned it.

"I've seen the files."

"What files?" His eyes were hooded now as he looked at her.

"I think you know the files I'm talking about."

"My son said your name was Lamberton. You're Lee Lamberton's sister, aren't you? I don't know what kind of blackmail game you're playing, but I want you out of my house." Singleton looked like he was trying to figure out how he could push her out the door.

"I think you want to talk to me," Kay said, aware that she was losing what little advantage she'd had. Singleton wanted her out of the house, no doubt so he could buy some time to learn what was going on and how much she and Lee knew.

"If you won't leave, I'll call the police." Kay could tell that he'd made up his mind to bluff his way through the conversation.

"We don't want money; we just want answers. If we don't get them, we'll let everyone know that they have a commissioner with a gambling problem." Kay moved on from Plan A's intimidation to Plan B's threats.

"People already know that I was quite the rake when I was younger. Everyone gambles a little." Singleton made it sound like a virtue. "Now, are you going to leave or do I have to call the sheriff and have you kicked out?"

Now Kay had to decide whether to go with Plan 9 from Outer Space and reveal the crazy story Ruby had told her in the kitchen. She had overhead them talking about Alton

Singleton and had given Kay information that sounded improbable at best, and crazy at worst. Kay had never been sure how many of Ruby's stories were Walter Mitty-type fantasies and how many were real, but she decided she might as well find out.

"Ruby Red Dress said to say hello," Kay said.

She was immediately rewarded by the shocked look on Singleton's face. His legs went wobbly and, if he hadn't reached over and grabbed for the banister, Kay thought he would have dropped to the floor.

CHAPTER ELEVEN

"Come into my study," Alton Singleton said in a whispered growl, pointing to a door down the hall.

Once they were inside, he shut the door and went over to the wet bar to pour himself a double shot of bourbon. "I don't know where you get your information, but I suggest you keep it to yourself."

"Ruby works for us," Kay said.

Singleton's eyes went wide and his face barely maintained the color that the bourbon had restored.

"That's impossible. I don't believe you." He stared at her defiantly.

"I assure you it's true."

"I need to sit down." He waved her to a leather sofa while he dropped down into a matching wingback chair. "It has been so long, I'd managed to push all of those dark days out of my mind. I'm a different person than I was back then," he said, clearly asking for her understanding.

"People change," Kay said, wanting to keep him talking,

even though she knew from personal experience that people rarely did.

"What did she tell you?"

"That she helped you get out of a tricky situation with some angry Cubans down in Havana."

Singleton held his hands out in front of him and looked at his fingers as he flexed them. "She helped me keep all of my fingers."

"You'd lost a lot of money."

"A lot."

"You got in the game by claiming that your father would back you."

"That's right. Dad had bailed me out in the past. Not with these guys, but with others in New Jersey and Vegas. I'd burned all my bridges with the people running the games in both those places, so I'd gone to Havana where I knew there would be high-stakes games. Once I got in… it wasn't long before I was in over my head, and I wasn't smart enough to stop. I just kept throwing money down the hole."

"And your father wouldn't bail you out."

"I called him with two goons standing beside me, listening in. When I asked him for the money, more than a hundred-thousand dollars, he told me no. Just that—no. I begged him. Nothing. When I told him they were going to kill me, he reminded me of all the times he'd told me what would happen if I kept gambling and incurring debts that I couldn't pay off. In the end, I heard him crying as he hung up the phone."

"Ruby said that they threatened to cut off your fingers."

"The two goons took me in front of Gimoaldo Perez. They called him The Confessor, not just because that was his name, but also because he could make anyone confess their betrayals of his trust. 'I don't want your dead body. I want my money,' he told me. When the goons said that my father wouldn't pay, he suggested that some of my body parts delivered to him might be more persuasive."

"How did Ruby become involved in all of this?" Kay couldn't believe that the story was true.

"When Perez lifted his knife **and** was going to chop off my pinkie, I screamed. Ruby had been dealing the cards while we played poker. She knew that I was in trouble and, when she heard me scream, she pounded on the office door. Perez must have liked her, because he stopped and told them to open the door. I can still see her, standing there in a halter top and a red sequined miniskirt. It's what she always wore while we played cards, so I called her Ruby Red Dress. Sometimes she was dealing; other times she'd serve the liquor."

"And she pounded on the door to save your life?"

"The Confessor made fun of her at first. He asked her if she was in love with me. Told her that I was a deadbeat and needed to be taught a lesson. She offered to go to my dad and ask him to send the money."

"This guy bought that?" Kay asked disbelievingly.

"I'm sure there was something going on between them. Anyone else, I think he would have killed them on the spot. Long story short, she traveled up here to meet with my father and convinced him to negotiate with Perez." Singleton held up his hand and wiggled his fingers. "Because of Ruby, I can still count to ten. I had no idea that she was living here."

"Almost two years now."

"I'd like to thank her. People think I'm an ass. Maybe I am, but I'm not an ingrate. I never saw her again. I asked Dad about it and he told me he gave her a reward, but that's the last I ever heard of her."

Kay looked at him levelly. "What she wants is for you to tell me about your relationship with Hubert Dobbs."

Singleton sighed and looked at the floor. "Bertie was a good friend. We knew each other for years, and he knew I was addicted to gambling. When he came to talk to me about it twenty years ago, I thought he was going to try to get me to quit cold turkey. That never would have happened. Instead, he offered me a deal. One night a week, I'd be able to play poker and bet on anything I wanted to with friends. A safe environment. This wasn't long after I'd almost lost all my fingers, so I was receptive to anything that might keep me in digits while allowing me to indulge my vice."

"You said friends? Who were they?"

"I'm talking about me, not ratting out other people."

"Then I'll tell *you*. It was Milton Campbell, Courtney Webber, Walt Lawson and Victor Pratt."

Singleton's eyes widened. "I guess you *do* know a few things. When you came in here, I thought you were just blowing smoke."

"You met on Wednesday night."

"Originally it was Thursday. Five years in, we changed to Wednesday. I don't remember why."

"What did you all do on… I was going to a call them your boys' nights out, but I guess Courtney changes that."

"Yeah, Courtney." His tone was odd and Kay wondered what he meant by it. "We met and played poker. The deal, pun intended, was that if any of us gambled outside the group, we'd get kicked out. Bertie set limits on how much we could lose too. Those were weekly limits and scaled to what we could afford."

"You all agreed to this?"

"We all have gambling addictions and were close to the bottom in our lives when Bertie came to us. He found us wallowing in the mud, looking for a lifeline, and he threw us one."

"What did he get out of it?" Kay asked, curious.

"That was my first question. Thing is, I knew Bertie. Nice guy writ large. I decided then, and still believe, that helping us was his main motivation."

"Main?"

"Bertie liked to play poker. I mean, he *loved* to play poker. One of us always had to call it a night, 'cause Bertie wouldn't. Four o'clock in the morning and he'd still be going strong. Five and he wanted a candy bar to get his energy back. Six and he wanted one more hand. The guy was the best too."

"Dobbs won?"

"It was a rare night that he didn't come away from the table richer. Don't get me wrong, one or two of us would walk away with some extra money too, but it was Bertie's game."

"So why did you all stick with this plan if he was always beating you?"

"That was why we stuck with it. If we won every time, what would be the point? Gamblers need to lose. The more we lose, the more we want to play. That's the mind game. That's why we get hooked. You go to Vegas, you lose. You go to Atlantic City, you lose. Horse racing, you lose. Winning is the endorphin hit, but the more you lose, the greater the hit when it comes. Understand?"

"That's kind of crazy."

Singleton nodded. "Of course it is. Doesn't matter. Just like a guy who keeps dating and marrying women who treat him like crap, or vice versa. They do it cause they like that feeling of hope. The belief that, just one time, it's all going to work out. It's the same with gamblers. We always believe that we'll get that big score and walk away happy. Is it ever going to happen? Never, 'cause that's not the way it works."

"Was there anyone else who played cards with you?"

"Over the years there were others that came and went.

No one that came to more than thirty or forty games."

"Anyone recently?"

"The same group has been playing for the last two years."

Kay took a deep breath and asked, "Who do you think killed Dobbs?"

"I've been trying to figure that out myself. I don't know," Singleton said, shaking his head and looking down at his hands.

"Could it be one of the five card players?"

"It wasn't me," he said, looking up at her. "That's all I can tell you."

"Of the other four, which one would you vote as most likely to be a killer?"

"See, that's another thing about addicts. They have this string built into them that, if it's pulled the right way, could cause them to do anything."

"Does that include you?"

"I'm an addict. I make no bones about it. There have been times over the last twenty years that the urge to grab a bunch of cash, mine or someone else's, and hop on a plane to Vegas has been strong. Real strong. And if you ever repeat that to anyone else, I'll call you a damned liar."

"What about Dobbs's girlfriends and their husbands?" Kay asked, wondering how much Singleton knew about what was in the little black book.

"Bertie loved women. I know that he got into more than a few scrapes because of it. It wouldn't surprise me if his death is related to his womanizing and not his gambling."

"Fred Goody?"

"No. I know Goody. He wouldn't kill anyone, at least not over the virtue of his wife. A land deal gone bad? That would be a different matter. Fred Goody married his wife to have children. When she didn't conceive, his interest in her went down the way it would in a prized heifer who was barren. He'd have divorced her if it wouldn't have upset his mother. He's always been a momma's boy."

"Do you have any idea why someone would kill Mrs. Goody and burn down Dobbs's house?"

"You don't have to be Sherlock Holmes to figure that out. The killer was covering his tracks. Ellen Goody knew something or was just in the wrong place when the killer decided to destroy whatever evidence was hidden in Bertie's house."

"Are you putting pressure on Sheriff Pratt to keep the investigation focused on Goody?"

Singleton laughed. "You forget that I'm a city commissioner. How could I influence the county sheriff? It's the county commission that has some control over the sheriff's budget, not anything I do."

"Don't pretend that you aren't an influential man in this county. You control a lot of votes that the sheriff will need to get reelected."

"Sure, I could put pressure on Pratt if I wanted to, but I don't. Now his brother… they're pretty close."

"Are you saying that Victor Pratt might have killed Dobbs?"

"I guess it's possible. But I don't think the sheriff thinks his brother did it."

"So what is the sheriff doing arresting Fred Goody?"

"He doesn't want his brother's name dragged through the mud. Does the sheriff really believe that Goody killed Bertie? I'd say he knows that Goody didn't do it. And he also knows that most of the *town* knows that Goody didn't do it. So he arrests Goody, or I should say, has that buffoon Sutton arrest Goody, knowing that Goody won't be convicted by a jury of his peers. Maybe the sheriff will even throw a few wrenches into the prosecutor's case. By the time the trial is over, everyone will be bored with the Dobbs murder. The sheriff can claim that the evidence they found pointed to Goody, so what more can they do? Goody isn't in jail anymore, so no harm, no foul there, and everything is swept under the rug."

"Is that what you think is happening?"

"When I heard that Fred Goody had been arrested, that's the first thought that came into my head."

"What's your opinion of Victor Pratt?"

Singleton frowned. "I don't like him."

"Why?"

"He's weak. Never done anything on his own. I know that I've relied on my family in the past. My father pulled me out of more than one fire, including one that would have cost me a few fingers and maybe my life. But I grew up. I started my own business. I own three Country Burgers in the county and they're all doing well. I employ twenty-five people full time. On top of that, I do my part for the city as a commissioner. I don't just phone it in like some of the other commissioners I could name. I know what I'm voting for or against. Pratt, though, that man hasn't done an honest day's work in his life."

Singleton abruptly stopped talking, his face red. Talking about Victor Pratt had obviously touched a nerve.

"Where's he get his money to gamble?" Kay asked.

"Oh," Singleton said, waving the question away, "technically he's the supervisor of the maintenance crew at the jail. Nothing but nepotism. I know that man doesn't do any real work. He's got three guys under him that do everything, including one that does all the work of the supervisor without the pay or the title."

"Why did Dobbs invite him to play with you all?"

"He was another of Bertie's rescues. Victor lost a ton of money betting on college sports and was drinking heavily. I think the sheriff came to Bertie and asked him to help

Victor, but I don't know that for sure. All I know is, he showed up one week about four years ago and hasn't gone away since."

"Did you all do anything other than play poker on Wednesday nights?"

Singleton didn't say anything for a few minutes. Kay let the silence draw out, knowing that there was more to the story.

"We're also allowed to make bets," he finally said.

"How's that work?"

He looked irritated by the question, but went on to explain, "If we wanted to bet on a game or an election or whatever, we would tell Bertie and he'd give us the odds, then we'd place the bet or not."

"How did he get the odds? Did he have a bookie that he worked with?"

Singleton nodded. "Yeah, he'd call him and sort our bets out before the poker game got started. That was all part of the routine. We'd show up at the game, spend some time making any bets we'd been thinking about, then play poker."

"Why did you do it that way? You could have worked through your own bookies."

"Don't you get it? This way we only had a limited time every week to make our bets. By channeling it through Bertie, there was a gatekeeper who could make sure we didn't get in over our heads. If one of us had been losing too much, he'd make that person take a week or two off to rebuild their stash. See, that's the worst part of being a gambler. Losing has a snowball effect. The more you lose, the more you want to bet. Bertie would interrupt that cycle and save us from our addiction."

Despite herself, Kay found herself feeling sorry for the man. He had an addiction, but once he'd admitted to himself that he had a problem, he'd found a way to control it and he'd stuck to it for twenty years. By the time she left his house, she still hadn't made up her mind about Alton Singleton.

"What did you learn?" Lee asked her when she got in the car.

"I'll tell you both everything as soon as we get back home."

An hour later, Lee and Alison were sitting across from Kay in the office, trying to decide what questions to ask first.

"*Our* Ruby did that?" Lee asked. Though he knew he should have been focusing on the things Kay had learned about the gambling ring, it was Ruby's history that he found most fascinating.

Kay nodded. "Apparently. Remember, she's the one who mentioned it to me in the first place."

"Ruby must have been quite the looker in her younger days," Alison said. "How did she end up working for this Perez guy?"

"According to her, she was dealing cards in Vegas when she met him. They hit it off and he asked her to come work at his place in Havana."

"Fascinating," Lee said. "So how much of what Singleton told you is the truth, do you think?"

"He came across as sincere." Kay shrugged.

"I know for a fact that he can lie to a person's face and make them believe it. He lied to Dad on more than one occasion." Lee frowned.

"I believe you. I'm just saying that, if he is lying, he's damn good at it."

"He *is* good. It's interesting that he doesn't get along with Victor Pratt. We might be able to use that to leverage Pratt or Singleton."

"Y'all are being too nice to ask the question, so I will," Alison said. "What was my father's real motive for doing all that? Did he just like to play poker and appreciated having a captive audience? Or was he really trying to help these addicts?"

"I can't see how helping gamblers to gamble is helping them," Lee said.

Kay leaned back in her chair. "I can understand it. I saw it in a lot of soldiers that got hooked on drugs over in Vietnam. They weren't able to kick drugs cold turkey, so if they had someone who had their best interests at heart acting as a gatekeeper to the drugs, they could at least function without killing themselves."

"But is that really helping them?" Lee asked.

"If you're keeping them alive, you are. Dobbs was keeping their addiction in check so it didn't drown them in losses. I get that. But like Alison said, what was her father's motive? Does it really matter? And would it help us find the person who killed him?"

"I wish Pratt wasn't off limits," Lee said.

"Leaving him to last was your idea, remember. But I agree. We can't confront him. At least not yet," Kay said.

"Even I can see how dangerous that would be," Alison seconded. "If his brother is protecting him, you wouldn't stand a chance."

"Courtney Webber, then," Lee said. "She's the second most vulnerable, politically at least."

"From what Lilly had to say, she isn't very nice," Kay reminded them, then pointed at Lee. "This is a job for a man."

"I think we've got enough information to get her to talk. The question is: Does she know anything more than Singleton?"

"My dad had a soft spot for women, so maybe they had a

connection, even if she's not in the little black book," Alison suggested.

"I'm game. As school superintendent, she doesn't want to be thought of as a gambler who's involved with some secret group of players. Especially a group where the organizer was murdered."

"There's your opening bid to her," Kay said.

"When?"

"Tomorrow. Our timeline is shrinking."

As if on cue, there was a knock on the office door. When Lee opened it, they were greeted by the sight of an unhappy Jerome.

"I don't want to be here. I told myself I was going to stay out of it and let you either sink or swim," he grumbled.

"So why aren't you?" Lee asked.

"'Cause I don't trust you to get this done by yourselves. And if it's not cleared up in time, no matter how hard I protest my involvement, I'm going to end up going down with the *S.S. Lambertantic.*"

"Thanks for the vote of confidence," Lee groused.

"And how confident are *you* that you're going to get this mess cleaned up before it sinks all of us?" Jerome asked.

The other three looked everywhere but at the deputy.

"Yeah, that's what I thought. Now tell me how far you've gotten."

They filled him in on what they'd found out.

"Ruby Red Dress, huh?" Jerome chuckled. "Funny thing is, I can see her all dolled up and dealing cards. Okay, so Singleton, Webber, Campbell, Lawson and Pratt were all involved in an illegal gambling ring. That's interesting. At least they aren't likely to just throw us onto the fire if we have that kind of information on them. I'm feeling a little better already."

"Have you heard anything else from Wade Sutton

concerning Mr. Goody?" Kay asked.

"The autopsy will determine if Mrs. Goody was killed by the fire or if she was dead first and then left to burn. I'm thinking it's going to be tough for even Sutton to peg everything on Goody if his wife was killed while he was in jail."

"I can call up my friend at the morgue in Gainesville and see if he knows anything. I need to check and see when Dobbs's body is going to be released anyway. Have they done his autopsy yet?" Lee asked.

"I haven't heard. No doubt it was murder, though. I saw that knife sticking out of his back. There was enough blood to convince me he wasn't dead until he was stabbed." He looked over at Alison. "Sorry."

"No, I want you to be frank."

"The main question the autopsy will answer when it comes to Dobbs is if he was intoxicated or drugged when the attack took place," Jerome said.

"If I'm talking to Webber tomorrow and calling the morgue, what's everyone else going to be doing?" Lee asked.

"I'll check out Walt Lawson. You said he owns the Fast Marts. I'll see if I can learn a little about him before I go asking questions about the murders. The more background info I can have, the better," Kay said.

"I'm going to call Mom and ask if she's willing to talk to me about Dad," Alison said.

"Aren't we a little group of meddling kids." Jerome gave them the first hint of a smile they'd seen since they'd told him about going into Dobbs's house. "There's one investigator with our department who might be able to help out. Martin Townsend wanted to be a violent crimes investigator when he entered CID two years ago. Instead, the sheriff gave Sutton that position and Townsend got stuck with auto thefts. He's still steamed about that. He might help me get some info about Sutton's incompetent investigation."

As they were leaving the office, Jerome turned to Lee. "You might find Webber at the elementary school tomorrow. They're having a harvest festival. I heard about it at roll call."

Ruby called everyone into the kitchen for a late-night snack of homemade chocolate chip cookies.

"You still got that red dress?" Jerome asked after finishing a cookie and taking a second.

"You'd be surprised what I still have," Ruby said with a smile that caused everyone to feel uncomfortable.

CHAPTER TWELVE

Kay opened the window a crack to let in the cool night air before she nestled down in her bed under her favorite comforter. When the phone rang thirty minutes later, the last thing she wanted was to get out of bed. Hoping Lee would get it, she lay there until the fourth ring, but then she gave up. *I should have known better*, she grumbled to herself. Lee was notorious for going to sleep instantly and taking an hour to wake up.

"Hello?" she answered as she glared at the clock on the wall that said it was just past midnight. She tried to think of the upside, that the call was probably business.

"I was calling for Lee Lamberton. He came over and was askin' questions. I'm Martelli, Hubert Dobbs's neighbor. His house burnt down early this morning." The man's New Jersey accent was a challenge for Kay's sleepy ears.

"I'm Lee's sister. What can I do for you?" She was curious in spite of herself.

"There was a light moving around over there a little bit

ago. I called the cops, but they just sent a car that drove by then, zoom, off they go again. So I figure, the daughter might want to know that there's someone prowling around her father's burned-down house."

Kay was wide awake now. "Are they still there?"

"I think so. I seen a flash or two after the cops drove off."

"Thanks, Mr. Martelli. We may come over and look around tonight."

"That's more than the cops did, I tell you."

After Kay hung up, she went over and knocked loudly on Lee's door. The only response she received was a muffled grumble. She opened the door and leaned her head into the dark room. "Get your butt out of bed!" she ordered.

Five minutes later Lee, with tousled hair and jeans but no shirt or shoes, came out of his room. "Where's the body?" he yawned.

Kay told him about the phone call.

"Why would someone be searching the burned-out ruins?"

"I think we should go over there and look around. Maybe it's the killer."

"That's supposed to make me *want* to go over to the creepy, burned-down house where a person was murdered?"

"Do you want to find the killer or not?"

Ten minutes later they were in Kay's car and headed toward the remains of Hubert Dobbs's house.

"It could just be some kids looking for souvenirs," Lee suggested, watching the road as Kay drove, in his opinion, way too fast through the dark streets.

They parked a block away from the house and walked toward the charred ruins, keeping to the shadows. The stench of the fire was heavy in the air and there was still a layer of smoke low to the ground near the smoldering remains.

They carried the same flashlights they had used the night before, but the streetlamps provided enough light that they didn't need to turn them on. Still, Lee found some comfort in the heft of the large Maglite.

What Lee didn't know was that Kay had taken one more precaution. Before leaving the house, she'd put on her shoulder holster and placed her Colt 1911 securely under her arm. She'd made sure that her coat covered it so she didn't have to argue with Lee about bringing it. *I'd rather have it and not need it than need it and not have it.*

"Let's stop over there and watch for a little while," she whispered.

They crouched in the shadows and watched the skeletal remains of the Dobbs house. When twenty minutes had passed and they hadn't seen a sign of anyone moving around the property, they stood up and inched closer.

All the surrounding houses were dark as Kay and Lee walked carefully around the damp and damaged structure. The walls of the first floor were mostly intact, with yellow crime-scene tape wrapped haphazardly around what was left of the doors and windows. The ground was still soggy from the water the firemen had used to douse the blaze.

"The place is such a mess, it's hard to tell if anyone's been here tonight," Lee mumbled.

"Just look for anything that looks… I don't know… different, I guess." Kay was as much at a loss as Lee.

After going around the house a couple of times and seeing nothing, Kay suggested, "Let's move out into the back yard."

Lee followed her into the yard. He was moving around a tree when his foot found a hole. "Damn!" he blurted, going down on his knees.

"What?" Kay whispered, hurrying over to him.

"There's a hole here." He turned on his flashlight and let it play over the area. "It's freshly dug too."

Kay looked around. "There's another one."

"What were they looking for?" Lee said, flexing his ankle to see if there was any permanent damage.

"Over there in the flowerbed," Kay said, pointing. A three-foot-high sundial had been knocked over and a hole dug where it had once stood. "They were sure looking for something."

"Something other than files, apparently," Lee said.

They spent another hour looking for clues but, finding nothing and feeling exhausted from their eventful day, they headed home to bed.

When a tired Lee came downstairs the next morning, Lester was waiting for him. "What's going on?"

"What?" Lee asked.

"I know y'all got together last night. Why are you leaving me out of everything?" Lester pouted.

"We're just trying to help Alison. We didn't intend to leave you out of anything." *It was just a happy coincidence*, he thought.

"Great. I move out and now I don't get to know what's going on or get chocolate chip cookies."

"Ruby saved you some cookies."

"Yeah, but they aren't fresh out of the oven."

"Your life is a living hell," Lee said with a dose of sarcasm large enough for even Lester to pick up on.

"That guy who was here yesterday is coming back this morning. I think he's going to book that funeral."

"Do you want to handle the final negotiations? I'll just sit in on it in case he has any special requests or questions you can't answer." Lee figured he'd better throw Lester a bone to keep him from deciding to move back into the house.

"That would be great. I can do it too. You'll see." Lester's enthusiasm was uplifting, especially when it wasn't fueled by a few hits of weed.

"Go get your suit on," Lee told him. Lester kept a black suit in the closet in the embalming room.

"I'll have to put off my confrontation with Webber until this afternoon," Lee told Kay when he went into the kitchen for a large mug of coffee. He explained about the future piece of business.

"We always have time to make a little money," she told him.

The Hartfield contract was sealed and in the filing cabinet by eleven-thirty. Lee changed out of his suit and into jeans and a flannel shirt so he wouldn't stick out at the school's fall festival. He hoped Courtney Webber would be there. It seemed like a better place to ambush her with their information than on her home turf.

Lee found the elementary school swarming with pilgrims, Indians and turkeys. There were carnival games raising money for various local groups and a stage set up for different performers to show off their talent... or lack thereof. Lee wandered through the groups of parents and children, looking for Courtney Webber. He found her pontificating to a dozen parents and officials about the importance of public education for the socialization of children and the future productivity of the nation. Lee waited twenty minutes for her to finish and was sure he'd never heard anything so bombastic in his life.

Her captive audience broke up when children came over and started pulling their parents away toward the games. Webber started off toward the stage. Lee took a deep breath and followed her. He didn't want to talk to her if she was getting ready to go up on the stage, as that would just give her a good excuse to put him off.

However, luck was with him. Instead of mounting the three steps up to stage, Webber stopped to talk to a teacher who was getting ready to take her class up to perform "If You're Thankful and You Know It."

With everyone's attention focused on the stage, Lee decided the time was right to approach the superintendent.

"Ms. Webber," he called out, picking up his pace to intercept her. She looked over at him with a smile that turned to mild annoyance when she sized him up as a non-parent. With what looked to be an effort, she put the smile back in place.

"Yes?" she asked, stopping and turning to face him. She stood five-foot-six, but four of those inches were high heels, and there were another few inches of dark black hair piled on top of that.

"I'd like to speak with you in private about a sensitive matter," Lee told her. He'd thought hard about what to say and had decided these words would add the best nonthreatening yet serious tone to his request.

"There's no one listening." She looked around as if to prove it. The closest person was fifty feet away, and the squawk of the sound system in conjunction with the excited singing and stomping of feet from the kids on stage would prevent anyone from hearing their conversation.

"It's about the murder of Hubert Dobbs," Lee said.

"You must have me confused with the sheriff. I'm the school superintendent. If you go that way," she said, pointing toward the town square, "a couple of blocks, you'll see the sheriff's office on the north side of Main Street."

"I want to talk with you because I know you were friends with Dobbs."

"He was a very nice man. Most people in town were his friends. Are you a reporter?"

"No."

"I don't understand… Wait, I recognize you. You're a Lamberton. Your father buried many family members and friends of mine. Why in the world do you want to talk to me about Bertie Dobbs?" The smile on her face looked frozen in place.

"Because you played poker with him every Wednesday night," Lee said in a slightly louder voice that caused her to look around again to see if anyone was listening.

"I don't…" Webber started to protest, but Lee shook his head.

"No, that won't do."

"Let's go into the building where we can talk in private," she said in a neutral tone, heading for the school without looking to see if he was behind her.

Lee followed her to a small conference room inside the building. The walls were covered with PSA posters warning parents and children about drugs, strangers and traffic accidents.

"Now what is this nonsense about?" Webber was trying to be aggressive as she faced him across the table.

"We know about your gambling and the games on Wednesday nights."

"Who is 'we?'"

"My sister and Dobbs's daughter."

The mention of Alison caused the first crack in her attitude. "I'm sure that Ms. Dobbs is very upset about her father's death, but I can't give you any information because I don't have any." She neatly avoided the gambling accusation.

"We need all the information we can get. Fred Goody didn't kill Hubert Dobbs."

"Like I tried to explain to you, I'm not the sheriff. If you or Ms. Dobbs have a complaint about the way they're handling the investigation, you need to take it up with them."

Lee decided to regroup. "Can we sit down?" He pulled out a chair and offered it to her.

"I don't need to sit because there's no reason for this conversation." Her jaw was set in a stubborn frown.

"Fine. I'll talk to a reporter with the *Gainesville Sun* about the illegal gambling ring that's associated with the murder of Santa Claus. With the holidays coming up, I think they'll like the hook." He pretended to move past her toward the door.

"Sit," Webber said, easing herself down into the chair that he'd pulled out.

"Tell me about your relationship with Dobbs," Lee said when he was seated across from her.

"It wasn't like that. Bertie Dobbs wooed women the way some men play golf, but I wasn't one of them. No, I was one of his lost ducklings. Bertie was friends with my Dad. Dad knew that if he ever needed help, he could count on Bertie."

"Your father asked him to help you?"

"Twenty years ago, I was married to a guy named Bud Waters. We lived down in Tampa. Bud was a super-nice guy. I was lucky to have met him when I was in college. We'd both gone to the University of Florida. I was studying early education and he was in the engineering school." She paused, looking off past Lee to some distant point in her memory.

"Let me guess, this isn't a happily-ever-after story," Lee said by way of encouragement.

"Not hardly. Bud got a job in Tampa working for a large construction company. Being the new guy on the team, he was expected to put in the long hours and extra weekends. Bud loved it. He didn't mean to ignore me. In college, I was always busy either with schoolwork or coming home to help Dad out with his business. I don't think Bud imagined me being bored.

"Thinking back on it, I don't think I'd ever been without something to do for more than an hour before that. The problem started when I couldn't find work right away. I tried. Before that, I'd always been a big fish in a small pond. I didn't know how to be a small fish. With no friends or family around, I was at a loss. I couldn't think of anything else to do but put in my applications and wait."

"Did you talk to your husband?"

"I tried and he tried to understand. He gave me suggestions, but by that point I was depressed and just wanted to go home. Six months in and fate knocked on my door by way of a bubbly woman named Cindy Zinn. What a name. She had just moved into the neighborhood and her moving company was late delivering her boxes. The clothes in her suitcase had gotten wet when we had one of those torrential afternoon thunderstorms and she was wondering if she could borrow some clothes. She offered to buy them if I wasn't comfortable loaning them to a stranger."

"That's pretty bold, to knock on a stranger's door and ask to borrow clothes."

"Bold would be a good description of Cindy. I never met anyone that was more daring. Anyway, her effervescent attitude won me over. I invited her in and took her back to look through my closet. We were close to the same size. She admitted that she'd seen me when I came out to check the mail and figured that my clothes would fit her."

"How did this…"

Webber put her hand up and stopped him. "I'm getting to the problem. It turned out that Cindy worked at the jai alai fronton on Gandy Boulevard between Tampa and St. Pete. After we met, she invited me to come out and watch some of the games. Being bored, I did. Biggest mistake of my life. I was sucked in after a couple of visits to the fronton. I started working there with Cindy. The place was exciting." She paused. "All those Latin men didn't make it less exciting. A few bets and I was hooked. Six months after going to work there, I was betting all the money I earned and then some. I started hiding things from Bud, which led to me growing more distant from him. I was soon hanging out with a player from Venezuela. Everything about it was exhilarating—the gambling, the romance, the sport. After the matches, I was going out with José, who liked to gamble. He knew every underground game in Ybor City."

"Didn't your husband notice?"

"He did, but he was working fourteen-hour days so he didn't have enough energy to fight me. Not until I started running up the bills. At first I was just taking the money for our bills and using it to gamble. When that ran out, I started getting lines of credit. A second mortgage on our house. Funny how you get pulled down into debt. I would win for a week and think everything was going to be fine, then I'd lose and lose and lose until I was in so deep that the only answer was to bet more. It's obvious from the outside that it's crazy, but from the inside everything makes sense."

"At some point you must have known that you were in trouble," Lee said.

"No kidding, Sherlock. The moment of real clarity hit when I came home and found all my stuff on the front lawn."

"Bud kicked you out."

"That was my first thought. Turned out the sheriff had kicked *both* of us out. I'd been hiding the eviction notices for months. On top of my clothes was a note from Bud. He wrote how he loved me, but couldn't live like this."

"And your dad had Dobbs come pick you up?"

"You're getting ahead of yourself, speedy. I wasn't anywhere near rock bottom yet. It took almost another year of living off and on with José. I even went to Venezuela with him once. It was a train wreck of monstrous proportions. Nothing like having two addicts egging each other on. The final straw was when I tried to steal the money out of a cash register at a Farm Store. The cops arrested me. My plan was to just hunker down and take my punishment. As far as I was aware, no one even knew I was in jail. José had taken off with some older woman who promised to keep him in fancy boots. And Dad? I hadn't talked to him in months. My guess is that the cops called him. Anyway, turned out Bertie knew some guys on the force down there, so Dad asked him to come get me out of jail. I must have looked awful."

"Now here you are, the school superintendent. That's a nice rebound."

"Bertie helped me out there too, beginning with a job at the local elementary school." Webber went on to tell the same story that Singleton had about the deal Dobbs had made with them.

"You make him sound like an angel," Lee said.

"Exactly. After all that, I *did* consider him my guardian angel. Every week I was reminded of how much I depended on him to keep me on the straight and narrow."

"What was it like when you found out he'd been killed?"

"I'm still in shock. *What am I going to do?* has been the refrain running through my mind ever since I heard he was dead. And I really don't know." There was a deep melancholy in her words.

"This wasn't an act of God. Someone killed your guardian angel, and I don't think it was Fred Goody."

"I know that," she snapped.

"So who did?"

"You think I wouldn't go to the sheriff if I knew?"

"Maybe you'd be too afraid to expose your elicit gambling," Lee said and was surprised when she burst out laughing.

"I'm sorry, but I'm not the least bit worried that the sheriff will expose us."

"Because Victor Pratt is part of the group?"

"You've done your homework. Precisely because Victor Pratt is a part of our group. The sheriff has been protecting his little brother since the day that spoiled brat was born. Do you think he's going to stop now?"

"Would he subvert a murder investigation in order to protect his brother?"

"In a heartbeat."

"Did Victor kill Hubert Dobbs?"

"I don't know."

"Forget what you know. What do you think?"

"It's not impossible. Victor is as selfish as a man can be. If Bertie was in his way and he thought he could get away with it, Victor is capable of killing someone."

"Who else?"

"I gave up looking into men's souls a long time ago."

"Where were you on Monday night?"

"Now you're playing detective. Lucky for me, I have a good answer. I was at the school board meeting. Dozens of people saw me there."

Lee knew that the school board meetings were held in the courthouse, which was only a five-minute walk from Dobbs's shop. Could she have slipped out for fifteen minutes? He couldn't rule out the possibility.

"Can you think of anyone else who had a motive to kill Dobbs?"

"That's the funny thing. For all of Bertie's weird eccentricities, he didn't have a lot of enemies."

"What about all the men whose wives he slept with?"

"It wasn't like that. He seldom slept with a woman who had a man who cared about her."

"What about women he dumped?" Lee realized they

hadn't discussed this possibility.

"Bertie was a great guy. Women liked to be around him… for a while. His optimism and good humor got old after a while. When he parted from a woman, she was usually ready to end the affair. Everyone went their own way a little richer, but glad to move on."

"Which brings us back to the gamblers."

"Point well made." She nodded.

"And you can't think of a motive for any of them?" Lee asked.

For a moment Lee thought that she hesitated, but then she said, very firmly, "No. Sorry."

"What about Mrs. Goody? Who do you think killed her?"

Again, Lee saw Webber hesitate. Finally, she just shrugged.

They heard the sound of footsteps in the hallway. "Ms. Webber, are you in here?" a woman's voice called.

"Yes, Amanda, I was just discussing some business." She got up and opened the door. A woman wearing a paper turkey hat stood there with a surprised expression on her face. Lee had the devilish thought to pretend like he was tucking in his shirt, but decided not to stir the pot any further.

As he drove home, he thought about his talk with Courtney Webber. It had gone better than he'd expected. *Still, did I get any useful information?* Webber had come across as honest, but like Alton Singleton, she was a politician and hypocrisy was part of her job description. In his head, Lee could hear his father asking him when he had become so cynical.

CHAPTER THIRTEEN

Lee was a block away when he decided not to go home. His other chore of the day was talking to his friend, Glen Doyle, at the morgue in Gainesville. If he went home, he might spend half the day trying to call him and never get through. On the weekend when the morgue was closed, Glen worked mostly as security and he seldom felt any obligation to answer the phone. He handled the occasional delivery or pick-up of a body, but only the most unusual homicides would bring the coroner out, so Glen spent a lot of his time with a book in his hands.

Lee figured that driving to Gainesville and knocking on the door would probably be quicker. A half-hour drive wouldn't be bad on a beautiful fall day. Lee rolled the windows down and turned up the radio. With Hall and Oates singing "Private Eyes," he eased his foot down on the accelerator as he left Lang behind.

The parking area behind the hospital where the morgue's

entrance was located was almost empty. Lee pulled up to the curb where he would normally park the hearse when picking up a body. Lee grabbed the package he'd bought on the way and stuck the funeral sign on the dash.

Two minutes after he pressed the buzzer at the loading dock entrance, the door opened and Glen Doyle looked out suspiciously. Doyle was a former pathologist who had lost his medical license due to an incident he'd never disclosed to Lee.

"My weekend just gets better and better," he said sarcastically, though the smile on his face gave the lie to his words.

"You know you love seeing me."

"For regular pick-ups, sure. It's these unscheduled visits that worry me."

"I want you to break some rules."

"And…" Doyle held out his hand.

"Your toll." Lee handed him the bag.

Doyle reached in and pulled out a bottle of Scotch. "Not top-shelf, but from a cheap bastard like you, I'm glad to get a solid middle-shelf label. Come in, my boy, and tell me what I can do for you."

They settled into the pathologist's office that Doyle used as his own on the weekends. He looked at the bottle and licked his lips before slipping it into his backpack. "Never a good idea to drink on duty."

"Have they done the autopsy on Hubert Dobbs?" Lee asked, getting right to the point.

Doyle opened a notebook and scanned the log inside.

"Did it yesterday." He sorted through a pile of files on the desk and pulled one out. He flipped through it, reading the highlights. "Seems he was literally stabbed in the back by a friend."

"Why do you say a friend?"

"Small knife, a single thrust through the back to the heart. Would you turn your back on an enemy or a stranger? You'd have to be a ninja to sneak up that close to someone in an empty store and stab him in the back."

"You have a good point. We'd assumed it was someone he knew, so I guess I'm glad the autopsy backs up that assumption."

"Let's see…" Doyle scanned the papers. "Some abrasions on his knees, and his forehead took a real knock. I'd say your friend was dead almost before he hit the floor. Not easy to do with a wound to the heart." He scanned some more, then tapped the paper with his forefinger. "There's part of the reason. He twisted a little as he was stabbed, which caused the knife to rip the heart open."

Doyle put the file down and pushed it across the desk to Lee, who opened it and read through the pages of medical jargon. He understood about half of it.

"A sudden, violent attack that killed the victim almost instantly," Lee said. "What's that tell us?"

"A couple of possibilities. Either the attack was planned and professional, or the killer struck out at his victim and was as surprised by the results as the victim. It's also possible that the person intended to kill…" He looked at the name on the file. "…Hubert Dobbs, but that the attack was successful more from luck than skill".

"I don't think any of our suspects is a professional killer, which leaves the last two options."

"You're wise to exclude a professional. Look at the knife." Doyle tapped a picture of the murder weapon. The knife had a black handle and, according to the ruler lying beside it, an eight-inch blade. "That's one of those Ginsu knives you see advertised on TV all the time. If the victim had put up a real fight like we often see in knife attacks, this weapon would have been broken at the haft. A decent enough kitchen knife, but not made for hand-to-hand combat."

"A Ginsu knife. Great, how many of those do you think have been sold around here?"

"How many lonely people are sitting in front of their TVs? You should be able to find out if Dobbs bought one, though. Most people who buy crap off the TV use their credit cards."

Lee nodded. "Good point. Of course, it could have been given to him as a gift. Probably a dead end. We'll be lucky if the detective investigating the murder even thinks to check his credit card records."

"If it was his, that'd tell you the murderer probably didn't plan on killing him when he or she arrived at the store."

Lee looked through the rest of the file without seeing anything that jumped out at him. He gave it back to Doyle, who straightened the papers before putting the file back in the pile on the desk.

"My next question is about Ellen Goody."

"Two bodies and only one bottle of Scotch?" Doyle raised an eyebrow. "Only for a friend." He looked in the log book again. "She's due to be autopsied on Monday."

"Can we take a look?" Lee knew that Doyle could determine a lot just by examining the body.

"Sure. I can pretend to be a medical examiner."

Lee followed him into the autopsy theatre where there was a wall of refrigerated horizontal cabinets.

"Look, they're finally using labels," Doyle grunted, finding Ellen's name on one of the drawers and pulling it open. The distinctly unpleasant odor of burned flesh wafted out of the drawer. When Doyle pulled back the sheet, it revealed an image straight out of a horror film.

Lee had seen worse. He wondered if he would be the one to embalm Mrs. Goody. No chance of an open casket at the funeral, no matter how skilled of a job he did. Most of her face and the right side of her body had been burned. Surprisingly, her left side was barely damaged.

"I've never liked fire victims. I don't know why they bother me more than the ones that come in waterlogged." As he spoke, Doyle snapped on a pair of gloves.

Doyle started by examining Goody's skull.

"I suspect that this is the cause of death," he said, tilting the head enough to show Lee a deep indentation at the back of the skull. "And while I'm not a detective, I'd imagine that the killer might have been trying to cover up the evidence of his attack by burning the victim."

"We'd wondered about that."

"And they were in a hurry, which explains the fact that they didn't even manage to burn the body completely. Not that a house fire is going to get hot enough to burn bones. The Sodder children aside, of course."

"Who?"

"Come on, surely you've heard of the Sodder children?"

"Not a clue," Lee said.

"Just after World War II in West Virginia, sometime around Christmas, a house burned to the ground. A large family lived there and only half of them escaped. There should have been the bodies of five children in the ruins, but no one ever found any trace of them. No bones at all. This led to the parents believing that their children had been kidnapped before the fire was started. I can't disagree. There is no way that five children—the oldest was fourteen—could have burned up completely in the fire."

"I'm glad Mrs. Goody wasn't burned any worse than she was. I wonder what the official version is going to be when the sheriff's office finds out that she was hit on the back of the head. Right now, their theory is that she was killed in the fire she started."

"That turkey don't fly." Doyle smiled and went back to examining the body.

When he was done, they slid the drawer back into place. "I didn't see any other obvious signs of trauma that couldn't be attributed to the fire," he said, stripping off the gloves.

After talking bodies and politics with Doyle for another hour, Lee headed home. Halfway there, he remembered that one of Ruby's cats had dragged home a playing card on the day of the Ward funeral. A chill ran down his spine. Did the cat know that gambling was an element of the murder of Hubert Dobbs?

Don't be ridiculous, he told himself, trying to dismiss the notion. Still, there was an air of weirdness around Ruby that was hard to ignore. The latest revelation that she had hung out in Havana during its pre-revolution heyday didn't do much to change that image.

The sun was sliding behind the trees as he pulled into the driveway. Lester was cleaning out the cabinets in the embalming room when Lee came in through the back door.

"Where have you been?" Lester asked.

"Over to the morgue. I had some questions for Doyle."

"Why don't you ever take me over there when we aren't going for a body?" Lester sounded like a housewife who never gets to go out to a restaurant.

"Sorry, next time," Lee promised.

"It was about the murders, wasn't it?"

"I wanted to check on the condition of the bodies."

"You know I can help."

"I appreciate that."

"I just don't like being squeezed out," Lester pouted.

"Didn't we have this conversation last night?"

"I'm just sayin'."

"What do you think of Ruby's cats?" Lee asked, wanting to change the topic and knowing that Lester hung around

Ruby and her feline friends more than anyone else in the house.

"Yin and Yang? They're smart, I'll tell you that. Sometimes I think they know what I'm saying. Why?"

"Nothing. I just got it into my head that… never mind."

Growing up in a funeral home had never bothered Lee, but now he was beginning to think that it might be messing with his head.

CHAPTER FOURTEEN

While Lee was taking care of his part of the plan, Kay was mounting her own assault on the local Fast Marts in order to get information about Walt Lawson.

There were four of the stores in town. They varied by location and the quality of their clientele. There were two on the main drag running through town, one on the north side and one on the south. Both of those dealt mainly in gasoline and commuters, though the one on the south side was a little less inviting. It had more than its share of people who hung out near the payphones, looking like the bad-guy extras from *Baretta* or *Hill Street Blues*. The third Fast Mart was the one Kay had frequented as a kid. It was located on East Main near the high school and had a steady flow of customers who lived within walking distance. The fourth store was at the interstate exit and dealt almost exclusively with travelers.

Kay decided she'd try her old haunt first. As soon as she walked into the store, a wave of nostalgia hit her. The smell of cleaner, candy and magazines was strong and took her back to the days when all she had worried about were her complexion, her hair and homework.

The woman behind the counter looked vaguely familiar. Kay walked around while the woman waited on a couple of kids buying comics and bubble gum. After they left, Kay picked up a Little Debbie Honey Bun and poured herself a cup of coffee before walking up to the counter. The blonde woman working the cash register was her age and was quick with a smile.

"That all for you, sweetie?" she said, ringing up the Honey Bun and coffee without looking directly at Kay.

"I think I know you?" Kay figured this was as good an opening line as any, whether the woman was someone she knew or not.

The woman stopped and gave Kay a real look for the first time.

"Yeah, you look familiar too," she said as if it were a great revelation.

"I went to school here," Kay prompted.

"Me too. Go Tigers!" She raised her hands in a mock cheer.

"Class of '66."

"Me too! Now I remember you! You're Kay Lamberton!" She pointed to her name tag that said: BEA. "I'm Bea Garland. Well, I'm Bea Matfield now. I should say *for* now, 'cause we're separated. So I'll be Garland again."

The bell over the door rang. Two teenagers came in and bought a six-pack of Mountain Dew and bags of chips. Kay recognized the scent of burned grass that she'd often smelled on the soldiers in Vietnam and suppressed a grin.

"I guess you all needed some snacks." Bea's naivete caused the two boys to start laughing. "I like to see kids having fun." Bea smiled, causing the boys to laugh harder. They managed to put their money on the counter and get their snacks without actually falling to the floor in hysterics.

Once they were out the door, Kay picked up the conversation again.

"You were in my typing class."

"We had driver's ed together too."

"That's right. Why didn't we hang out together?" Kay asked, though she knew the answer. In high school, Bea was part of the cheerleaders while Kay had drifted between the nerds and athletes.

"You're being too nice. I was on the cheerleading squad, and those girls had a list of rules longer than your arm. They practically told me who I could hang out with and who I couldn't. It was sooo stupid. But my momma wanted me to be in that crowd, with all the belles, pompoms and beauty pageants. Momma thought that was the way to a good man and a better life. More the fool her, God bless her."

"I kind of had my own crowd."

"You ran with those smart guys. Vince Edwards, Millie Jessup and Rick Bruhn." Her face took on a look of horror and she put her hand over her heart. "The murders this spring! That's right, you were kinda involved in all that. It was awful!"

"So you're working at our old Fast Mart," Kay said, not wanting to talk about any of that. Besides, she wanted to get the conversation back on track before more customers came in. As if the mere thought had conjured them, two cars pulled up outside.

Fifteen minutes later, Kay and Bea were alone again.

"That's the way it is sometimes. Customers always come in waves," Bea said.

"When did you start working here?"

"Almost a year now. Just after my husband moved out. My momma watches the boys while I work. I actually kinda like it."

"Isn't it kind of a hard job?"

"Honey, this is miles above the Fast Mart on the south side. I told Walt after a week down there that I couldn't do it. Drunks coming in all hours of the day. I was always dealing with one mess or another. This is like home. I live four blocks away, so I can walk if the weather's nice."

"Walt?" Kay asked innocently.

"He's the owner."

"If he moved you to this store, he must not be too bad of a guy."

"Yeah, for a boss. I could do a lot worse. I've *had* worse. Let. Me. Tell. You."

Bea looked ready to share stories of former bosses when Kay was only interested in the current one. "Did Walt own the Fast Marts when we were in school?" she asked quickly.

"No. It used to be the guy that runs the real estate office downtown. About eight years ago, he got tired of running things and sold the stores to Walt."

"I don't think I've ever met Walt… What's his last name?"

"Lawson. He's related to the Lawsons who own the FRM mill south of town."

"How old is he?"

"Forty-something. Older than us, but he carries it very well." She winked.

"Is he married?"

"Don't think that wasn't the first question I asked." Bea gave her a big smile. "Unfortunately, not only is he married, but the wife is a looker."

More customers came in, and Kay figured she'd milked Bea for as much information as she could without making her suspicious. Considering the odds, Kay thought she'd done well. It was time to move on. She made promises to talk to Bea again soon, then left the store.

The Fast Mart on the north side of town was her next target. That proved a bust when the two clerks working there were juggling restocking with waiting on the numerous customers who constantly came and went. Kay left without having a chance to speak to either clerk.

She chose the south side store for her next scouting attempt. She didn't want to spend a lot of time there, but felt the need to stop in out of a sense of completeness.

The store was on the end of a mini strip mall that also had a coin laundry and a pawn shop. There was the expected group of odd and suspicious characters hanging out by the payphones as she got out of her car and hurried inside.

The man behind the counter looked to be in his thirties with brown hair and a cleft chin that reminded Kay of Kirk Douglas. When she entered, he was busy handling customers who were almost exclusively buying beer or cigarettes.

She watched him work, looking for an opportunity to engage him in conversation. The opportunity presented itself in the form of a coffee machine that was out of coffee. Kay walked to the counter holding an empty cup.

"Could I get some coffee?"

"The pot is in the back," he said while he placed a beer can in a bag and handed it to a customer who looked like he'd already had his share that day.

"It's empty," Kay said apologetically.

The man looked up. "Give me a minute."

"No problem," she said and wandered back toward the coffee machine.

A lull in customers arrived five minutes later. The clerk hurried out from behind the counter and over to where Kay waited by the empty machine.

"I appreciate this," she said while he dug out coffee and some clean filters from a cabinet under the counter.

"Coffee isn't this store's biggest seller," he said, refilling the machine as he talked.

"The owner must do pretty well… depending on the profit margin for beer." Kay smiled.

"We do all right," he said, which she thought was an odd way of phrasing it.

"We?"

"Sorry." He looked at her and stuck out his hand. "Walt Lawson, owner."

She shook his hand, trying to reconcile Bea's statement that the owner was in his forties with the man in front of her, who didn't look much older than herself.

"You look mighty young to be running this business."

Lawson grinned. "I'm forty-two."

"You must jog or something."

"Hard work. The stores keep me busy."

"I'm Kay Lamberton," she said, sticking out her hand. He took it and gave her a couple of shakes.

"You aren't one of the funeral home Lambertons?"

"I confess I am. Funeral homes don't scare you, do they?" She knew he was married, but there was no harm in flirting.

"I've always respected the business. I've gone to several funerals that… I guess your father handled. They were well done."

Their conversation was interrupted by a middle-aged woman buying Coke and potato chips.

"We're handling the Dobbs funeral," Kay said when he'd finished checking out the woman. Kay watched him closely for any reaction to the name. He never flinched.

"Dobbs was an interesting guy," was all he said.

"I'd like a chance to talk to you when you aren't running a cash register," Kay said.

He looked at her curiously. "I'm flattered, but I'm married."

"You have no reason to be flattered. I want to talk to you about Hubert Dobbs's murder." As soon as the words were out of her mouth, Kay could feel the temperature between them drop twenty degrees.

"I don't know why you would want to talk to me about that." He tried to make it sound casual, but failed as she watched his fists clench and unclench.

"Because you played poker with him every Wednesday night, and that's not all…"

"This is…" He started to protest before a look of resignation took over. "Fine. My regular clerk was running late and should be here in a couple of minutes. We can talk in back when he gets here."

Twenty minutes later, Kay and Lawson were face to face in a cramped office in the back of the store.

"I don't know what you think you know, but I'm not one to put up with threats."

"All we want is to find Dobbs's killer."

"We?"

"Me, my brother and Dobbs's daughter."

Kay saw his muscles relax. "Alison. Bertie talked about her sometimes. He helped me with a… problem I had. I always thought that someday I might be able to repay him by getting them together. Bertie never talked about regret except when he talked about her. I'd like to meet her."

"I don't see why not. I would assume you'll be at the funeral."

"I hadn't thought about it."

"You were friends, weren't you?"

"This may sound odd, but I never thought of him as a friend. He was more like a mentor… or maybe a fellow traveler. We had some of the same vices."

"You can stop beating around the bush. I know about your gambling problem." Admittedly, Kay was making an assumption, but after hearing Alton Singleton's story, she figured it was a safe one.

"I was kicked out of my family because I gambled away a savings account and stole money from the business. They were going to have me arrested. My own parents. The only thing that stood between me and public humiliation was Bertie Dobbs. My mother was related to him, second cousin by marriage or some such. Anyway, he came to some of our family get-togethers. At one of these, he overheard my parents arguing about my problem and he offered to talk to me."

"Let me guess. He said he'd let you gamble at his place every week if that was the only time and place you gambled."

"Yes, and he held the purse strings when it came to betting. I didn't have a choice, so..." He shrugged.

"Seems you've done okay for yourself."

"That's another funny thing about it. I wasn't even interested in running a store until I helped him out with the appliance store for a year. He showed me how to keep the books, do my taxes, figure out what price I needed to sell items to make a profit. He put me through a hometown MBA."

"I'm surprised that he was able to convince all of you to only gamble under his watchful eye. Weren't you tempted to place a few bets with your own bookie, or go to a card game that Dobbs didn't run?"

"Tempted maybe." Lawson shrugged.

"It's almost like he had some hold over you." Kay thought she saw him give her a sideways glance. Suspicion? Guilt? She couldn't tell what he was thinking.

"After the first year, it was clear to me that I needed him. My life had completely turned around. I owed that to him, and the steady hand he used to guide me on the right path."

He sounds almost like a cult member talking about his guru, Kay thought. Aloud, she said, "You must want to find his killer as much as we do."

"I thought the sheriff had arrested some guy and that his wife was killed trying to cover up evidence."

"That's what the sheriff says," Kay said dismissively.

"And you don't believe it?"

"You do know you play poker with the sheriff's brother, right?"

Lawson looked like he'd eaten a very large sour pickle.

"You're suggesting that the sheriff is protecting his brother?"

"Is that hard to believe?"

"No."

"Do you know anyone who had a grudge against Dobbs?"

Lawson shook his head. "He didn't hurt people. The womanizing was a... flaw. Still, he was careful. When I worked in the store and some customer came in with an unreasonable complaint, you know what he told me to do? He told me to do whatever they wanted, but then to never do business with them again. That avoided the conflict and got rid of the problem. It worked, and I've told my clerks and store managers to do the same. Solve the problem in their favor and then don't do business with the person again. Be non-confrontational."

"It's still difficult to get away from the jealous boyfriend or husband angle," Kay mused. "What about your group? None of your fellow gamblers had any issues with him?"

"Not that I know of. We're all worse off now that he's dead. We have to find a way to handle our addiction without his help."

Kay thought he looked genuinely melancholy at the prospect of not having Dobbs in his life anymore.

They talked for a few more minutes and Kay had him

promise to call if he thought of anything that might help.

"I'll be at the funeral," he assured her as she left the store.

Kay was conflicted as she drove back home. After talking to the gamblers that Dobbs had taken under his wing, she wondered if they *should* have been concentrating on that little black book. However, the thought of tracking down all those women was overwhelming. How long would that take? *Way past Jerome's deadline, that's for sure*, Kay thought.

Then there was what they had found last night. Who was digging up Dobbs's yard and why? How did that fit into the murders?

When she got back to the funeral home, she went into the office and closed the door. Over the last six months she'd found that going over the business's accounting books was soothing, even if the totals didn't always add up the way she wished. But the numbers were the numbers; there was nothing subjective. No people to figure out or emotions to deal with. It was oddly relaxing.

CHAPTER FIFTEEN

Hours later, there was a knock on the office door.

"Can I come in?" Lee asked.

After the siblings compared notes, they grew quiet.

"So what now?" Kay asked.

"Maybe we've shaken the tree and a clue will fall out."

"I'm not sure we're shaking the right tree. I've been wondering if we need to look harder at all those affairs Dobbs had."

"I wondered that myself. But if the murderer is in the black book, it's going to take a long time to ferret him out," Lee argued.

"And what the hell is up with those holes in Dobbs's back yard?"

Lee snapped his fingers. "I've got an idea."

"I don't like that look in your eyes."

"I'll be right back."

Lee found Lester trying to fix one of the lamps that stood on either side when a casket was in the viewing room.

"Leave that and come with me," Lee told him, directing Lester toward the office.

"We need you to help us out tonight," he said, once they were both standing in front of Kay.

"Sure, anything," Lester said eagerly.

Lee explained about the intruder who had been in Dobbs's yard the night before. "I want you to stake the place out and let us know if someone comes around again tonight."

"Coooool," Lester said. "Is someone going to loan me a gun?"

"No!" Lee and Kay said in unison.

"You just watch, see if anyone comes back, then call us," Lee instructed.

"How do I do that?"

"I think Mr. Martelli, one of the neighbors, might let you use his phone. I'll check."

"Thanks! I won't let you all down. Ummm… who am I looking for?"

"Anyone walking around the Dobbs ruins," Lee said.

"Okay." Lester nodded.

After they'd sent him out of the room, Kay gave Lee a questioning look. "You think this is a good idea?"

"I don't think he can do too much harm."

"It could be dangerous."

"I'll give him specific instructions. I know he acts like a big kid most of the time, but he's not."

"No weed."

"That will be part of the specific instructions," Lee assured her.

Ruby came to the office door and shouted through it. "Alison is here! She said you invited her to dinner." There was mild chastisement in her words. Ruby's rule was that if someone beyond the usual suspects was expected at dinner, she was to be told ahead of time.

"Sorry. Tell her to come in." Lee tried his best not to sound like a ten-year-old caught with his hand in the cookie jar.

When Alison came into the office, Kay took note of the look that passed between her and Lee. *Cupid has been tossing arrows around*, she thought.

"I talked to Mom," Alison said. "She still won't talk about Dad, but she did give me the name of a distant cousin. They live in Tennessee. I'm going to see if I can find them."

Lee and Kay filled her in on what they'd learned and the plan to have Lester stake out what was left of her father's house.

"I don't know what they could have been looking for," Alison said. "Will he be safe?"

"Sure," Lee said, giving her a reassuring smile. "Lester isn't very tough, but he's resilient. I've seen him do crazy stuff and come out without a scratch. As long as he doesn't confront the person, he'll be fine."

Moments after they sat down to dinner, Jerome popped in through the back door.

"What a surprise. It's dinnertime and you show up," Lee said good-naturedly.

"Us bachelors need to eat too. Besides, I got some…" He tapped the side of his nose.

Lee and Kay looked at each other while Lester and Ruby did a poor job of pretending not to care.

"Do you have time to eat first?" Lee asked, taking note of the fact that Jerome was still in uniform. Normally, he only wore it if he was still on duty.

"I'll grab something and we can go somewhere to talk," Jerome said, filling a bowl with Ruby's thick, hearty chili.

"That's just fine. I do all the cooking, but I don't need to be in on the secrets," Ruby said with half a smile.

Lee looked around the table and realized that Lester and Ruby had managed to insinuate themselves into the investigation, despite his and Kay's best efforts.

"What the hell," Kay said, having come to the same conclusion. "You may as well tell everyone."

Lee looked around the table and said, "Nothing about the murders or our little private investigation leaves this room. Cross your hearts and hope to die."

Ruby nodded while Lester did the full heart-crossing gesture.

"Okay, tell us what you've got, Jerome," Lee said.

"All of your gambling friends have serious money problems of one sort or another," Jerome said before spooning chili into his mouth.

"I guess Bertie's rehabilitation program didn't work so well," Lee said

"It's not like the economy is on fire. A lot of people are having problems right now," Kay pointed out.

"True," Lee said, then looked at Jerome. "How did you find out?"

"I told you Martin Townsend would be willing to help if he thought it would trip up Sutton. Actually, he was beyond enthusiastic. We ran a credit check on all of them. They're all at least five figures in debt and have missed payments on different credit lines in the past two years. Lawson's credit is the worst, but he also has the most assets. Singleton has been propped up by his family. I got that by talking to a confidential informant I've got at the Lang State Bank. All of them are living on the financial edge."

"Seems a little thin. The funeral home is on the edge too," Kay said, then noticed the looks that everyone was giving her. She backpedaled a bit. "Not really, really close to the edge. As long as we keep business coming in we'll be okay." Everyone leaned back in their chairs. "What I meant was, being in debt doesn't give you much motive to kill a guy who's been helping you out with your gambling problem."

"Unless the person felt like they were being cheated, or they just wanted to be able to go on a gambling binge without all the judgment," Jerome said.

"We're still missing a piece of the puzzle," Lee sighed.

"Several pieces," Kay said. "Why was Ellen Goody at Dobbs's house and why did someone kill her? Who's digging up the yard and why?"

"Maybe those two questions are related," Alison suggested. "Like maybe he hid something valuable."

"Or something incriminating. Like the little black book. Goody might have known about the book and wanted to get it back because it had her name in it," Lee said.

"One of the others might have wanted the book to use as a tool to blackmail someone," Jerome said.

"I don't like that," Kay argued. "Because if the black book is what everyone is looking for, then I'm the reason Mrs. Goody couldn't find it and possibly the reason a frustrated killer hit her over the head."

"But if the killer wanted to use the black book, then why burn the place down? That looks more like it was another person whose name is in the book. If they couldn't find it, they might have burned the house down to make sure it was destroyed," Lee said.

"The Holy Grail," Ruby murmured. "It destroyed all those who looked for it."

"I don't think we're looking for a golden chalice," Lee said.

"It may be made of wood. That's what a humble carpenter would have had at the Last Supper. I saw an episode of *In Search of* and Leonard Nimoy was talking about all these different grails that people think are the real one," Lester said.

"That's true," Ruby agreed, and the two of them began an animated discussion about the Holy Grail. Lee and Kay exchanged looks, amused at how the conversation had gone off the rails, but happy enough not to be talking about murders for a while.

When everyone had finished eating, Lee told Jerome of their plan to leave Lester out by the Dobbs house that night.

"Sure, why not?" Jerome said, looking at Lester appraisingly. Lee couldn't tell if he was being sarcastic or not.

"I need some kind of weapon," Lester insisted. His original enthusiasm had worn off a bit.

"A piece of pipe. That'd be the best thing," Jerome said. Lee still couldn't tell if he was being serious, but his face implied he was.

"We'll find you something in the carport. But remember, it's for defense only. You want to stay hidden and call me if you see anything," Lee said.

Lester nodded.

"I'm going out for a few hours. If you need me, I'll be back by midnight," Kay told them.

"A date?" Ruby asked archly.

"Nothing so exciting. I'm going to see *Dead & Buried* with Zach," Kay said. She'd become reacquainted with Zach Terrill, an old high school friend, when she'd returned home in the spring. Since then, they'd been exploring a relationship, but Kay was insistent on taking things slow and she wasn't yet ready to consider him a boyfriend. Unfortunately, everyone else already was.

"Nothing exciting. I hope none of my dates describe me that way," Jerome snickered.

At ten o'clock, Lee and Alison drove Lester over to Mr. Martelli's house. He was more than willing to let Lester use his phone if he needed.

"Sure, no problem," Mr. Martelli told them. "I don't like no one creeping around the neighborhood. Bad enough we've had a murder and fire next door. Come on, I'll show you the phone that I got in the garage you can use."

He walked them around the side of the house and opened the door into the garage. "I'll leave the light off so they won't see it when you come inside. The phone's right here on the wall."

After Martelli left them alone, Lee looked Lester up and down, assessing his readiness for the stakeout. He was wearing a coat against the chilly November night and carried a bag generously stuffed with snacks from Ruby, as well as a flashlight. Stuck in his belt was an eight-inch piece of lead pipe they'd found in the funeral home's carport.

"You remember what I told you," Lee said. "Stay out of sight and call if you see anything."

"Yep," Lester said confidently.

"Do you think he'll be okay?" Alison asked once they'd left Lester hunting for the perfect observation point.

"He'll be fine," Lee said, trying to convince himself that what they were doing was safe. *Lester isn't as dumb as he acts most of the time, but he can overestimate his own abilities. That and the fact that he has a strong desire to prove himself could get him into trouble,* Lee thought. *On the other hand, odds are no one is going to come tonight so we're worrying about nothing.*

"I'll probably stay awake all night listening for the phone," Lee finally admitted. Alison took his hand and squeezed it. In an instant, all concerns about Lester left his mind.

Lee went to bed around midnight. He'd spent an enjoyable evening with Alison, discussing her father's funeral arrangements. To most people, that wouldn't have been a way to spend a romantic evening, but for Lee it felt very intimate to show Alison what his job entailed.

He left his bedroom door open a crack so he'd be better able to hear the phone ring if Lester needed help. As he climbed into bed, he heard Kay come up to her room. Glad to know his sister was home, he fell into a deep sleep that wasn't interrupted until the phone began to ring at two o'clock.

Stumbling into the hall, he picked up the phone and heard Lester's hushed voice.

"Someone is walking around the house with a flashlight."

"Just one person?"

"I think so. I don't know where he came from. I didn't see a car."

"Stay close enough so you can keep an eye on them without being caught. I'll be there in a minute." Lee hung up, then jumped when Kay spoke behind him.

"I'm going with you."

Five minutes later, they were backing out of the driveway.

"We need to be careful," Lee said, stating the obvious, as much as a reminder to himself as to Kay.

As they had the night before, they parked down the road from Dobbs's house. This time they were careful to look around, knowing that the trespasser must have parked somewhere close by. Silently, they crept down the sidewalk toward the ruins of the house.

"I see a light!" Lee said excitedly in a hoarse whisper.

"Quiet."

Suddenly the light ahead of them flipped right and left, then came straight at them. They were only about a hundred feet from the house and the figure running toward them was closing the distance quickly.

Another person came barreling down Martelli's driveway.

Lee was distracted by the second figure, who turned out to be Lester, pinwheeling his arms and running at breakneck speed.

"He saw me!"

Meanwhile, Kay had kept her eyes on the light, which started to veer away from her. She moved quickly to intercept it. Her timing was off, but not by much. She put her shoulder into the figure and sent the man sliding across the asphalt road and into the opposite gutter. Off balance, she hit the pavement on her knees.

When she looked up, Lee and Lester were standing over the man, whose flashlight had blown apart when it hit the street.

"What the hell were you looking for?" Lee asked Alton Singleton, who was slowly trying to stand up.

"Anything that might implicate me in the gambling ring," Singleton told him.

"I'm fine, if anyone cares," Kay said, still on the ground as she flexed her ankle and brushed some of the dirt off her clothes. Standing up, she said, "We should probably step out of the road." She heard a car in the distance, but the street was quiet and deserted.

"She's right." Lee reached down and helped Singleton up.

"I know who killed Mrs. Goody," Singleton told him matter-of-factly.

Lee had been ready to step out of the gutter and into the street when Singleton dropped this revelation on him. He stopped and stared at the other man, the sound of an approaching car not registering with him. They were under a streetlight and not in the road. The car slowly came closer, but Lee ignored it as he waited for Singleton to elaborate.

In a flash, everything changed. Lee caught the motion of the car behind Singleton as the vehicle swerved toward them and accelerated.

Lee moved toward the curb, pulling Singleton with him. If the car hadn't been trying to run them down, this probably would have been enough to get them both in the clear. However, the Chevy Nova—Lee thought it strange that he noticed the make of the car as it plowed toward him—corrected for their evasive tactics. It caught Lee's side and flung him into an azalea bush.

Alton Singleton wasn't that lucky. He was tossed onto the hood of the car and rolled off the passenger side, only to be sideswiped by the rear of the vehicle as it accelerated and made its escape down the street.

CHAPTER SIXTEEN

Lee lay dazed and tangled in the azalea bush. After what felt like seconds but was actually more than five minutes, he became aware of a sharp pain in his side and the sound of someone calling his name.

"Lee, can you hear me?" It was Kay.

"Yeah, I'm okay," he mumbled, struggling to get out of the bush. He gritted his teeth and stumbled. "My hip is killing me."

"Take it easy. Here, lean on me."

"What about Singleton?"

"He's dead," Kay said flatly. "I did what I could, but..." What she didn't mention was the old rush of adrenaline and anxiety she'd felt, reminding her of all the times in the Army when the casualties had demanded miracles that she couldn't give them.

"Son of... He was going to tell me who killed Ellen Goody."

"It's okay. He told me before he died. He said he saw

Courtney Webber going into the house after we left that night."

Lee shook his head. "Webber? She wouldn't have been my first choice."

"I don't think he was lying," Kay said as they hobbled across the street. Lee looked down at Singleton's body as they passed it. He was lying on his side with blood pooled around him and his legs bent back at an impossible angle.

"The cops?" Lee asked.

"Lester's already called them." As if on cue, the sound of sirens rang out in the distance and grew steadily louder.

"What are we going to tell them?" Lester asked, shifting his weight from foot to foot nervously.

"The truth. Or at least, most of it," Lee said. "Martelli called us about lights at Dobbs's house. We came over to investigate last night and decided to watch the place again tonight. From there, we just tell them what happened."

"What about the part where he told me who killed Ellen Goody?" Kay asked.

"Give it to 'em. If they can solve this, more power to them. I'm not sure how gung-ho I am for another round with our killer." Lee's hip was throbbing, along with his head.

Half a dozen patrol cars and a depressingly familiar unmarked Crown Victoria rolled up to the scene. An ambulance wasn't far behind. Lee could hear Wade Sutton's voice bullying the patrol officers.

"Great," Kay muttered.

"What the hell hap—" Sutton started to say before he saw Singleton's body. "Mother of all the freight trains coming down the tracks, that's Alton Singleton. Damn it!" He yanked his radio off his belt. "Eli, get the sheriff and tell him we need him out here. It's a four alarm if ever there was one." After a little back-and-forth, he clipped the radio back onto his belt.

"What's his problem?" Sutton asked Kay, pointing at Lee.

"He was hit by the same car that killed Singleton."

"Hey, I'm right here. I can talk for myself," Lee said.

"Oh yeah, you're goin' to do some talking. What are you all doin' out here in the middle of the night?"

Lee told him.

"There were lights in the back yard?" Sutton sounded unconvinced. "Why didn't anyone call us?"

"Mr. Martelli did."

"Bullshit!" Sutton jerked the radio off his belt again. "Eli, have there been any calls about trespassers at the Dobbs house?"

Eli answered in the affirmative and gave the date and time, as well as Martelli's name as the person who'd called it in.

"Why in the holy hell wasn't I told about that?" Sutton shouted loud enough that Eli probably could have heard him without the radio. "Never mind."

Eli informed him that the sheriff was en route. The yelling got going for real once he showed up.

"You two," Sheriff Tom Pratt said in disgust as he stared at Lee and Kay. Lee was lying on a stretcher with Kay standing by his side. The EMT tending to him discreetly backed away. "I heard the flimsy story you gave to Sutton. What's clear is that you're meddling in another murder investigation."

"We're just trying to help out Dobbs's daughter." Kay met his eyes, refusing to back down.

"You're morticians, not detectives. Stay out of my business."

"If you did your business, we would." Kay knew she shouldn't be poking the bear, but Pratt and Sutton had her hackles up.

"How dare you! I can arrest both of you right now for obstruction of justice and probably several more things."

Listening to their exchange from the stretcher, Lee just prayed that the sheriff wouldn't arrest him until his hip had been X-rayed. His sister's next comment did nothing for his hopes.

"I don't think you want to do that," Kay said, her voice low.

"And why not?" Pratt leaned toward her, his nose less than a foot from Kay's.

"Because then it would become common knowledge that your brother is mixed up in three murders and a gambling ring," Kay said menacingly.

The sheriff looked like his head was about to explode. His cheeks were puffed, his face flushed and his mouth clenched tight. "What are you talking about?" he said in a surprisingly soft voice.

"You know exactly what I'm talking about. That's why you assigned your chimpanzee to the case." Kay flung her hand out in the general direction of Sutton, who was overseeing the liberal application of crime-scene tape.

Sheriff Pratt looked indecisive for the first time that night. His eyes darted right and left and he licked his lips.

"Okay, smartass, let me make this clear. If one word of this libel gets out, I'll know exactly who to come hunting."

"No."

"What the hell do you mean, no?"

"We aren't going to play it that way. Here's what's going to happen. You're going to let Lee and me look into these murders without interference from you or that." She nodded toward Sutton.

"What right do you have to be digging into my murder investigation?" the sheriff demanded.

"The killer just tried to murder *us*. So I think that gives us some rights. Let me ask *you* a question." Kay's hands were on her hips now. "Do you seriously think Wade Sutton is going to solve anything?"

The sheriff's jaw worked back and forth. He seemed stymied by the question.

"I'll take that for a no. If your bother isn't involved, then the best thing that can happen is for the real murderer to be caught. We can do that. I'll add that we can do it without any media scrutiny. We find the murderer, he's yours. As long as he or she is prosecuted, we don't care what story you spin. We won't mention your brother if you don't."

Sheriff Pratt took some time considering this. Lee knew he was trying to figure out all the angles. Lee also knew that, if the sheriff determined that the best thing for the Pratts would be to lock Lee and Kay up and throw away the key, they'd be in the back seat of a patrol car within minutes.

"You have until the end of the week," the sheriff said, pointing a finger at Kay. "I want to see some results by then. If my brother's name gets associated with this mess…"

"We need to talk with him and Milton Campbell," Kay pushed.

"Do it! And I'm going to come by the funeral home for a report whenever I damn well please. Is that understood?"

"You're always welcome." Kay kept the sarcasm to a minimum, not wanting to screw up the concessions she'd managed to secure.

"Sheriff, can we get to the body?" The coroner's assistants had arrived and were snapping on latex gloves.

"Our photographer isn't done yet," Sheriff Pratt snapped. He turned back to Kay and Lee. "I've got my eye on you two. Sutton will need to formally interview you about the hit-and-run. You said it was a Chevrolet Nova?"

Lee nodded. "Blue. I didn't notice anything else as I was

flying through the air."

The sheriff ignored Lee's comment and went off to talk to Sutton.

"You were taking quite a chance," Lee said to Kay.

"Not much of one since he was already threatening to throw us in jail."

"True."

The EMT walked back over when he saw the sheriff leave. "You need some X-rays." He turned to Kay. "We're taking him to Alachua General."

"I'll be right behind you," she assured Lee.

After two hours in the emergency room, it was determined that Lee was badly bruised, but not broken, so they gave him a mild painkiller and kicked him out of the hospital.

"We've got a lot of work to do," Kay said as she drove back to Melon County. "You really didn't get a look at the driver?"

"I was a little busy trying not to die. You had a better opportunity to see the driver than I did."

"Remember that I was still recovering from tackling Singleton. I'd just gotten out of the road myself, and by the time I turned around, it was too late."

"It happened really, really fast," Lester said from the back seat.

"Why didn't you drop him off at the funeral home before you came to the hospital?" Lee asked.

"I wanted to make sure you were okay," Lester said, stung.

"Besides, I didn't know if I'd need someone to help lift you into or out of the car," Kay added.

"Did you get any good painkillers?" Lester asked.

"Stay away from my drugs," Lee warned. He turned back to Kay. "I noticed you didn't tell the sheriff about

Singleton's deathbed accusation against Courtney Webber."

"What's the point? It's hearsay and, at least for a few days, we're the ones looking into the murders."

"I'm feeling very rogue." Lee nodded, also feeling a bit woozy from the painkillers. "Do we go straight to Webber?"

"I was thinking we should talk to Pratt and Campbell first. The more background we have when we approach her, the better."

"I really didn't have Webber pegged as a killer. Do you think Singleton could have been wrong?"

Kay looked thoughtful. "I believe that he saw Webber come out of Dobbs's house after we'd been over there. I'm not sure that makes her a killer."

"A lot of people sure are interested in that house, even now that it's burned down," Lester observed.

"You're right. I wish Singleton had been able to tell us what he was really doing there." She glanced over her shoulder at Lester. "You haven't told us what he was doing or how he saw you."

"I saw his light going over the back yard and up around what's left of the house. I thought I could tell who he was if I got closer. I guess I got too close."

"I guess you did." Kay shook her head.

"Who do we talk to first, Pratt or Campbell?" Lee asked.

"You take Pratt and I'll take Campbell," Kay said.

"Ladies always go for the firemen." Lester chuckled.

"I'll show you who's a lady," Kay said, holding her fist in the air. "Fine, Lee will talk to Campbell."

"I hope I'm able to move tomorrow," Lee said, rubbing the spot on his hip where the car had caught him.

"It *is* tomorrow," Kay said, pointing to the blue line emerging across the eastern horizon as they drove into Lang.

Lee sat up in bed, but the pain caused him to drop back down almost immediately. He'd passed out as soon as his head hit the pillow and he'd only woken up when the clock radio he'd set for eleven started blaring KC and the Sunshine Band. He made another attempt to get up, groaning through the intense pain as he stood and hobbled to the bathroom.

Dressed, he walked slowly down the stairs, gripping the banister for support and hoping that he could get some food and have a little time to wake up before people started talking to him. But luck wasn't on his side.

"I was just coming up to get you. Mr. Hartfield died in hospice this morning. We need to go pick him up." Lester met him at the bottom of the stairs and spoke in a voice several decibels louder than Lee was prepared for.

"Crap," he moaned. "I'll get ready in—"

"You don't have to go. Jerome is here."

Jerome came out of the kitchen carrying a cup of coffee.

"Y'all are really trying to get me fired now. But when I heard you had put on your own private Evel Knievel show last night, I figured you might need a little help."

"Thanks, Jerome. I'll fill you in on everything when you get back."

"Don't bother, I told him what happened," Lester said.

"I'll tell you my side of the story," Lee said and limped toward the kitchen. He turned back to Jerome. "I *do* appreciate you coming over."

"I'm on the clock," Jerome said and handed him his empty coffee cup before following Lester into the embalming room and out the back door.

"Take Bertha!" Lee yelled to them. Lester and Jerome had a bad habit of using the new hearse when Bertha could do the job just as well.

Ruby was cleaning the kitchen when he came in and stumbled to the pot of coffee. As he poured a cup, he heard the new Cadillac engine roar to life and cursed under his breath.

"I heard you went dancing with a car last night," Ruby said.

"You should see the other guy." Lee regretted that comment as soon as he said it. "That's the drugs talking. It was pretty awful. I know that Singleton really wanted to meet you again. I'm sorry that didn't happen."

"We all have a destiny. Though a part of me would have liked to talk with him and reminisce about Havana in the old days."

"I think it was quick, if that's any consolation."

"Kay told me all about it."

"She's up already?" Lee was impressed.

"Said she had some chores to take care of."

"Good for her. The woman's a tank." He groaned as he sat down at the table. His hip was on fire.

"You have two messages, both of them from your lady friend, Alison. She wants you to call her as soon as you get up."

"You didn't tell her about the… accident?"

"I just said that you'd had a little accident and were resting. Go call her before I put the bread in the toaster."

Painfully, he got back to his feet and went over to the phone. He gave Alison the broad outlines and told her to come over for dinner.

As he dropped back down in the chair, Ruby asked, "Eggs?"

"No. Just toast and cereal."

Ruby busied herself at the sink. "Two of the gamblers are dead now. You've got to ask yourself what sort of stakes they were playing for. My friend, Sandy, has a weight problem. Always dieting. The only way she can convince herself to stay on her diet is to give herself a little reward when she meets her goals. Thanksgiving is just around the corner. I've got most of the menu done, but if there's anything special you want, let me know in the next day or two."

"Hopefully you won't have to bring it down to the county jail," Lee said, not even bothering to try to make sense of the rest of what Ruby had said.

An hour later, with breakfast and another pain pill in his belly, Lee was feeling better.

Jerome and Lester had returned from the nursing home with Mr. Ron Hartfield. Lee had given them a hard time about taking the new hearse as they guided the client safely into the cooler. He'd embalm him that afternoon. His nephew just wanted a small graveside service the next day. Closed casket. Nothing that demanded too much multitasking.

Lee had expected to be grilled by Jerome about everything that had happened the night before, but he'd hurried away for Sunday lunch with his mother. He'd left Lee with the promise of a full debrief later.

"Where have you been?" Lee asked Kay as he passed her in the hall on the way to get his keys.

"I did a little recon. Drove by all of our suspects' houses to see if there was any sign of a blue Chevy Nova." She held up her hand. "You don't need to ask. No luck. I didn't expect any, but you never know."

"It was a good idea."

"I half wondered if our killer might not try to frame one of the other players by leaving the car at or near their house."

"We're in Florida," Lee reminded her. "That car is probably at the bottom of a river or sinkhole by now."

"I wonder where it came from."

"Stealing a car isn't that hard. Question is: Did they go to

Dobbs's house planning on killing Alton Singleton?"

"Maybe they followed him," Kay speculated.

"Could be. Or they were there and saw Singleton and decided to take advantage of the situation."

"If Courtney Webber is the killer, did she know that he had seen her the morning of the fire?"

"Another murder and all we've got are more questions. I'm going to try and track down Campbell," Lee said.

"I'll go talk to Victor Pratt later this afternoon. Depending on what we find out, we should talk to Courtney Webber sooner rather than later. We can use what Singleton told me as leverage."

CHAPTER SEVENTEEN

Milton Campbell's house was a brick ranch-style, built in the middle of a two-acre lot with sprawling live oak trees and azaleas that would burst into a riot of pink, purple and red come spring. No one answered the door, so Lee waited in his car, hoping that Campbell was only out to church and Sunday lunch and would be home shortly. He decided to give him until one-thirty before he checked at the fire station.

Lee had his hand on the wheel, ready to drive away, when a Ford Econoline van pulled into the driveway and Campbell's family piled out. They looked like an advertisement for the modern nuclear family. Campbell was six feet tall with blond hair and a nice tan, even in November. His wife was a petite brunette who laughed at least three times between the van and the house. The boy and girl carried Bibles and a few pieces of paper each. No doubt some artwork they'd done during Sunday school.

Lee decided to give them twenty minutes to change and

relax before knocking on the door. Just as he opened the door of the car, the garage door rose and Milton Campbell, dressed in jeans and a T-shirt now, stood looking out at the neighborhood. Behind him was a CJ-7 Jeep and an assortment of boy toys.

He noticed Lee and watched as he approached. Lee lifted his arm and waved. Campbell gave him a hesitant wave back as Lee made a beeline toward him.

"Hi, I'm Lee Lamberton. I own the funeral home in town." Lee decided that a full introduction was called for.

"The funeral home guy. Yeah, okay." Campbell gave him a genuine smile and came forward with his hand out. "I know being a fireman is dangerous work, but I didn't expect the local funeral home to send out the boss to solicit my business." He was pumping Lee's hand now.

"I'm not here on funeral business. I wanted to ask you some questions about Hubert Dobbs's murder." Lee watched the smile drop off Campbell's face as he released his hand.

"I don't understand why you would be asking me any questions about that," Campbell said, his face wide and innocent.

"Because you played poker with him every Wednesday night."

Campbell stared at Lee while he let the silence draw out. He wanted to force Campbell into addressing his connection to Dobbs.

"Playing poker with someone doesn't mean you know everything about them."

"Mr. Campbell, I'm not trying to give you a hard time or disturb your comfortable life. I just want you to answer a few questions."

Campbell looked like he wanted to argue some more, but instead he said, "Come into the garage."

Lee stepped into the garage. As soon as he was inside, Campbell pulled the door down.

"I don't know what you think you know about me and my connection to Hubert Dobbs, but I'll tell you this: I won't be intimidated or blackmailed."

"Dobbs's daughter came to me and asked if I'd help bury her father. That's where my involvement started. It grew to helping her find the person that killed him. While looking into the case, I learned that a group of people got together every Wednesday to play cards. That group included you."

"So?"

"I've talked to the other people in the group. They all had gambling issues."

"You haven't talked to Victor Pratt." Campbell smiled. "I know what's been going on. We're friends. Sure, I did a little gambling when I was younger. Could it have gotten out of hand? Maybe. Dobbs talked to me and invited me into the little card club he ran. I admit it helps to scratch the itch." As if to illustrate his point, he reached over and scratched and stretched his left arm.

"Do you think that any of the players could have been the one who killed Dobbs?"

"Why? What'd be the motive? Dobbs ran a nice game that was helping us stay on the straight and narrow."

"Does your wife know about the gambling?"

Lee thought he might have stepped over a line when Campbell gave him a hard look and took a step forward, but Campbell relaxed almost immediately.

"She knows I go and play cards every week."

"Have you heard about Alton Singleton?"

"Everyone in town is talking about it. I won't say that it doesn't worry me that two members of our card game have been killed in the last week."

"Where were you last night?"

"Working at the fire academy." Campbell paused. "The department has ten acres on the edge of town next to the county landfill where we do a lot of our training. We were doing some night exercises with new recruits. Oh, and if you want to know where I was on the night that Dobbs was killed, I was called out for a dumpster fire."

"They call the deputy chief in for a dumpster fire?"

"How many firefighters do you think we have in this town?" He smiled. "This was in the business district, and just 'cause the caller says the fire is in the dumpster doesn't *mean* the fire is in the dumpster. So dispatch did a full call-out."

Lee nodded. "Who do you think killed Hubert Dobbs?"

"I thought it was a cuckolded husband or boyfriend until Singleton was killed."

"What about Ellen Goody?"

"She was probably just in the wrong place at the wrong time. The fire was part of the killer's revenge and Goody just happened to be there."

"Is the fire department investigating the fire?"

"Of course. It was an amateurish arson. I think the same person who killed Dobbs set the fire. Which, I guess, means it was the same person who killed Singleton."

"So what do you think now?" Lee asked, wondering if he was pushing his luck with Campbell.

"I'm puzzled. Maybe Singleton had a clue to the killer and they murdered him to keep him quiet."

Lee thought about Singleton's last words to Kay. Was it that simple?

"What about Fred Goody?" he asked.

Campbell gave a snort of derision. "Not Goody. I know Fred. I doubt there's a more passionless man in the county. And he has a perfect alibi for his wife and Singleton's murder."

"How did you meet Hubert Dobbs?"

"That's ancient history," Campbell said. Lee thought he was going to leave it there, but Campbell sighed and went on: "After high school, I went into the Navy and learned to fight fires. When I got out, I looked around for a local fire department to join and ended up here. Firefighting wasn't the only thing I learned in the Navy. Gambling was a big thing on the carrier I served on. Not allowed, of course, but a lot of stuff goes on that's not allowed. I learned everything from Acey Deucey to poker to dice. I came out of the Navy with less money than I went in with. After a couple of years working here, the boredom led me right back into my bad habits."

"So Dobbs helped you out?"

"One day we were both sitting at the same card table and I'd been losing all night. I didn't always take losing well, so there was a fight. I got the worst end of the stick, and I do mean stick, though it was more like a sawed-off baseball bat. Dobbs picked me up and took me to the hospital. We got to talking and he told me about his game night with friends. The games were safe and they monitored each other's debts."

"You went for that?"

"The fact I'd gotten a concussion and three broken ribs helped to convince me. Also, I was seeing Darla at the time. She wasn't impressed with my rat-eaten apartment or beater car, so I figured I needed to start saving my money if I wanted to marry her."

"What were those game nights like?" Lee asked.

"We'd play poker mostly. If there was a game that night, then Dobbs would have it on the TV in the background. Most of us put some bets down on any games being played that night. Baseball, basketball, you name it. It was our splurge night."

"But Dobbs held the reins on the amount of the bets?"

"He kept a tally. We were allowed percentages of our salaries. Whenever we'd win, that money could be rolled over into what we had available to bet the next week."

"Did any of you keep the money you won?"

"Of course. If we needed it for bills or anything else."

"There was a recent credit check run on all of you that showed each of you being close to insolvent." Lee watched Campbell go scarlet as the words struck home.

"I don't know one person at the fire department that's not on the edge of a financial cliff. The economy sucks. Most of us have kids. What do you expect?"

"Trust me, I'm not that good with money either," Lee sympathized.

"I'm about done answering questions," Campbell said, stretching his arms. "I'll open the door and let you out."

Satisfied that he wasn't going to get any more useful information, Lee thanked him and left.

Kay wasn't sure what approach to take with Victor Pratt. Having met his brother, she was prepared for a younger jackass. On top of that, none of the other players seemed to like him much.

Pratt lived in a duplex on the north side of town. It was well kept and set back on an acre lot that was mowed and would have been shaded in the summer when the sweetgum trees were full of leaves.

A Chevy Blazer was parked on Pratt's side of the duplex. It wasn't new, but it wasn't ragged-out either. The neighborhood was quiet and she wondered why no one was moving around on a nice Sunday afternoon. When she parked in the driveway behind the Blazer and got out of her car, the answer became obvious. From inside the duplex she could hear the sounds of football and guys cheering and groaning.

Great, testosterone overload, Kay thought, walking up to Victor Pratt's door. She had to knock a dozen times before she was heard over the game.

"Who ordered the pizza?" someone inside yelled and received laughter in reply. When the door opened, the man standing there was clearly not Victor Pratt. Black with an even blacker mustache, the man gave her a broad smile. "This is better than pizza!" he yelled back to the other guys.

"I'm looking for Victor Pratt," Kay told him.

"Ain't we all," he said. Seeing her look of frustration, he added, "He's sitting out back on the patio. You can come on through. Those idiots on the couch won't bite unless you want them to."

She followed him through the living room. There were two other guys on the couch eating snacks, drinking beer and half watching the game. They took time to nod and smile at her without any construction-worker leering.

A sliding glass door led out to a small concrete slab where there was a smoking grill and a man in a lawn chair holding a fire iron. He looked surprised when he saw her, but not too surprised.

He stood up. "I got this, Lewis."

"Lucky you," Lewis said and went back inside.

"They've already had a few beers," Pratt said. He looked like his brother, only smaller-boned and with a softer jawline. "My brother said that someone from the funeral home was coming over to talk to me about Hubert Dobbs's murder."

"I'm Kay Lamberton." She held out her hand. There was a vulnerability about the man that she hadn't expected. He took her hand and gave it a gentle shake.

"Honestly, I didn't understand when he told me. Why are you asking about the murder? I thought Wade Sutton was handling the case. And why someone from the funeral home? I'm confused." He stepped over to the side of the house and got another lawn chair. "Sorry, have a seat. And being confused is a natural state with me."

"My brother and I are working with Dobbs's daughter," Kay explained. "Both with the funeral and with trying to find the person behind his murder."

At the mention of Alison, Pratt leaned forward and looked more interested.

"I never met Alison. I'd like to. Dobbs helped me a lot and… I guess I'd just like to tell her that."

"I'm sure she'd be glad to talk to you."

"When's the funeral going to be?"

"The sheriff hasn't released the body yet."

"Don't mind my brother. He was born with a stick up his butt."

"I suppose you heard about Alton Singleton."

"That's why I'm out here instead of in there watching the game. It's all so crazy. I've never known someone who was killed before and now I know three." He shook his head in disbelief.

"You knew Ellen Goody?" Kay asked

"I met her one day when she was out with Bertie. Funny thing, it was in Gainesville at Skeeter's. I guess they were trying to be discreet by meeting up there. When I walked in, I saw them and went over to say hi to Bertie. Turned awkward real quick. Then, when I saw her at the produce stand a couple of days later, she asked me not to tell anyone about seeing the two of them in Gainesville. I told her I wouldn't because I cared a lot for Bertie, which sort of got us talking."

"When was this?"

"I guess about five months ago."

"And you've talked to her since then?"

"Yeah. I got in the habit of stopping by the produce

stand and chatting with her. She was a nice lady. I think she was kinda bored."

"Did she talk about her relationship with Dobbs?"

"Some. She thought he was fun."

"Do you think it was serious on her part?"

"No. She told me a few times that it was just something to do."

"What about her husband?"

"That part was really sad. She said they were more like business partners than a married couple. He'd lost interest in her when she couldn't have children."

"Do you think she could have had anything to do with Dobbs's murder?"

"No." Pratt shook his head emphatically.

"Did you see her after Dobbs was killed?"

Pratt didn't answer at first. He just looked at the burning coals in the grill for a minute. Kay let the silence draw out.

"Yeah, I did," he said eventually. "I knew she'd be torn up over it, so I came out to the produce stand on Thursday. One of their workers was running the stand and said that Ellen wasn't feeling good, so I went up to the house. I felt funny doing it since she'd never invited me there before, but I did it 'cause I wanted to make sure she was all right."

"Was she?"

"Not really. She was angry as much as she was grieving. I got it. I wanted to find the guy who did it too. She seemed like she wanted to make a big deal of it. Like she was at a point she didn't care anymore about anything else."

"Who was she angry at?" Kay thought she might be on the verge of learning something truly helpful. What had Ellen Goody known?

Pratt looked at his feet. "She was angry at us. The gamblers. She was sure it was one of us that killed him. She didn't blame me 'cause she knew me, but she was sure one of the others was responsible for his death."

"Did she know something?"

For the first time, Kay had the feeling that Pratt was hiding something when he just said, "No."

"Still, that's what she thought?" Kay pressed.

"I shouldn't be telling you this 'cause it was just her and me talking. I think she might have gone to his house looking for clues."

"And someone was there and killed her?"

"Which makes it my fault. I knew she was upset and I should have talked to her more about it. I was just so upset myself."

"If one of the group murdered Hubert Dobbs, who would you say it would be?"

"Everyone can… commit… despicable acts if they're pushed against a wall." The words sounded rehearsed.

"Who in the group has been pushed to the wall?" Kay persisted.

Pratt just shook his head, staring at the fire.

"What is everyone looking for at Dobbs's house?" Kay asked, switching gears. The trick seemed to work. There was a flicker of indecision in his eyes, but Kay was disappointed to see him recover his composure.

"Clues, I guess."

"Clues to the murders?"

"Sure, what else?" Pratt said, and Kay was sure he was lying. She'd expected him to be a jerk like his brother, but instead she'd found a vulnerable man who was not good at lying.

"I don't know. You tell me." Kay stared at him until his eyes shifted away.

It was clear that he wasn't going to tell her what was so important that people were willing to take such risks to dig up a dead man's yard.

"Why do people not like you?" Kay asked, trying to jar him into revealing what he knew.

"People think I'm... worthless. That I just leech off my brother." Pratt continued to stare at the flames in the grill. "Of course, they're right. The only person that trusted me was Bertie. The only person who thought I could make something of my life. Now he's dead."

"Maybe this is an opportunity for you," Kay said, not sure what she felt about this sad man.

"I'm going to have to start grilling the steaks soon." He leaned forward and spread out the coals, effectively ending the interview.

Kay stood up. "If you want to help find your friend's killer, call me at the funeral home anytime," she said with an edge to let him know that she thought he was letting people he cared for down by not telling her all that he knew.

He stood and walked her back through the house to the front door without another word.

CHAPTER EIGHTEEN

Kay got home a little after Lee. She could hear him and Lester in the embalming room working on Mr. Hartfield. She decided to wait until Lee was done preparing the body before comparing notes, so she headed for the kitchen to grab a Coke and a snack.

Ruby was at the stove, stirring a pot of thick vegetable soup and humming softly to herself. "How's your day been?" she asked as Kay opened the refrigerator.

"Interesting. We'll see how productive it was," Kay said, popping the cap off the bottle of Coke.

"I'm a dollar richer," Ruby bragged, pulling a worn dollar bill out of her pocket. "Now where do you think Yin found this?"

"Looks like it's been out in the weather. Tell him to look for bills with more zeroes on them next time. Do you think you could teach him to recognize the presidents?" Kay joked.

"Now you're teasing. The question is: What does it

mean? Those two never bring me anything unless there's an underlying meaning to it," Ruby said in all seriousness.

Kay swore that whatever crazy web surrounded Ruby drew in everyone else in close proximity. Despite herself, she felt pulled into the madness.

"Didn't one of them find a playing card?" Kay remembered Lee mentioning that the cat had found a six of clubs in the cemetery. How odd was it that they were now dealing with a club centered around a group of gamblers? …Six gamblers, to be exact.

"I'm sure he was pointing your investigation toward gambling," Ruby said earnestly.

"The dollar bill could be a different clue pointing in the same direction," Kay reasoned against all logic.

"Why would he have to point you toward gambling? You've already figured that out." Ruby made Kay's suggestion seem ridiculous.

"Then what do you think the dollar means?" Kay asked. Half of her thought the question was stupid and the other half was listening intently to see what Ruby's answer would be.

Ruby looked at the bill. "Washington is on the bill, so maybe something related to Washington. Though it was printed in Philadelphia. Brothers, maybe?"

As soon as she said it, Kay felt lightheaded. Could Yin have been pointing a finger at the Pratts? She shook herself. Investigation by cat wasn't a thing.

Ruby chattered on a while longer about everything from the menu for Thanksgiving to being worried about Lester's new accommodations. On this last point, Kay was pretty sure that Ruby just liked to have Lester around all the time so she could feed him. It was a symbiotic relationship. She wanted to tell Ruby to shut up and leave Lester alone. She had all her hopes set on Lester's new place working out.

"What's going on?" Jerome came in through the back door with an odd smile on his face and a large file folder under his arm.

"What are you doing here?" Kay asked. Jerome usually spent his Sunday afternoons off with his mother.

"I had to cut Momma a little short this week. A funny thing happened." He dropped the file folder on the table.

"What's all this?" Kay asked, thumbing through the papers inside. As soon as she looked, she knew the answer. "These are the reports on the murders."

"Yup."

"I've got peanut butter cookies over there," Ruby said, pointing to a tray on the counter.

"Where did you get them?" Kay asked.

"That's the really strange part. Muriel, the sheriff's secretary, called me into the office on a Sunday afternoon. She'd come in to make copies for me. This note was paper-clipped to the file."

Jerome handed Kay the note, which read: *Sheriff wants you to assist your "friends" in clearing this up. Also wanted to remind you that employees work at the pleasure of the sheriff and can be terminated without cause.*

"That last line seems heavy-handed," Kay said.

"Why do you think he wanted us to see these reports?" Jerome asked. Lester had already told him much of what had happened early that morning, but Lester hadn't heard Kay's conversation with the sheriff.

When Kay had finished filling him in, Jerome whistled. "So keeping my job depends on our half-ass investigation coming up with the right answer. Let's hope the answer isn't the sheriff's brother, 'cause that dog won't hunt."

Kay remembered the dollar bill and dismissed the thought. "I talked to Victor Pratt this morning. He doesn't seem like the type to kill anyone."

"Anyone can be the right type. Though I got to admit that Victor isn't an aggressive guy. He's annoying, but not… tough. The sheriff tried to get us to train him as a deputy a few years ago. Victor was too timid and naïve."

Kay was flipping through the reports.

"I already went through most of them," Jerome told her. "I was especially interested in the alibis."

"Of who?"

"Surprisingly, they talked to all of the card players except Victor."

"That is surprising, since Sutton seemed to be ignoring that angle."

"Sheriff Pratt isn't stupid. And if you hadn't figured it out, he's the puppet master behind Sutton. If things go south, Sutton will be the fall guy, but the sheriff is telling him what to do. I suspect the sheriff wants to know who the killer is as much as anyone. The longer this goes on, the more likely it is that the whole county is going to find out that his brother has ties to the murders."

"And his brother could be a target of the killer."

"You aren't wrong," Jerome admitted.

"Have you read through *all* of these?" Kay was looking at several of the reports spread out in front of her.

"The ones written by deputies I trust," Jerome said.

"What'd you find?"

"Why don't I call Lee in so I don't have to go over everything twice?"

"Good idea. In fact, we ought to wait until Alison gets here so everyone can talk it out."

"Dinner now, talkin' later. I'm on board with that," Jerome said with a grin.

"It'll be ready in half an hour," Ruby told them.

After grabbing a couple of Ruby's peanut butter cookies, Jerome went to the embalming room to tell Lester and Lee to get ready for dinner.

"Would you take this out to Yin and Yang?" Ruby set two bowls of cooked hamburger meat on the table next to Kay.

"They eat well," she said, taking the bowls and heading for the door.

"Dinner, guys!" she called up the stairs that led to Ruby's apartment. The two tabbies popped through the cat door on the landing and bounced down the steps.

"If you two were really psychic, you'd have been waiting down here when I came out of the kitchen," she told them.

Yin purred as she put the food down in front of him while Yang acted as though being served was only to be expected. He even took a sniff at the bowl to make sure it met his high standards. Once he was assured that the meat was prepared to his satisfaction, he dove in with the same gusto that Yin was already showing for his food.

"Tell me what you know about the murders. You brought us a playing card and a dollar bill. What's it mean?" Kay asked as she petted each of them in turn and knowing they'd never answer.

After dinner, Jerome, Lee, Kay, Alison and Lester met in the office. Kay gave them a quick briefing before Jerome spoke up.

"I went over the best of the reports. What I got out of them was that none of the gamblers have an ironclad alibi. Since none of them live more than ten minutes away from the store and Dobbs's house, they wouldn't need a large window of opportunity."

"Webber was at a school board meeting," Lee pointed out.

"And they established that she would have had plenty of

time to walk down to the store and kill Dobbs."

"Since we don't know exactly when Dobbs was killed, I'm not sure Campbell's dumpster fire rules him out either," Lee said.

"The only murder we have a precise time for is Singleton's," Kay pointed out.

"The problem there is that it happened in the middle of the night. All of the suspects except Campbell were at home asleep. At best they have a spouse to vouch for them, but what does that really mean?" Jerome asked.

"Campbell said he was at the fire training center," Lee said.

"He was. Again, it was dark and he wasn't directly training the recruits. No one was sure if he was at the training facility at the exact time Singleton was run over," Jerome said. "None of the reports and interviews have any smoking guns, which is why the sheriff is flapping in the breeze. Giving us all of this is a sign of how desperate he is."

"So what are we going to do next?" Lester asked.

"You don't think y'all did enough harm last night?" Jerome shot back.

"Man, I didn't cause that. We were going to get something for sure when that car came out of nowhere," Lester argued.

"He's right. I never saw it coming until it was on top of me," Lee told them.

"We should keep an eye on Courtney Webber. That's the only solid lead we have," Kay said.

"The lead was made more credible by the fact Singleton was killed trying to tell me about her." Lee was still shaken up from the night before. He'd tried to act like it was no big deal, but every time he thought about it, his hands started shaking. Even now, he had to force them down to his sides. "She may make another move tonight."

"Just because Singleton saw her leave Dobbs's house doesn't make her guilty of murder. You all were in the house that night too," Jerome reminded them.

"Can you think of a better course of action?" Kay challenged him.

Jerome pursed his lips and looked thoughtful for a minute before shaking his head. "Your surveillance needs to be better than last night. You know, like no one gets killed."

"Hey, man, I told you, I—" Lester started to defend himself, but Jerome spoke over him.

"I'm not blaming you. I'm just saying there needs to be some professionalism."

"What about you?" Kay asked.

"I'm working tonight."

"I take the blame for last night. I shouldn't have sent Lester out by himself," Lee said. He felt Alison take his hand.

"Forget last night. Jerome is right. We just need to do better tonight," Kay said. "I'll go and watch Webber's house."

"You might want someone else with you," Jerome suggested.

"I'll go," Alison volunteered.

"No, I'll go," Lee insisted.

"You need to get some rest so you can take care of Mr. Hartfield's funeral," Kay told him. She wasn't sure she wanted to sit in a car with Alison for hours on end, but Jerome was right. She shouldn't do it alone and the only other choice was Lester. "Alison can keep me company."

"Okay, we'll see what happens tonight. If nothing does, then we should confront Webber tomorrow with the allegation that Singleton made," Lee said.

"Agreed. Anyone have anything else to add?" Kay asked.

"I finally got ahold of Dad's lawyer today. He'd been on a

fishing trip down in the Keys. He told me that Dad's will names me as his heir." Alison sounded embarrassed. "The lawyer lives in Tampa, but he said he'd drive up this week to go over the details."

Kay and Jerome exchanged looks. They were both thinking that Alison had one of the best motives of any of the suspects. *Where was she last night when the car tried to run us down?* Kay wondered.

At midnight, Kay and Alison were parked on the street half a block from Courtney Webber's house.

"Ruby made us a care package," Kay said, lifting the bag that Ruby had filled with sandwiches, drinks and a canister of Pringles.

"Do you think Webber really killed my father?" Alison asked.

"I think it's possible. But it could be also Pratt, Lawson, Campbell or someone else."

Kay looked over at Alison. After everyone had gone their separate ways earlier that evening, Kay had dug through the reports until she found the one from Deputy Henry Booker. He'd done the background check and follow-up on Alison's alibi for her father's murder. He'd left open the thin possibility that she could have driven from Pensacola and killed her father before driving home in time to be seen by her roommate the next morning, and to take the call from Sutton informing her of her father's death. But that timeline was razor-thin. Was it possible that this quiet, nerdy woman could have killed her own father for whatever inheritance she was going to get?

"You and Lee get along well," Alison observed, jarring Kay out of her thoughts.

"We haven't always. There's a big gap in our ages and...

he was my parents' favorite," Kay admitted.

"Parents always say they don't have favorites, but that isn't true, is it?"

"I think it's hard not to be more attached to one of your children. For my parents, Lee came along when they were older and could enjoy being parents more than they could when I was a baby and they were struggling to get the business off the ground. You're an only child, right?"

"My mother got remarried and the man already had a son. Not that I lacked for attention. Truth is, I would have preferred it if Mom had given me more space."

"Do you get along with your stepfather and brother?"

"They're okay. He's older than Mom and my stepbrother Nick was in college when they got married, so he wasn't around much."

"You like Lee?" Kay changed the subject.

"He seems really nice."

"With Lee, what you see is what you get, which is one of his best qualities."

"I don't like people who pretend to be something they aren't," Alison said.

"Amen, sister," Kay said, wondering if Alison was pretending. "Did the lawyer give you any idea how big your father's estate is?"

"Just that there are several pieces of property, as well as his bank account."

"The house was probably covered by insurance."

"I don't know. Even if it was, they might not pay if it was arson."

Kay opened the can of Pringles and offered Alison one.

"How do they get them stacked so neatly without breaking any?" Kay asked as she pulled a couple of chips apart and popped one into her mouth. "It's a modern miracle. Speaking of which, Lee said you worked for an airplane factory or something?"

"I did statistical analysis for a company that makes turbines."

"That sounds… interesting," Kay lied through her teeth.

"Only to a nerd like me. With the economy in a mess, the company got sold and laid me off, so now I'm working as a projectionist at a movie theatre," Alison admitted.

"Probably don't make as much money," Kay sympathized.

"Not nearly. But I love getting to watch all the movies. Every cloud…" Alison steered the conversation away from herself. "I know you keep the funeral home's books. You must be good with numbers."

"I'm better at it than Lee, that's a fact," Kay said dryly.

"He told me how grateful he is that you came back to help out with the business."

"He did?" Kay didn't quite know what to think. She felt oddly grateful that her brother appreciated her help.

"What was it like in Vietnam?" Alison asked.

"Terrifying, boring, horrifying, uplifting, basically the worst and best moments of my life." Kay paused and decided that Alison deserved more of an answer than that. "I went over there with silly ideas filling my head. Growing up here in Lang was not good preparation for being in a war zone in Southeast Asia. The only thing it prepared me for was the humidity. Once I got my… war legs under me, I was able to do a little bit of good amongst all the horror and chaos. But worse than being over there was coming back. For years I felt like this," she nodded to the world outside the car, "was all some sort of lie. It didn't feel real after being someplace where life and death coexisted side by side."

"But you were still a nurse when you came back."

"Yes. And death walked the halls of the hospitals and nursing homes where I worked, for sure. But sometimes the reaper came as a friend who was taking away a patient's pain, and not as an enemy who was stealing away decades of a life half-lived."

Alison nodded and they drifted into silence. The hours slipped by as they kept watch over Courtney Webber's house. It was just after three, as Kay's eyelids were slipping closed, when movement across the street startled her awake.

"There!" Kay said, causing Alison to sit up with a start. Kay pointed to the red taillights of a car backing out of Webber's driveway.

"Is it her?"

"I don't know, but I'm going to follow them," Kay said. She started the car without turning on the headlights. Then she yelled, "Get down!" as she saw that the car was coming in their direction.

The two women bumped heads as they both ducked out of sight.

"Son of a…" Kay said, rubbing her head as she sat up and whipped the car around to follow whoever had left Courtney Webber's house.

They followed the car through the dark streets of the sleeping town until it turned onto a road that headed west into the more rural parts of the county.

"Where do you think they're going?" Alison asked.

"I don't know, but I'm glad I filled up the gas tank." Kay was intently focused on the red taillights of the car ahead. She didn't want to get too close. The roads were deserted at this hour and it wouldn't take long for the other driver to realize that they were being followed.

Live oaks and pines caught the headlights of the two cars as they sped past them. Five miles out of town, Kay was getting nervous.

"I wish we could call someone," she muttered to herself.

"What are we going to do if they stop out here in the

middle of nowhere?" Alison asked.

"I haven't a clue." Kay was gripping the steering wheel tightly with her hands at the ten-and-two position.

She barely had time to react when the other car's taillights flared bright red as the driver applied their brakes. "Damn it!" Kay put her own brakes on harder than she intended, sending both of them sliding forward in their seats. She heard hands slamming into the dash as Alison caught herself.

The car in front of them turned left onto a dirt road.

"What now?" Alison's voice was soft and unsure.

"We follow them." Kay dug down inside herself and came up with a dose of firm determination. "We're going to find out what's going on."

"Even if it kills us?"

"I doubt it will come to that," Kay said with a grim smile.

CHAPTER NINETEEN

The road was narrow, but well maintained. Kay drove past a couple of mailboxes, and they were able to see a few small houses and trailers set back from the road. Her car's headlights struggled to find the car in front of them as it stirred up a layer of dust.

"Can you see the taillights?" Kay was scanning the windshield, but the dust was acting like a fog and making it impossible to see more than a hundred feet in front of them. "I'm going to turn the lights off."

"What!"

Kay cut the headlights, but left on the running lights. This made it easier to see the car they were following, but it also meant that they hit every rut and hole in the road without warning.

After a mile, the other car turned again. Kay slowed and watched as the car moved slowly down a lane of trees. Kay drifted to the side of the road and stopped the car. "It looks like a private drive."

They could see the other car's headlights briefly illuminate a white clapboard farmhouse. Kay looked around for a safe place to park.

"Ah! We're in luck." She pulled into a short, neglected driveway with a gate across it and turned off the engine. The gate's hinges were rusty and there was a large lock on it. "Doesn't look like anyone comes here much."

In the distance, they saw the lights of the other car go off.

"Are we walking up there?" Alison asked, sounding both nervous and excited.

"Now you're learning." Kay reached up and took the cover off of the cabin light, pulling the bulb out before opening her door.

"Are you sure you weren't a spy in the Army?" Alison asked.

"I read all of the Parker Family mysteries when I was a kid." Kay gave her a smile.

The moon provided enough light for them to walk up the driveway while sticking to the shadows.

"What would the Parker Family do when they got close to the house?" Alison whispered.

"Watch. At least for a little while. We don't even know how many people were in the car."

"I didn't think about that."

They could see a light moving through the house, flashing from window to window.

Kay had a thought. "Could this be one of your father's properties?"

"Maybe. The lawyer just said that there were several properties as part of the estate, but he didn't say where they were."

The road opened up into the large yard that surrounded the old house. Now that they were closer, they could see that the house needed painting.

"Doesn't look like anyone lives here." Kay didn't see signs of any vehicles other than the car they had followed. "That looks like Webber's car. I saw it in her driveway the other day when I was looking for the Chevy Nova that ran Singleton down."

The light was upstairs in the house now. It had stopped in a room facing the yard.

"I wish we knew what she's looking for," Kay muttered. "I'm going to throw a monkey wrench into Webber's plans."

"What?"

"Wait here. I'm going to let the air out of her tires."

"Why?"

"Just to mess her up. And she'll have to get out of here somehow, and that will probably leave a trail if we need to prove she was here. Finally, if something goes wrong, she won't be able to chase us."

"Good idea." Alison nodded.

Kay slipped out of the shadows. Crouched over, she hurried across the part of the yard that was bathed in the light of the moon. Once she got up next to the car, she took the cap off the valve stem of one of the tires and began to let the air out.

The night was still, the silence broken only by a dog barking miles away, and the hissing sound of the escaping air was very loud to Kay. When the tire was flat she thought about heading back to Alison, but then she decided that if one flat tire was good, then two would be better.

Before she could start on the second tire, she heard Alison scream. Turning, she saw an object on a straight trajectory toward her face and flinched backward. This saved her from taking the full brunt of the blow. Still, she was clobbered hard enough to send her head flying back into the side of the car. Alison screamed again, closer this time.

Kay tried to regain her senses, but the ringing in her ears and the pain in her head had left her mentally staggering. She could see that two people were rolling around on the ground in front of her. Still confused, she scooted away from them.

As she heard the grunts, growls and cussing issuing from the combatants, Kay's mind started to clear. She felt the 1911 pistol rubbing against her armpit and was glad she'd thought to bring it with her again. She pulled her flashlight from her pocket and slowly drew her gun.

Clicking on the flashlight, she saw that Courtney Webber and Alison were pulling each other's hair, butting heads and spitting at each other. The light startled the pair, who stopped their struggling for a second before diving back into the fight.

"Stop!" Kay yelled, but it didn't have the same effect as the light. "I swear someone will get shot if you two don't stop fighting."

Kay kept her distance. At this point, she wasn't even certain which one of them had hit her. She saw the shovel on the ground near the two wrestlers, but who had swung it at her?

Kay stepped over and kicked the shovel into the two women, which finally got their attention.

"She attacked you!" Alison said, holding both of Webber's wrists in a death lock as they struggled on the ground.

"You two are going to kill me!" Webber grunted, still trying to get the upper hand.

"If we wanted to kill you, you'd be dead already," Kay said, indicating the gun in her hand. "Now, both of you stop struggling."

Alison and Webber both stopped moving and let go of each other.

"Now put some distance between you." Kay motioned

with the gun in her hand. Each of them slid cautiously backward. "Now, let's figure out what the hell is going on."

"I was watching and she came creeping up on you with that shovel," Alison blurted.

"I was defending myself," Webber said indignantly.

"How's that?" Kay asked.

"I saw you sneaking around my car. You were going to strand me out here and do God knows what to me."

"No, we weren't. I just didn't want you to get away scot-free like you did from the murder scenes," Kay argued.

"I wasn't at… not when anyone was murdered."

"What are you doing here? And what is this place?"

"Nothing." Webber was dusting the dirt off her slacks.

"Don't lie to me. I'll remind you I still have a gun and one hell of a headache." Kay felt the tender spot on the side of her head.

"Are you going to kill me?"

"That's nonsense," Kay said, then realized that she was still pointing a gun at the woman. Slowly, she re-holstered the pistol. "There, feel better?"

"Can I get up?"

"Slowly," Kay cautioned.

Keeping a wary eye on Kay and Alison, Webber got to her feet. She wobbled a little before getting her legs under her. "Why did you two follow me?"

"Because someone is going around murdering people, and they tried to kill my brother yesterday."

"What's that got to do with me?"

"Don't play stupid," Kay growled. "I know that Lee talked to you, and I'm convinced it's one of Dobbs's gamblers."

Webber tried to straighten her hair with her hands. "You may be right."

"Did you go to Dobbs's house and dig up his garden?"

"I didn't dig all those holes!" she declared with a shake of her head.

"But you did dig *some* of them."

"Maybe."

"What's everyone looking for?"

"I guess I don't have any choice. But if I'm gonna tell you, I need to lean against the car for a while." She limped over to the vehicle and slumped against the door. "You're quite the little tigress," she said to Alison, who gave her a wry smile as she rubbed at her own sore arm. Both women's clothes were torn and dirty.

"So?" Kay prompted Webber.

"Bertie kept us in line with more than the camaraderie of the game. From the very beginning, he would take a share of everyone's winnings and put them into one pot. The deal was that, one day, we would all split the money among us. It would be a reward for sticking with the program."

"How much money are we talking about?" Kay asked.

"A month ago the pot was up to 1.1 million and change."

Kay whistled. "And no one knows where it is?"

"No. Bertie didn't trust us."

"Imagine that," Kay said, raising an eyebrow.

"So you're all just digging a bunch of holes hoping to find it?" Alison asked.

"What else are we going to do? Just let more than a million dollars go?"

"Did it ever occur to you that maybe he did something crazy like put it in the bank?" Kay asked.

"The money can't go in a bank. It's all… under the radar."

"You mean the IRS doesn't know about it," Kay said.

"Not most of it. And the stuff that came from bookies isn't exactly… legal."

"He could have kept it in a safe deposit box," Alison

suggested.

"I thought about that, but I don't think so. Bertie wasn't a guy who liked banks. Always said that he didn't like the idea of having to wait for someone to open the door before he could get his money. Bertie said that, if he wanted his money at three in the morning, then that's when he wanted it."

"But why would he bury it in the yard?" Alison asked.

"I don't know. But a couple of weeks ago, when we were asking him about it, he told us he kept it safely planted next to the garden."

"You all need money now," Kay said, thinking about what Jerome had told them about the gamblers' credit reports.

"That's why we were asking about the money. We wanted him to split it up now."

"Were any of you more insistent than the others?"

"We're all hungry at this point. Do you think I'd be digging around this old place if I wasn't? By the way, I can tell that I wasn't the first person to think of it. There are lots of footprints in the dust and someone has been tearing out the paneling to look in the walls."

"Over a million dollars," Alison said. "I can't believe my dad had that kind of money sitting around."

"It cost him his life," Kay reminded her. "And it might have all burned up with his house."

"I have nightmares about that," Webber admitted, looking at the ground.

"Could the killer already have the money?" Kay suggested.

Webber shrugged. "All I know is that *I* don't have it."

"If the killer didn't find it, then why burn the house down?" Alison asked.

"Maybe the fire was an accident. Or the killer was so

desperate to cover up the murder of Ellen Goody that he just took a chance that the money wasn't in the house," Kay mused.

"Well, this has been a fun night, but I need to get home. There's school tomorrow," Webber said, standing up and wobbling a little as she smoothed down her blouse. "Damn," she said, looking at the flat tire. "You can help with this."

"Who's going to help fix my head?" Kay muttered.

"This house was my father's?" Alison asked Webber as they moved to the trunk of her car.

"I asked a friend in the property appraiser's office to look up what he owned. There are six pieces of property in the county. Three of them have houses on them. Well, only two now. This one and a little place in town that he rented out."

"We need to talk to all of you about this money," Kay said, helping her dig in the trunk for the spare tire and jack.

"Be my guest. I'd love to know if one of my buddies is hiding anything. Believe me, if you find the murderer, no one will be happier than me." She looked at Alison. "Of course, I know you will be."

"At least we know the motive now," Kay said.

"But if one of us did kill him, then why do it without knowing where the money is?" Webber dropped the jack on the ground by the tire. "That's what I can't understand."

"Maybe the killer does have the money and is pretending he doesn't in hopes of throwing the rest of you off his trail," Kay said.

"I guess. But it's going to be obvious when all their debts magically disappear."

"Maybe they just thought they knew where the money was," Alison suggested as she held the flashlight on the flat tire.

Kay got down on the ground and put the jack in the right spot under the axle.

"Or it was an impulse decision," Webber said. "We were all upset the night we were discussing the money. It's possible that one of the others could have gotten pissed enough and just… stabbed him."

"Gamblers are gamblers because they lack impulse control and like the thrill of the game," Kay said, then looked at Webber. "No offense."

"None taken. Your points are valid."

They got the car jacked up, the bolts loosened and, with some effort, the tire off.

"We *are* going to find out who murdered Dobbs, Goody and Singleton," Kay told Webber.

"I told you, I'm on your side. Having said that, I also want my money."

"You can't go around digging up Dobbs's property," Kay told her.

"If it's not me, it's going to be one of the others."

"I don't want the money," Alison said.

"That's beside the point. The money is part of your father's estate. Plus, it's evidence in three murders," Kay said, her voice rising.

"Still, that money was promised to us."

"And one of you killed for it," Kay said bluntly.

"Maybe." Webber grew thoughtful. "Look, we need to talk to the others and declare a truce. Maybe we can figure something out. It will take some of the pressure off if they know that Alison doesn't want to stake a claim to the cash."

"Tell them to be at the funeral home tomorrow at three. We have a funeral in the morning, but we'll be free by then," Kay told her as they hoisted the spare tire into place.

Twenty minutes later, Alison and Kay were headed back to the funeral home. Kay was letting Alison drive.

"Bed. I just need to get to my bed," she said. "My head feels like it's on fire."

"Do you want me to take you to the hospital?"

"No. Good grief, that's all I need is to spend what's left of the night sitting in an emergency room. I had enough of that *last* night. I'll be fine as soon as I get to a bed."

"Do you really think there's a pile of money hidden somewhere?"

"I guess there is if your father didn't spend it. Or if one of those idiots didn't burn it up in the house."

CHAPTER TWENTY

"The note said what?" Lee had just come into the kitchen when Ruby told him she had found a note from Kay.

"It said to wake her up at ten to make sure she isn't dead."

"What the hell is that supposed to mean?" Lee looked at his watch and saw it was only eight o'clock. He wondered what had happened during the night's surveillance of Webber's house. He'd call Alison a little later and get the details. "Look, if I'm not here at ten, will you go up and make sure she's all right?"

Ruby nodded. "Eggs, bacon, sausage and toast?"

"Just some bacon and toast today. I've got a lot of work to do." He looked around, surprised to see that Lester wasn't already stuffing his face. As the thought entered his head, he heard the rattle of Lester's latest junker pull into the back driveway.

"What time is Mr. Hartfield's funeral?" Lester asked two minutes later when he came in.

"Noon. But we need to go out to the gravesite and set everything up." Lee wasn't expecting a large group. The man had lived in a nursing home for years and most of his family was dead or had moved away. Still, even if no one was there but themselves and the client, Lee wanted it done with dignity. That had been his father's way.

"I just need to grab some food."

"Don't give him the full breakfast treatment," Lee said, wagging his finger at Ruby.

"Man has to eat." Ruby was already cracking eggs.

"If a man wants to eat, he needs to show up early," Lee grumbled.

"If I lived here—" Lester started, but shut up at a glare from Lee.

Kay heard the knocking, both from her bedroom door and from inside her head. Bleary-eyed and with her head thumping, she turned and looked at the clock radio. The red numbers showed it was ten o'clock on the dot.

"You alive in there?" Ruby asked, with a hint of real concern in her voice.

"Barely," Kay answered while trying to get up the gumption to roll out of bed.

A hot shower and aspirin helped subdue the pain. She put on a little make-up over the abrasions at the edge of her hairline that had been left by the shovel. "I hope Webber's guilty as sin," Kay mumbled to herself while feeling the tender area under her hair.

Before going downstairs, Kay stopped at the phone in the hall and made a call to the motel.

"How are you feeling this morning?" she asked when Alison answered.

"My arm is sore and I've got a black eye. Other than that,

just a few scratches. I hope I left some marks on Ms. Webber." Kay was surprised to hear such tough talk coming from Alison. "How are *you*?"

"I'll live. I'm going to call Webber and make sure she's going to round up the gamblers and have them all here by three."

"Have you told Lee what happened?"

"Not yet. Here, you can do it." Kay put the phone down and yelled downstairs, "Lee! Phone."

"I don't have time," he called back. "We've got to get the body in the hearse."

"It's Alison!"

Lee appeared at the bottom of the stairs, dressed in his funeral clothes. "I'll grab the phone down here."

I thought so. Kay smirked to herself.

When she reached the bottom of the stairs, she could hear Lee saying things like: "Wow. Really? No kidding?" He glanced over at Kay with his eyebrows raised.

"What can I get you to eat?" Ruby popped her head out of the kitchen.

"Not everything can be fixed with food," Kay told her, but she allowed herself to be lured into the kitchen.

"Don't talk nonsense," Ruby said, then added, "What happened to your head?"

"I guess the make-up doesn't hide it very well." She gave Ruby the quick version while pouring herself a cup of two-hour-old coffee.

"You don't need coffee," Ruby said, taking the cup out of Kay's desperate hands. "I've got some special tea that will help take some of the sting out." She was already pulling a tea canister down from the cupboard.

"This better be good," Kay warned her. The only reason she hadn't grabbed her cup of coffee back was that Ruby had proven capable of curing some ills with her homebrews, so she was willing to give her a chance.

Once again, Ruby knew what she was doing. After only half a cup of tea, Kay was already feeling better.

"You look awful," Lee said, sticking his head into the kitchen. "I wish I could have seen you and Alison battling the school superintendent!"

"I'm trying to get all of our gambling buddies here at three." Kay paused thoughtfully. "I should probably ask Jerome to be here."

"I should be done and back by two. We can talk then and see if we can come up with a game plan. Got to go!"

"We're having company?" Ruby raised her eyebrows.

"Four people plus the regulars, which seems to include Alison these days. Oh yeah, and one of them is most likely a murderer three times over, so you might want to hide the sharp knives." Kay winced as she tried to smile.

"I got ahold of them," Courtney Webber told her on the phone a few minutes later. "Walt and Milton weren't happy. They think it's some sort of setup. When I explained to them that you already knew about the money, both of them blew up over the phone."

"Are they going to come?"

"You couldn't stop them now. I just can't promise they're going to be very cooperative."

"You did your part."

Kay hung up and thought about how much they still didn't know. *We know more than we did yesterday*, she assured herself.

A dozen people showed up at the Hartfield funeral. Lee and Lester had stopped off at Lang Florists, where they picked up several arrangements of flowers that were too close to their sell-by date for Ann to use in any arrangements for full-price customers. Lee's father had known Ann for twenty years, and he had always supplemented funerals he knew would be small with some discount arrangements. It was another custom Lee meant to maintain.

Lee saw two people he knew at the funeral. One was an older man who had been one of Mr. Hartfield's neighbors before he'd moved into the nursing home. The other was a nurse from the home. Lee had gone out on a few dates with her. She had always struck him as a compassionate person, and seeing her at one of her patient's funerals confirmed his impression of her.

Lee walked over to her when the funeral was done.

"Mr. Hartfield always had a smile for me. Even when I knew he wasn't feeling very well," Liz English told him.

"I'm sorry I never had the chance to meet him," Lee said.

"It's the worst part of working at the home. It hurts to see the ones you like finally go. The only consolation in Mr. Hartfield's case was that he went downhill fast. Some of them suffer for years." Her eyes were damp.

"Do you need a ride back to the nursing home?" Lee asked, feeling a little uncomfortable due to his budding relationship with Alison.

"No, I've got my car here. Besides, it always upsets the residents to see the hearse drive up." She gave him a sad smile.

"I guess it would. I'm so used to driving around in a hearse that I never think about it."

"It's good seeing you again," Liz said.

"Is that a cat?" Lee had been looking past Liz when he saw movement near one of the graves.

"Where?" Liz turned to follow Lee's gaze.

"Right over there near those headstones. My housekeeper has a couple of fat tabbies, and I'm pretty sure one of them has been coming over here. He brought home a playing card from here the other day."

They watched for a minute, but didn't see anything else. Lee said goodbye to Liz and went back to wait in the hearse with Lester until the mourners had gone.

Lee and Lester had everything from the funeral put away with half an hour to spare before the three o'clock meeting. Lee was cleaning up the embalming room when he heard Alison's voice from the doorway.

"Hi," she said, smiling at him.

Oddly, he felt embarrassed at having her see him in the embalming room. *At least there isn't a body*, he thought. It had been a while since he'd felt any awkwardness over his profession. Still, he'd had more than one woman get turned off at the idea that he handled dead bodies for a living. Others had *thought* they were comfortable with the idea until they saw the reality of the funeral home.

"This is where the… gruesome work is done," Lee said in a self-deprecating manner.

"Interesting." Alison took a single step into the room. Lee half expected her to see the steel embalming table and all the tubing, then turn around and run. But Alison didn't run. Instead, she started to walk slowly around the room. "I've never thought about how the body is prepared for the burial. I guess the roots of your profession go back to the mummies of ancient Egypt."

"Dad used to talk about the art of mummification. There are a dozen books upstairs on mummies and the pharaohs." Lee moved beside her and walked with her as she looked at everything in the room.

"I guess that isn't for food." She pointed to the stainless steel door of the walk-in cooler where the bodies were stored.

He pulled the door open, knowing that today it held only a gurney and nothing else.

Alison turned away from the refrigerator and did a small spin as she looked around the room. "You could make a great horror movie here."

"I can't see anything spooky about it," Lee said, a little insulted.

"Think zombies, or maybe *Frankenstein*. I love movies. Horror movies most of all. They give me a special chill that makes me feel at home. After Mom and I left Dad, I wasn't interested in too much. But the one thing that I always loved was Spook Theatre on Saturday afternoon. The Spook, the host, was crazy. He'd always make up these stupid jokes and sing crazy little songs." Her eyes had gotten wistful and faraway.

"I'd like to watch a horror movie with you." Lee regretted the words as soon as they were out of his mouth. *You're moving too fast*, he scolded himself.

"That might be fun," Alison said to his surprise.

"Come on, let's go find Kay." He guided her back into the hallway.

Kay was pacing around the office when they walked in.

"I wish I knew the right approach to the meeting," she told them.

"It's difficult to have a plan when there are so many variables," Alison agreed.

Kay nodded. "For the most part, we've met our four suspects only once. One of them is a killer and the others are just desperate people looking for a brass ring."

"Y'all waiting on me?" Jerome came in wearing his uniform.

"The uniform was a good idea." Kay was grateful.

"Yeah, I thought it couldn't hurt. Wouldn't be wearing it if we didn't have the sheriff's under-the-table approval for your half… um, half-hearted attempt at an investigation."

"Thanks for the vote of confidence," Lee joked.

"What are we hoping to get out of this shindig?" Jerome asked.

"A feel for who isn't telling the truth. I'm going to lay some of our cards on the table and hope they'll do the same," Kay explained.

"Nothing wrong with a fishing expedition as long as you don't set the hook in your own finger," Jerome said.

Lester came into the office. "Can I sit in on the meeting too?"

Kay sighed. "Sure. Just don't say anything."

Lester nodded obediently.

A few minutes later, they heard a loud rap on the front door.

"I asked Ruby to answer the door and usher them back here," Kay said.

"Nice touch." Jerome nodded.

"Like an Agatha Christie story," Alison said with a hint of excitement in her voice.

"I'm here to meet with Kay Lamberton." Walt Lawson's voice could be heard as he stepped through the front door.

"Ms. Lamberton is in the office." Ruby sounded like the downstairs in *Upstairs, Downstairs.*

"What's this…" Lawson started to say as he entered the office before stopping and looking around at the others. "Quite a crowd."

"We're expecting the rest of your friends too," Kay told him. "Have a seat." She waved toward the extra chairs she'd brought in from the parlor.

"I won't be here that long," he said through clenched teeth.

The doorbell sounded and Ruby could be heard letting more people into the front hall. Kay recognized one voice as

Courtney Webber's and assumed the other belonged to Milton Campbell.

"I don't understand why we're here." Campbell looked around the room as he entered.

"I told you why," Webber said, coming in behind him.

"I know what you said. It just doesn't make a lot of sense for us to be here. I already explained my part in the card games," he said, looking directly at Lee.

"Why don't we wait for the last member of your party to arrive?" Kay suggested and he gave her a curt nod.

Victor Pratt looked nervous as he entered the room. "I hate to be the last one to arrive for a meeting, but I never seem to be able to get to one early." He gave them all a small smile.

"You damned sure never arrived early to our card games." Lawson frowned.

"We're all here now. Can we get started?" Campbell asked.

"First tell us why we're here," Pratt said.

"We asked everyone here so we could talk about the… digging you've been doing on Hubert Dobbs's property," Kay explained.

Campbell, Lawson and Pratt all looked down at their feet.

"Ms. Webber said she told you that we know what you're looking for," Kay added.

"Fine. It's our money. Bertie intended for us to split it up at some point," Lawson spoke up.

"Actually, it's Alison's property," Lee said.

"I don't want the money." Alison's words caused everyone to stop and look at her. "Really. If it's part of Dad's estate, you're welcome to it."

"The point is that someone killed Dobbs to get that money," Kay interjected.

"You don't know that!" Campbell argued.

"Know? Maybe not, but I think it's a good bet. Pun intended." Kay stepped into the center of the group. "There's a good chance that one of you four killed Dobbs."

"Wait a minute! I didn't come here so you could accuse me of murder. Even if we had a motive to kill Dobbs, why would we kill Ellen or Singleton?" Pratt asked.

"I'm not sure about Ellen Goody. Maybe she went there and found one of you rummaging through the house, or maybe she found the money and was killed for it."

"That's crazy. If Dobbs was murdered for the money, then why did the killer need to take out anyone else?" Lawson asked.

"I think the killer thought he could get the money by killing Dobbs, but found out that the money was better hidden than he thought," Kay said.

"That's nonsense," Campbell said. "Okay, I admit I've been looking for the money. I've seen the rest of you looking too. But I think that just proves we didn't kill Dobbs. How stupid would we have to be to commit murder without being assured that we could get our hands on the money?"

"Desperate. That's what you all are. Every one of you needs money. Whoever the murderer is thought they knew where the money was, had the chance to get Dobbs out of the way and took it," Kay argued.

"Ridiculous," Campbell tossed back.

"Maybe the killer has the money. Maybe all of that shovel-work is just a smokescreen." Jerome was leaning casually against the back wall as he spoke. His words had a noticeable effect on the four gamblers. Each one looked suspiciously at the others.

"Yeah, that's a bone to chew on, isn't it? Y'all might want to keep an eye on each other and take action if you see one of the others start packing for a lifetime stay in Central America." Jerome maintained his cool air of indifference as he looked at each of them.

"You aren't going to turn us against each other," Pratt stated.

"It's been everyone for themselves since we all started hunting for the money," Webber reminded him.

"This is insane. I'm not going to stand here and be accused of crimes by… by a bunch of detective wannabes," Lawson said.

"He's right," Campbell agreed. "Call me when the real investigators want to talk to us." He turned toward the door.

"I expected this to be more of a cooperation thing." Pratt shook his head.

"Are we all going to go our own way and risk getting picked off one by one by the killer?" Webber asked.

Campbell stopped walking toward the door and turned toward her. "Do you really think these guys are going to solve these crimes?"

"Well…" Webber looked around the room. "Then we need to come up with our own strategy." She started to follow him out the door.

"Wait!" Lee shouted, then looked a little embarrassed by the volume of his voice. "What if we had a high-stakes poker game? Would you talk to us then?" He had their attention now.

"What are you talking about?" Lawson asked.

"We'll put up five thousand dollars of our money to play you all in a poker game. Each of you put up the same and we'll have a pot worth twenty-five thousand dollars. The only requirement is that, during the game, we get to ask you all questions."

Kay's mouth was hanging open. Was Lee really going to toss five thousand dollars of the funeral home's money into a poker game? She'd played poker when she was a nurse in the Army, but the maximum bet had been a quarter. Pots seldom rose to more than five dollars. She'd heard stories of high-stakes poker games in Saigon gambling parlors, but she'd also heard of soldiers playing Russian Roulette. In her mind, one was as insane as the other.

From the looks on their faces, it was clear all four of the gamblers were considering Lee's idea.

"I'll put up five thousand dollars for a seat," Alison said. Everyone in the room turned to stare at her. "That makes the pot worth thirty thousand."

"I'm in," Lawson said.

"When do we play?" Campbell asked.

"Wednesday, your usual night, seven o'clock," Lee told them.

"I'll be there." Campbell nodded.

"Count me in." Pratt smiled.

"I won't be the odd one out. Where are we going to play?" Webber asked.

"Here," Lee told them.

"Have the money with you," Lawson said to all of them, then the gamblers filed out of the office.

CHAPTER TWENTY-ONE

"Are you out of your damned mind?" were the first words out of Kay's mouth after the door shut behind the last of the four suspects.

"I couldn't let them slip away without another chance of talking to them," Lee said.

"Five thousand dollars! Have you ever played poker for real stakes?" Kay was shouting now.

"No… but it's not about the money," Lee said, trying to defend himself.

"The hell it isn't!" Kay stormed.

Jerome and Lester leaned against the wall and enjoyed the show.

"I can beat them," Alison said, causing Lee and Kay to turn and look at her. "I'd prefer to play five-card stud."

"You've played high-stakes poker?" Kay was incredulous.

"No. But our math club played it in high school."

"Your math club! We're talking about losing ten thousand dollars between us," Kay said, exasperated.

"Were you any good?" Lee asked Alison.

"It's statistics and probabilities. Five-card stud is the best. With six of us playing, there will be twenty-four cards showing. I'll know where half the deck is. All I have to do is look at each person's four cards and figure out the probabilities for the possible hole cards." She made it sound simple.

"You can do that in your head?" Lee asked.

"Pretty close."

"You aren't serious?" Kay asked.

"I won most of the time. Obviously there was luck involved, so the time it took for me to win all the chips varied depending on how the cards fell."

"Do you understand that these are semi-professional poker players?" Kay asked.

"Math doesn't care. I'm playing the odds. The odds don't change depending on who's playing. They might be able to hold out longer, but if they're relying on reading other players and on bluffing, I'll win in the long run 'cause I'll be betting based on the odds, not my intuition or some attempt to intimidate others. Plus, they can't intimidate me 'cause I know that the numbers will favor me."

"Why don't all the math wizards go to Vegas?" Kay asked.

"I had a friend from school who went. He could count the cards in blackjack in his head. They kicked him out of every casino on the strip."

"Did he work the small joints?" Lee was fascinated and impressed.

"He was scared they'd do more than just kick him out. There are stories of card counters getting lost in the desert. Forever."

"I can see why. Do you seriously think you can pull this off?" Kay was warming to the idea.

"And I promise I'll give you back all your money," Alison assured her.

"What if they won't play five-card stud?" Kay asked.

"Then it will be harder."

"Five-card stud it is."

"We could also play with seven."

"Okay, leave the game to me," Kay said. "We'll at least argue them down to dealer's choice."

"Y'all are crazy." Jerome smiled and pushed off the wall. "You've got yourselves some wicked suspects."

"Do you think one of them did it?" Lee asked.

"They're so hungry for money they'd eat their young for a dollar," Jerome said. "Motive isn't a problem. Unfortunately, opportunity and means isn't either. I read the reports. All of them had the time to commit the murders and none of the murders required any great feat of strength."

"Any luck finding the car?" Lee asked, rubbing at his hip. It had felt better this morning, but working the funeral had been more than he was ready for and the pills he'd taken afterward were starting to wear off.

"No. Patrol was told to keep their eye out for a car matching the description, and I got the watch commander to include a heads-up to keep an eye out for any smoke that could be coming from a car fire. My bet is the car will end up a burned-out wreck down some dead-end trail in the woods. The intrepid Inspector Sutton did call all the body shops in Gainesville and the surrounding area to tell them what we're looking for."

"Some bad guys burned a car on *The Rockford Files* the other night," Lester informed them.

"We need to be better prepared for our suspects Wednesday night," Kay said, ignoring him.

"We'll make up a list of questions," Lee said.

"I just thought about the fact that these are people whose

hobby is suppressing their emotions," Kay pointed out.

Jerome nodded. "We need to find evidence. The real deal if we're going to break down our killer."

"There must be clues in the murders," Kay said. "I read through the reports and interviews and didn't see anything that I could put my finger on. One thing that did occur to me was that the fire set in the house was amateurish. The fire investigator even used that word. Like the killer just splashed a little gasoline around and lit it on fire."

"Which is why only part of Goody's body was burned. The murderer was just lucky that there was enough mess to obscure any physical evidence," Jerome said.

"The report also said that the house might have been saved if it hadn't been built out of wood and materials that were highly flammable," Kay added.

"Did the killer come to the house intending to kill Goody?" Lee asked.

"According to the reports, the gas cans were brought there from the Goody farm," Kay said. "They found similar ones in Goody's garage."

"Wait. So does that mean that Ellen Goody brought the gas?" Lee asked.

"They found evidence that the cans had been in her hatchback," Jerome answered.

"So was she coming there to burn the house down?" Alison asked. "Why?"

"Trying to hide the evidence of her affair? Or out of anger at Dobbs. People can be angry at the dead," Lee pointed out. "It's that or the killer drove Goody to the house in her car."

"Which is not impossible. Maybe the killer was trying to stage a death scene for Goody that would further implicate her husband in the murder of Dobbs," Jerome said.

"That doesn't make sense. He'd have to make it look like

suicide." Kay's head was pounding again.

"If the arson had been more professional, it might have been impossible to tell if she'd been murdered or committed suicide," Jerome said.

"That's a lyrical story. A woman whose lover was killed by her husband commits suicide by burning herself up in her lover's house," Alison said, looking off into the distance as though she were watching the story unfold on a movie screen.

"If the killer set the fire, that would seem to eliminate Campbell. He knows how fires work. They're his business," Jerome said.

Kay nodded. "I think if the murderer set the fire, then he or she already has the money and any searching they're doing is just a charade to deflect suspicion."

"'Cause you'd be crazy to burn down a house that might have a million dollars hidden inside," Jerome said.

"I've got a question. Why was my father killed in the back room of the shop?" Alison asked.

"So the murder wouldn't be seen from the front part of the shop. Or maybe so the body wouldn't be discovered too soon," Lee suggested.

"But they didn't even bother to lock the front door. And if the body had been behind the counter or in his workshop, it would have been hidden as well as it was in the back room."

"The door to the back room wasn't closed either, which wouldn't have taken any time to do. I agree with Alison. The killer wasn't that worried about the body being discovered," Kay said.

"What's in the back room?" Lee asked.

"It's mainly just a utility room. Mops and buckets, a utility sink, the heater, the fuse boxes, nothing anyone would want to steal," Jerome said.

"There's a back door, but the report said it was bolted from the inside, so the killer didn't escape that way. So that doesn't explain why the killer led Dobbs back there to stab him," Kay said.

"Maybe Dobbs kept the million dollars hidden back there," Lester said and everyone looked at him in surprise.

"Where did that spark of insight come from?" Lee asked him and got a big grin in return.

"I feel like we should throw him a Scooby Snack." Jerome shook his head. "I think one of us should go to the shop and look around the back room."

"Didn't Sutton and the deputies search it?" Kay asked.

"They weren't looking for a hidden compartment or a trapdoor. Even if Sutton had thought of it, I wouldn't trust him to do a thorough search."

"We can go when we get done here," Lee said.

"You're going to have dinner before you go anywhere else," came Ruby's voice from the other side of the door.

"Ruby, just open the door!" Kay yelled.

The door opened and Ruby stepped in. "Thank you. These doors are thicker than you'd think." She tapped on the old oak door.

"Fine. We'll go after dinner," Lee said.

"You'll be glad you ate first. I've fixed green beans and ham hocks with fresh biscuits, and peach cobbler from preserves I put up this summer."

Kay saw Lester actually drooling.

"I've never eaten so well in my life," Alison said.

"Honey, feeding these people is my job. If they aren't getting fatter, I'm not working hard enough," Ruby told her.

"There's one more murder. We can't forget about the hit-and-run," Kay said, focusing everyone's attention back on the matter at hand. "If that was the murderer's car, then we've got this all wrong because none of our suspects owns a car like that."

"We can check the DMV. It's possible that it's a relative's car or a friend's. If that's the case, I don't see how it can be kept a secret for long. Most people aren't going to let someone drag them into a murder, family or not," Jerome said.

"What about stolen vehicles?" Kay asked.

"That's been checked. Nothing so far, and that includes all the surrounding counties."

"Maybe it's as important to find where the car came from as where it went," Lee said.

"For all we know, the car could have been stolen from someplace like the Gainesville airport's long-term parking. Which means it's not going to be reported missing until the owner comes back for it," Jerome said.

"Why kill Alton Singleton?" Kay asked.

"And me!" Lee added.

"Lee has an interesting point. Maybe the driver *was* trying to hit him." Jerome patted Lee on the shoulder.

"That's not comforting." Lee frowned.

"Look on the sunny side. He missed you."

"*Almost* missed me," Lee reminded him. "My hip is killing me right now."

"I doubt that Lee was the target. Let's assume the driver got his man. Why run down Singleton?" Kay asked.

"It could be as simple as the fact that Singleton knew the identity of the killer—Webber," Lee said.

"I'm just not convinced Courtney Webber is the killer." Kay wasn't satisfied with that answer.

"She almost killed you," Alison reminded her.

"There is that," Kay admitted, feeling the knot on the side of her head.

"If it was Webber, then she's come close to killing both of us," Lee said. He didn't like the thought that they were targets of the murderer. "We need to be more careful."

Alison reached over and took his hand in hers.

Kay said, "Finding the killer as quick as possible is our best defense."

"The cemetery," Ruby said and everyone looked at her. They were all used to her making odd comments, but it was still hard not to pay attention when she did.

"What about the cemetery?" Lester asked.

"The cats have been going to the cemetery and bringing back trinkets. I'd say that's important. I'm going to put the biscuits in the oven. Dinner will be ready in fifteen minutes." She turned and left without another word.

"What was that about?" Kay asked the universe.

"I've got to go on duty." Jerome looked at his watch, then added, "After I get some of those green beans, ham hocks and biscuits." He turned to Lee and Alison. "Put the crime-scene tape back up when you leave the store. We're done with it, but it might make some people think twice before breaking in."

Lee and Alison got up from the table, having eaten a few bites too much.

"We're going over to the store. Anyone want to go with us?" Lee asked, rubbing his stomach and stretching.

"I'm going to read through the reports and interviews again," Kay said.

"I'll come." Lester's answer took Lee by surprise. The invitation had been meant for Kay. Lee cursed himself for not making that explicit.

"Sure. Let's go." Lee couldn't think of a way to un-invite Lester.

"My parents bought me an eight-track player for Christmas from your dad's store when I was twelve," Lester told Alison as they walked down the street to the store. "I guess going to the place your dad was murdered is going to be tough for you?"

"Yes," Alison said in a quiet way that made Lee feel protective of her.

"You don't have to talk the whole way there," Lee said peevishly.

"Okay." Lester started whistling instead.

They walked around to the back of the building.

"How are we going to get in?" Lee asked.

"Dad's lawyer told me where Dad hid a spare key."

There were two doors at the back of the store. Along the wall of the building were paving stones, which turned into tarmac several feet from the building. Alison started counting stones from the door on the left. When she got to the twentieth paving stone, she kneeled down.

"Do you want help?" Lee had followed along beside her.

"No, I think I can get it." With just a bit of effort, she pulled the stone up. Underneath it was a small, rusted metal box. "The key," she said after popping off the lid to reveal a fob with a single key attached.

They were able to unlock the first door they tried, but couldn't push it open. Assuming that it was bolted from the inside, they moved to the second door, which opened easily.

Lee reached up and took down the yellow crime-scene tape from the doorway. He put it aside so they could replace it when they left. Alison felt along the inside wall and found the light switch. The door opened into a workshop that had two long, wooden tables filled with TVs, radios and phonographs in various states of repair.

Lester had been following along behind with a mopey expression on his face.

"Okay, I'm sorry that I snapped at you. You can talk now," Lee told him, causing Lester's face to break into a huge grin.

"Look at all this stuff!" Lester went over to the table.

"Talk, but don't touch anything," Lee said.

"I'm not stupid," Lester said, looking at everything with a fascinated expression.

"I want to go look at the utility room," Lee told Alison. "You don't have to come if you don't want to."

"I can handle it," she said and followed him out into the front part of the store.

"Wow. All of this is yours!" Lester had joined them and was staring at the displays of electronic equipment that had been for sale.

"Lester!" Lee chastised him.

"I didn't mean anything. I know it's horrible about your father," Lester said to Alison, who gave him a small smile.

"It's all right. When we get this settled, we'll have to go through all of this."

"There's the door to the utility room." Lee pointed to an open door on the south side of the store. They had to go around the counter to get to it.

Lee reached behind him and took Alison's hand as they approached the opening. There was just enough light from the store to show him the string hanging down from the bare bulb in the ceiling. He tugged on it and the dim light did its best to push back the darkness.

The room was ten-by-ten, with a hot-water heater and a gas furnace in one corner. The furnace was giving off a slight hiss and a fan was pushing air through the duct work that fed into the store and workshop. There were breaker boxes against the outside wall of the room, with a dozen stickers showing that the store had been inspected by various officials for conformity to city codes. On the left-hand side of the door was a professional-grade fire extinguisher.

Even in the dim light, they could still see a dark stain

covering most of the pine floorboards. There was no theatrical chalk outline showing where the body had lain, but there didn't need to be. The stain made it clear.

Lee felt Alison tighten her grip on his hand as she saw the spot where her father had died. Lee knew from seeing the autopsy report and talking with Doyle that Dobbs had died almost instantly, but that didn't make it any easier for Alison.

"He was facing the breaker boxes," Lee observed.

"What a sad place for him to die." Alison's voice was melancholy.

"From what they learned at the autopsy, it was very quick," Lee said.

"I guess that's a small mercy."

"There's not much to search," Lester said, poking his head into the room.

He was right. The walls were covered in cheap paneling and, other than the mop and other cleaning supplies, there was only a steel rack that held some bathroom tissue and cleaning products.

"Maybe behind these shelves," Lee said, looking at the steel rack.

Finding nothing behind the shelves, Lee grabbed a chair and asked Lester climb up and lift one of the panels to look at the space above the drop ceiling.

"Really dusty and dirty. I think I could tell if anything had been up here," Lester said, using a flashlight they'd found in the workshop to peer into the dark corners of the narrow space between the drop ceiling and the store's roof.

They spent another half hour knocking on the walls, looking behind the hot-water heater and the furnace, as well as checking to make sure the fire extinguisher was real and not a dummy stuffed with money. All the while, they tried not to stand on the bloody stain on the floor.

"Nothing," Lee said. "I'm sure the money isn't in this room and, as far as I can tell, it never was."

"So why did Dad's murderer bring him back here?" Alison asked.

"I don't know." Lee shook his head.

"If we're done back here, I'm going to go look around the store." Lester looked at Alison. "If that's okay with you."

"I wouldn't mind looking around myself." She gave him a light punch in the arm that caused him to blush.

"I'm going to look around the workshop and see if there's anywhere the money might have been hidden in there," Lee said.

As he looked under the tables, behind doors and in cabinets, he could hear Alison and Lester talking about all the electronic gadgets and gizmos her father had had in the store.

"Which is better, Betamax or VHS?" Lester asked Alison.

"Betamax has a slightly better resolution and sound quality, but VHS is cheaper and the tapes are formatted for a full two hours." Alison's voice was excited. "It's just too cool to think you can watch all the movies you want at home."

"The movies are like ninety dollars each. I want one so I can record TV shows," Lester told her.

They chattered away like kids discussing what toys they wanted for Christmas until Lee came in and told them they should take one more pass around the store and call it quits.

When they got back to the funeral home, Kay was sitting on the couch in the office with her feet propped up, watching *Little House on the Prairie* on the nineteen-inch color TV their dad had bought six years earlier

"You caught me. I confess I've got a thing for Michael Landon… ever since he was Little Joe on *Bonanza*. I'd love to run my hands through those curls."

"I didn't need to know any of that." Lee put his hands up

and covered his ears.

Alison elbowed him. "Women can look too."

"La, la, la! Not listening," he said, laughing. This led to Alison chasing him around the room and out toward the kitchen.

Kay smiled, feeling a sense of family that she hadn't had in a long time.

CHAPTER TWENTY-TWO

"The morgue's on the line for you!" Kay yelled, rapping on Lee's door the next morning.

"I'm up!" he lied and rolled out of bed.

"It's a Tuesday morning special," Glen Doyle said cheerily when Lee got to the phone. "I was told to release two bodies to you."

"Two?"

"Yep. Hubert Dobbs and the very toasty Ellen Goody."

"Really?" Goody's body was a complete surprise. "Are you sure about Goody?"

"Authorized by her husband."

"He's in jail."

"So I heard. Apparently he used one of his phone call privileges to authorize the Lamberton Funeral Home as the recipient of his wife's body. Lucky you."

"We'll definitely be over to pick up Dobbs's body this morning, and I'll double check on Goody just to make sure there hasn't been a mistake."

"Take your time. They aren't going anywhere on their own and we currently have plenty of vacancies."

After he hung up with Doyle, Lee stood and stared at the phone. He needed to talk to Fred Goody, but he had no idea how to make a call to someone in jail. He briefly considered calling Jerome until he remembered that his friend had worked the late shift. Lee valued his life too much to bother him now.

Deciding that in-person would be best, he dressed in his best professional-but-not-conducting-a-funeral clothes.

"I'm going to the jail and talk to Fred Goody," Lee told Kay, explaining what Doyle had told him.

"Do you really think he wants us to conduct the funeral?"

"Someone does. Maybe they've got other family. Not that anyone contacted us."

"Are you going to ask him any questions about the murders?"

Lee nodded. "If I get the chance."

It was chilly that morning, so Lee drove the Lincoln with the heat on high. With the jail less than a mile away, he was still feeling the cold down deep in his bones when he walked up to the front doors. Inside the lobby were a dozen people waiting to talk to family members.

The deputy manning the reception desk had a face carved out of granite. He looked like he was tired of listening to stupid stories from stupid people.

"I'm Lee Lamberton from the funeral home. I need to talk to Fred Goody about the arrangements for his wife's funeral."

"Put your name on this list," the deputy said, pushing a clipboard filled with the names of visitors and the prisoners they wanted to see.

Lee looked at the deputy's name embroidered on a patch sewn to his shirt. "Deputy Fisher, I'd really appreciate it if you could let me talk to him for just a second. I need to pick his wife up from the morgue this morning."

Lee didn't think the deputy had blinked since he walked up to the counter. Without making eye contact, the deputy tapped the clipboard.

Lee decided to go for shock value in hopes of getting the deputy to reconsider his case. He leaned forward and lowered his voice so that the other people sitting around wouldn't hear him. "Her left side was burned so bad that the skin is peeling off, and I'm going to have to replace the eye with a glass one just to make her… viewable."

The deputy swallowed and, for the first time, looked directly at Lee. "You don't need to bother on Fred's account. He won't be getting out to see her."

"I'm sure they'll bring him to the funeral." He remembered at least three different funerals where prisoners had been allowed to attend with law enforcement escorts.

"He killed his wife's lover. I don't know why he'd want to," the deputy sneered.

"If I could talk to him, I'd be able to better assess his wishes," Lee said.

The deputy sighed, obviously tired of dealing with Lee. "Sure, what the hell." He pressed a button on a large phone console on his desk. "Chuck, I'm going to let this guy from the funeral home in. Show him to a table and go get Fred Goody. The guy needs to talk to him."

A loud buzzer sounded as Fisher hit the door release. A short, older black deputy with a grey afro met Lee at the door. He ushered him over to a wall of lockers where Lee was made to surrender all of his worldly goods and submit to a quick pat-down. Once the deputy was sure that Lee wasn't sneaking in any nail files, he escorted him into the jail proper and over to a long row of tables with chairs on both sides and a Plexiglas shield dividing them in half. Most of the chairs were filled with prisoners and family members. Chuck pointed to an empty chair and left without a word.

Five minutes later, he returned with Fred Goody, who was wearing both wrist and ankle restraints. Lee recognized the tall, broad-shouldered man from his many visits to the produce stand.

Goody sat down across from Lee. "You got her body?" he asked without preamble.

Lee shook his head. "Not yet. But I got a call from the morgue saying that we're supposed to pick up your wife."

"That's right."

"Have we made any arrangements? Did you have an agreement with my father?"

Goody looked confused. "Didn't my nephew call you?"

"No one has contacted us."

"That good-for-nothing…" Goody took a deep breath. "It's hard to get anything done when you're locked up in jail. I want you to take care of Ellen."

"What do you mean, take care of her?" Lee saw the exasperated look on Goody's face and hurriedly added, "I know you want me to bury her, but there's a lot more to it than that. The type of coffin, service, obituary, who you want to conduct the funeral. What about a viewing?"

"Geez, nothing's easy." Goody's frustration seemed on the verge of turning to anger.

"If it's any consolation to you, I don't think you killed Hubert Dobbs," Lee told him.

Goody raised his eyebrow. "You don't?"

"No. Someone murdered your wife and Alton Singleton too. I was hit by the same car that killed Singleton."

Goody's eyes narrowed. "I heard about that. I know why my wife was killed."

Lee's heart began to beat faster. "You do?"

"I know why she went to that house."

"I'd be interested to hear about that," Lee said, trying not to sound too anxious.

"Yeah, and I'd like a ZERO bar."

Lee was baffled. "Huh?"

"The candy bar. A ZERO bar. I want one. I've been eating this crap prison food for days. I got a sweet tooth and want a candy bar. Is that so hard to understand?"

"No."

Goody pointed over Lee's shoulder. "There's a vending machine right over there. If you buy one, the guard will give it to me." Now he was pointing to a female deputy who looked like she weighed twice what Lee did.

Lee dug into his pockets and came up with the required quarter. Soon, Goody was savoring his candy bar as Lee asked him why Ellen Goody had gone to Dobbs's house.

"Ellen was going to burn that sucker down," Goody said, leaning back in the metal chair.

"Why?"

"'Cause she liked that stupid Santa guy and didn't want those gamblers to get their hands on that money."

"Money?" Lee asked, playing dumb.

"Sure, there was a pot of money. Dobbs told her about it. The gamblers had been bugging the hell out of him for weeks about it. He thought that they needed to keep their promise of not gambling outside of his weird little circle. I guess with the economy in the pits, they needed the money now."

"Ellen told you all this?"

"Yep. Soon as she heard that he'd been killed."

"She admitted to the affair?"

"What choice did she have? Ellen wasn't stupid. She knew it was all going to come out anyway. Her and I weren't in love with each other. Still, we were friends. She even knew that the cops were going to come down hard on me."

"Why didn't she tell the police about the gamblers and the money?"

"I told her not to," Goody said calmly.

"Why would you do that?"

"Save it back. I went to school with the sheriff. Tom Pratt is the most conniving snake I've ever met. Best to guard any information you got and use it when it's to your own advantage." The farmer looked through the Plexiglas with eyes that were used to staring a hundred yards across a plowed field. Lee wondered if he was thinking he'd badly miscalculated the situation.

"Did you know that she would burn the house down?" Lee asked.

"No. I did know that she thought one of the gamblers killed him, which made her angrier than I'd ever seen her. I feel a little bad now about asking her not to tell the sheriff. If she had, she might have felt like she was doing enough. As it was, she needed a way to reach out and hurt them. Destroying that money was the best she could do."

"Why are you still in jail? Haven't they set bail?"

"I'm better off here. Realized that when Ellen was killed. If I'd been loose, they would have tried to pin that murder on me too."

Lee knew he was right.

"Did she know that the money was in the house?"

"No. Dobbs never told her where it was. Before he died, she didn't care. It just became important to her after he was murdered."

"Did she have any idea which of the gamblers might have been the killer?"

"I think she had her suspicions, but we didn't exactly have a calm, rational conversation at the time."

"Did you know about the affair before she told you?"

"Nope. I figured she had a friend 'cause she had perked

up the last six months or so. Ask me then, I'd have told you that, as long as it was kept quiet, it was a good thing. Like I said, we were friends more than we were husband and wife. She was a disappointment to me, not being able to have children. I just lost interest in that sort of thing. Too much work to be done to be wasting energy rolling around in the bed." Goody's tone was dismissive.

Remembering that he had other business, Lee pulled out a few brochures that he'd brought with him. "We need to talk about Ellen's funeral."

They settled on the arrangements, then Lee bought Goody another candy bar and left the visiting area.

In the lobby of the jail, Lee used the payphone to call Alison at her motel.

"They're releasing your father's body. If you meet me at the funeral home, we can settle all the details before I pick him up."

Thirty minutes later, Alison was signing off on the forms for everything they'd previously discussed.

"I'm sorry we have to go through all these formalities," Lee told her.

"I understand. I guess we should have a viewing for him."

"Absolutely. He was a popular figure in town and folks'll like the opportunity to say goodbye. When do you want to hold the funeral?"

"Soon. Can we do it Thursday?"

"Sure. We can hold the viewing tomorrow evening."

"What about the poker game?"

"We said the game would start at seven. The viewing can be from five to seven. The gamblers would want to be at the viewing anyway." Lee felt odd scheduling a viewing around a poker game, but nothing about this situation was normal.

When they were done, Lee walked with Alison out to her

car.

"I'm sorry to rush off, but I need to go pick up Mrs. Goody and your father," Lee told her, wishing he could spend more time with her.

"I know. I'm sorry to want to get everything done so quickly."

"It's okay. My dad and I did five unrelated funerals in three days once. There won't be a viewing for Mrs. Goody, and her husband is fine with the funeral being on Friday, so everything will work out. But I need to go ahead and get the bodies." He didn't want to go into the gory details of cleaning up what was left after an autopsy.

Before Alison drove away, they exchanged a gentle kiss that had Lee feeling light as air as he went back up the driveway to find Lester.

"I can drive the new hearse," Lester whined as Lee got behind the wheel of the Cadillac and pointed Lester toward Bertha.

"I'm sure you can, but you aren't," Lee told him in no uncertain terms.

"It's almost two years old. It's going to get a scratch on it eventually."

"That attitude is exactly why you won't be driving it anytime soon. Now go get Bertha and follow me."

The next day, Lee worked nonstop until noon. He'd embalmed Dobbs after they'd brought both of the bodies from the morgue, so he still had to work on Ellen Goody, as well as manage the final preparations for Dobbs's viewing that evening.

When he finally had a chance to take a break, Lee went looking for Kay and found her in the office with two new decks of cards.

"Working on your game?" he asked, walking over to the desk.

"I hope we aren't going to drop five thousand dollars tonight," she told him.

"You picked up the money from the bank?"

She tapped a manila envelope on the desk. "Makes me nervous having that much cash around."

"Want me to put it in the safe?"

"I'll do it in a few minutes. What about Alison's share?"

"She emptied her bank account and she's bringing it with her this afternoon."

"Do you think she knows what she's doing?" Kay asked.

Lee hesitated. "She's nervous. What worries her most is how you're going to get them to agree to five-card stud."

"I've got a plan. I'll talk to her about it before the viewing. A lot will depend on how good of an actor she is."

"Maybe they'll surprise us and *want* to play five-card stud."

"Or they'll insist on draw poker," Kay said darkly. "Let's hope my plan works."

"At least we now know for sure what Ellen Goody was doing in that house."

"She knew about the money. Makes you wonder if anyone else knew about it," Kay mused.

"That's a scary thought. We don't need any more suspects."

Alison arrived at four-thirty. The black dress she wore was simple, but she still took Lee's breath away.

"I feel so wrong telling you how beautiful you look at your father's viewing," he said, taking her hand in his.

"You're sweet," Alison said and hugged him.

"Would you like to see your father before anyone else arrives?"

"Please."

"I hope you like the suit I picked." With his home destroyed, there hadn't been any of Dobbs's clothes to dress him in, so Lee had used one from a small selection of funeral clothes he kept, just in case. "I think Mrs. Mathis did a good job on his hair too. She was a friend of his and spent a bit of time to get everything just right." Lee realized he was rambling. "I'm sorry. Not everyone wants to hear all the details."

Alison squeezed his hand as they approached the coffin. "It's fine. Thank you. He looks very peaceful."

Lee left her alone with her father. He knew that every family member's grief was different, and he could only imagine how hard it was for Alison when she thought about all the time she had missed with her dad.

The viewing was crowded. Lee told Alison that it was a testament to how well-liked her father had been. While that was true, he also knew that a fair number of the people present were gawkers who'd come solely to see a murder victim at the center of an ongoing investigation.

The four gamblers showed up and maintained a wary distance from each other. More than once, Kay saw them look at each other with something less than charity in their eyes. *This is going to be a fun poker game*, she thought. *We should probably frisk them for weapons.*

Jerome, looking official in his uniform, was helping with parking and security. He was surprised to see Wade Sutton walk past him up the drive to the funeral home.

"Whatever you've told the sheriff doesn't mean a hill of beans to me," Sutton said to Lee when he came inside, strutting like the proverbial bull in a china shop. "You're going to be sorry for sticking your noses into my investigation."

"You're a brave man, trying to push your weight around, not knowing what I've got going with the sheriff," Lee responded.

This took Sutton a minute to digest. "What do you mean?"

"Think it through, Einstein," Lee snapped. "And a word of advice: If you know what's good for you, I'd suggest you don't go over and threaten my sister like that." Lee nodded across the room to where Kay was stationed at the head of the coffin, guiding the line of mourners.

"Why, what you goin' to do about it?"

Lee laughed. "If you think it's me you have to worry about, then you're really going to step in it."

Lee left Sutton standing in the middle of the room looking angry and confused. Secretly, he hoped that Sutton *would* go over and say something to Kay. He changed his mind when he thought about a scuffle breaking out at Alison's father's funeral. That was the last thing he wanted. So he went over and called Kay away from the coffin long enough to tell her what Sutton had said and to warn her that the man seemed to be looking for a fight.

"I've got enough to worry about with this card game tonight." Kay looked more distracted and nervous than Lee had ever seen her.

"Did you talk to Alison?"

"We have a strategy. Just keep your fingers crossed. What's Sutton doing here, anyway?"

"I guess he's hoping the murderer will throw themselves on the coffin and beg for forgiveness so he can step in and make the arrest."

"That's the only chance that lummox has to solve the case."

Kay returned to her station next to the coffin so she could observe each of the suspects as they came up to pay their respects to Dobbs. She looked hard for any indication that one of them felt some remorse or guilt for his death, but if one of them was guilty they were able to look on the dead man without any outward signs that they had stabbed him in the back.

At a quarter to seven, everyone had left the viewing except for the four gamblers.

"I'm going to take Lester and set up the office for the game," Kay told Lee, who was standing by the front door, watching the driveway in case any last minute mourners showed up.

"Fine. I'll start closing things down in a few minutes and join you at seven."

Jerome came in from the driveway as Kay headed for the office.

"Looks like the crowd is thinning. Are you ready to lose all your money to our suspects?" Jerome grabbed Lee's shoulder and shook him playfully.

"I wouldn't want to be me if we lose," Lee joked weakly. "Seriously, Kay will kill me if we end up five thousand dollars poorer."

"Oh, I know she will."

"Thanks for your support."

Alison joined them. "I'm a little nervous."

"Your boyfriend here was just saying the same thing." Jerome chuckled.

All Lee heard was the word "boyfriend." He looked at Alison to see how she took it and noticed a small smile on her face that lit a fire in his gut.

"They look nervous, but I don't think it's the game they're worried about," Jerome said, nodding toward the four suspects who were still standing apart from each other.

"Looks like 'trust' isn't the word of the day," Lee observed.

CHAPTER TWENTY-THREE

When the hall clock struck seven, the four gamblers started toward the door of the office as one.

"I'm going to close up the casket, then I'll join you. Kay has everything set up for the game," Lee said as they passed him.

"I hope y'all brought your money," Walt Lawson responded.

"Would you like to say a final goodbye?" Lee asked Alison.

"I think so."

Alison followed him back into the viewing room. Lee stood back to let her have her last moment alone with her father. She reached out to touch his hand, but stopped just short before mouthing the words, "I love you."

When she backed away, Lee stepped up and lowered the lid of the casket and locked it. After turning off the lights, they left the room and closed the doors behind them.

Kay and Lester had brought a large round table out of

the parlor and into the office. Now, with six chairs around it and the four gamblers dressed in black standing behind their places, Lee thought it looked oddly ominous.

"I don't get a chair," Lee said, half in jest.

"No one sits at the table who isn't playing," Milton Campbell said with the air of a drill instructor.

"And you can't wander around behind us either," Courtney Webber added.

"Let's see the money," Lawson said. As an example, he pulled out his own five thousand dollars and laid it on the table. The rest of the gamblers followed suit.

"Here." Kay handed Alison an envelope of cash as they joined the others around the table. Alison had wanted it kept secure during the funeral, so they'd put her portion in the office safe with Kay's share.

"I brought chips." Victor Pratt held up a small case.

Alison opened her envelope and was sorting through her money when she said, "I've only played poker a few times. We're playing the one where you lay one card face down and then deal the other cards face up, right?"

Everyone looked at her as she continued to fiddle with the stack of cash she was holding.

"We usually play five-card draw," Lawson said flatly.

"Oh." Alison had her money spread out in front of her on the table. "I don't know about that. I... just assumed... I didn't even know there were any other types of poker."

"We'll explain it. A couple of hands and you'll know what you're doing," Webber said. Her voice was kind, but Kay thought she could detect a little greed as the woman stared at the cash spread out in front of Alison.

"Easy-peasy," Pratt told Alison, also keeping an eye on her cash.

Slowly Alison began to gather up her money. "I don't know. That doesn't sound very smart to play a new game for all this money. I think maybe I'll just sit this out and watch." With all four of the gamblers watching intently, she started to put her money back in the envelope.

"What the hell! Five-card stud is fine with me." Lawson smiled.

"Sure. For the little lady, we can play stud," Campbell agreed.

"I'm game." Webber nodded.

"You know I'm easy." Pratt opened the case of poker chips.

As everyone took their seats, Jerome and Lester came in.

"We took down the signs and locked everything up," Jerome told Lee.

"If you all are going to stay, you need to keep away from the table," Lawson said to Lester and Jerome. They joined Lee in three chairs set against the wall.

"The game is five-card stud." Pratt put a deck of cards in the center of the table. "We'll cut. High card deals."

Webber won the deal, but the first two hands went to Lawson.

"The agreement was that we get to ask questions during the game," Kay said, shuffling the cards.

"We're here, aren't we?" Campbell told her.

Kay dealt a card down and a card up to everyone. "We'd like to go over where everyone was on the night that Dobbs was killed," she said.

They bet on the first two cards. As the cards were dealt and bets placed, each of the players went over their lack of an alibi for the night that Dobbs had been killed.

"So you all had the opportunity to kill him," Kay said.

"This is a small town and it's easy to get across in ten minutes. Three of us could walk to the shop in ten minutes. You know I was at a school board meeting and still could have gone to the shop and gotten back without being missed. Not having an alibi doesn't make us guilty," Webber said as Pratt pulled the pot in and stacked his chips.

The next two games went to Alison and the players started to look at her differently. Campbell won a hand, then Alison pulled in two more pots and the looks on the players' faces turned sour. Kay had worked them around to talking about the murder of Ellen Goody, but their minds were clearly focused on their diminishing supply of chips.

"I was at the house after you, but before Ellen Goody showed up," Webber told them.

Campbell tossed chips into the pot. "I was at home. My wife can vouch for me. Anyway, if I'd started the fire it would have been done professionally, not like that half-ass effort." He looked around at the others as though to imply they were more likely to have done the sloppy arson job.

"I don't really have an alibi," Lawson said. "I got called out to the north side store because the clerk was worried about a couple of... ladies who were hanging out. He thought they might be trying to pick up... gentlemen. He called me around six that morning and I drove over there and chased them off."

"Why did he call you? Why not the sheriff's office?" Kay asked.

"I want to open a new store near the Pine Grove neighborhood. It doesn't help me when the homeowners who don't want it can go to the commission and show how many calls for service my stores have generated. So I've told my clerks that unless someone is bleeding or threatening them or a customer, to call me before they call the sheriff."

"After you went by the store, where'd you go?"

"Back home eventually, but I stayed out so I could drive by the store a couple of times and make sure the women didn't come back. When I got home, I heard the fire engines headed for Dobbs's house."

Kay pulled in her first pot. As she was stacking her chips, she said to Campbell, "Ellen Goody started the fire, so that part of your alibi doesn't fly."

Campbell gave her a sharp look. "Where'd you hear that?"

"Fred Goody told me she intended to burn the house down," Lee said from his seat against the wall. The four suspects looked at him as though they'd forgotten anyone else was in the room.

"Seems she knew about the money and suspected that one of you had killed Dobbs," he continued.

"No way." Pratt looked at Lee, wide-eyed.

"She wanted to destroy the money to punish all of you."

"Ha!" Webber said. "That sounds like Ellen."

"I never would have thought that Bertie would have told her about the money," Lawson said thoughtfully.

Five more hands and the stacks of chips in front of Alison had grown to impressive heights.

"What kind of con are you all playing?" Lawson growled, pointing a finger at Alison. "She's played a lot more poker than she let on."

"I played in high school. Never once have I played for more than pennies." Alison neatly moved her stacks of chips to the side.

"High school. I bet!" Campbell huffed.

"Shut up, Milton, and deal," Webber told him.

As the night drew on, the four gamblers became more sullen as their chips diminished. Jerome was stretched out on the couch. Lester, bored, had gone home. Kay continued to mix a few questions with periods of silence.

"I'm about done answering questions." Lawson tossed his cards across the table at Kay. She gathered them up and shuffled the deck.

"I just want to go over where you all were when Alton

Singleton was run down," she said.

"They ran me down too," Lee reminded them.

"Ask your damn questions before we go bust," Campbell grumbled.

"That's it. Where were you that night?" Kay dealt everyone a card down and one up.

"I was at the academy working with new recruits on night training." Campbell looked at his hole card. "Seventy percent of the house fires we fight occur at night, which is a world of difference from fighting a fire during the day."

"At home in bed that night," Lawson said.

"Anyone with you?" Kay asked.

"Sadly, no. My wife and I are separated, and I can't afford a girlfriend." Lawson's words came out in an angry burst.

"I broke into Dobbs's store that night," Webber said and everyone looked at her. She glared back while tapping her cards. "What? Does it matter anymore? I didn't find anything, if that makes you happy."

"I was with a woman in Gainesville. She works at the Purple Porpoise Pub. You can have her name and number if you want," Pratt said.

Two more long hours passed and the clock in the hall struck three. Webber was out and sitting on the arm of the couch while Alison, Kay, Campbell, Lawson and Pratt struggled on. Lawson was the only one of the three with more than a hundred dollars in chips left in front of him.

The deal was Alison's. She tapped the deck a couple of times and yawned. "I'm done," she said.

"You can't just say you're done and walk away," Lawson snapped.

"We've asked all our questions," Kay said, shaking herself awake.

"I'll give you a choice," Alison said. Her eyes were cold and steady. "We can finish the game and I keep all the money, or we can quit now and I return everyone's stake."

The gamblers stared at her, trying to decide if she was serious.

Lawson looked like he'd eaten a lemon. "What kind of joke is this?"

"It's a deal," Webber said.

"I'm good with that." Pratt sounded relieved.

"You suckered us into this game anyway," Campbell grumbled.

"Wait. That's not… screw it! Whatever." Lawson covered his face with his hands.

Everyone took their money back almost reluctantly.

After Kay and Lee walked them to the door and watched them leave, Lee said, "I don't understand. You would have thought they would have been more grateful to get their money back."

"Alton Singleton explained it to me. They don't mind losing. In fact, that's the part of the game that gives them a thrill. By giving them the money back, they felt cheated," Kay said.

"That's just weird." Lee shook his head. "Did we learn anything from the game?"

"I found it interesting that Campbell likes to insist he couldn't be the killer."

"Protests too much?"

"He made me want to check up on his alibis," Kay said.

"I'm out of here." Jerome had walked up behind them, headed for his motorcycle.

"Where's the fire academy?" Kay asked him. "Where was Campbell training the night that Singleton was hit?"

"And me. I'm still walking with a limp and you can't even remember that I was hit too," Lee said. Kay and Jerome ignored him.

"It's out by our shooting range, next to the county

landfill," Jerome said.

"I can show you where the landfill is on a map," Lee told Kay.

"I better head back to the motel," said Alison, joining them at the door.

"You can stay here," Lee said. When he saw everyone looking at him, he added, "We have a spare room."

"Stay," Kay urged her. "You were amazing tonight."

"It's just math," Alison said, blushing.

"You'd be surprised how few people can do probabilities in their heads," Kay assured her, putting her arm around Alison's shoulder and pointing her upstairs.

CHAPTER TWENTY-FOUR

Thursday morning was hectic. The funeral was scheduled for noon at Lang Methodist Church. After finding out about all the womanizing and the gambling, Lee had been surprised when Alison told him that her father had requested his funeral be held at the church. He'd even left a small bequest to them. When Lee contacted the minister, he'd confirmed that Dobbs was a semi-regular congregant. Lee wondered how many Methodist women were in Dobbs's little black book.

The funeral would be followed by a short graveside service. Dobbs owned four plots less than fifty yards from where Lee had buried Mr. Hartsfield.

"Polish the Cadillac and the family cars," Lee told Lester when he found him in the kitchen, nursing a large cup of coffee. "And lay off the coffee. Otherwise you'll be going to the bathroom every five minutes."

"It's really cold out there," Lester grumbled.

"The cars are clean, so it shouldn't take long. Just make

sure there are no smears and no trash inside."

"I hear that Alison is pretty sharp with a deck of cards," Ruby said, pushing down the lever on the toaster. "And I know she stayed here last night. She stopped to say hi before heading back to her motel this morning. You two make a cute couple."

Lee blushed all the way down to his toes.

"Couple." Lester chuckled.

"We're just friends. No big deal. She doesn't even live here," Lee said, hoping that all three things wouldn't be true for long.

Kay came into the kitchen and went straight for the coffee. "I'm going on a little scouting mission this morning. I want to see how far the fire academy is from Dobbs's house. What do you need me to do when I get back?" While Kay ran the money side of the business, she deferred to Lee when it came to the actual service and burial arrangements.

"Help man the door at the church and seat mourners at the graveside. You can ride with me in the family car. I'm going to let Jerome drive the hearse," Lee said.

"How does he get to drive the new hearse and I don't?" Lester asked, crunching through a piece of toast.

"Gee, I don't know. Maybe because he has no traffic tickets and you could paper the walls with yours."

"Most of them are parking tickets," Lester defended himself.

"You're lucky you get to drive Bertha. Today you ride with Jerome. Which reminds me." Lee went to the phone on the wall and called Jerome to make sure he'd arranged for two deputies to escort the funeral procession from the church to the cemetery.

"You can't just have coffee," Ruby told Kay, who was waving off Ruby's attempts to fill a plate for her.

"When I've been up half the night, I can't face a big

breakfast. I'll grab something before the funeral. Gotta go."

Kay was anxious to check out the fire academy. Something about Milton Campbell's attitude at the game when they'd been discussing Singleton's murder had made her suspicious. Of course, he'd been losing at poker, so his attitude might have been all about that. Still, she figured it wouldn't hurt to drive out and see what she could learn.

The directions that Lee had given her to the landfill were straightforward. Two miles south of town was the appropriately named Dump Road, which turned into a dirt road half a mile from the landfill. Not long afterward, the sheriff's department's gun range appeared on the right side of the road and the fire safety academy on the left.

When Kay pulled up to the farm gate at the entrance to the fire department's property, she got out of the car to see if she could see anything on the other side of the gate. The sky was bright blue and the sun was burning off the morning frost as she walked up to the gate.

"Now that's just temptation in a nutshell." Kay looked at the padlock that wasn't locked. Someone had just wrapped the chain around and hooked the lock without snapping it shut.

"What the hell," she said, trotting back to her car.

After driving through, she got out of the car and closed the gate behind her. *They would have locked it if they didn't want anyone coming back here*, she told herself.

The dirt road was wide and well-traveled. A quarter mile from the gate, the woods gave way to a hundred-acre field that had a dozen buildings spread across it. Most were shells that looked like half-built homes. There was a five-story wooden tower in the middle of the field, and off to the side were various cars and trucks in different states of dereliction. All around the area were fire hydrants of various shapes and sizes.

Kay cursed when she saw the C10 Chevy pickup by the tower. Before she could think about turning around, a man came out of the tower and looked her way. She drove over and parked next to the truck.

"I didn't think anyone else would be coming out here this morning," the man said, walking over to her car.

"I'm doing some work with the sheriff's office and wanted to come out and look around." Kay stuck as close to the truth as she could.

"The sheriff?"

"I'm just looking into something for him."

"It involves the fire academy?"

"I'm Kay," she said, sticking out her hand. Automatically, the man shook it.

"I'm Seth. I just wanted to get in some practice." Seth was in his early twenties with red hair and broad shoulders. He wore a pair of dark blue BDUs and a flannel shirt.

"Practice?"

"For the physical." He pointed to a coil of fire-hose near the door. "Part of our test. We have to carry the hose up the four flights of stairs while in full gear."

"I'm impressed."

"A couple of us guys have a side bet on how fast we can do it."

"I heard y'all were doing some training Saturday night."

"That's the good stuff, when we get to work with real fires. It's amazing when you start learning the different types of fires and techniques for battling them. Fires are like living things. They grow and spread, almost with a purpose." Kay wondered if he talked that enthusiastically about any women he dated.

"What types of fires did you fight on Saturday?"

"After dark, we learned some practical points about electrical house fires. We used that house over there." He pointed to what was left of a two-story frame.

"That's realistic."

"Come on. I'll show you around."

Seth was so excited to share what he knew about the fire academy that he forgot that Kay hadn't explained what she was doing out there in the first place.

Kay tried to look interested in the building and Seth's running commentary on various types of fire. She truly was impressed with the realism of the training facility. The model house even had furniture.

"Careful. You shouldn't go in there unless you've got the right equipment," Seth said when Kay went up to a doorway and peered in. She winced at the pungent odor of burned fabric, plastic and wood.

"They start a fire and y'all have to put it out?"

"That's part of it. We also learn to recognize burn patterns so we can tell if the fire is being ventilated. They showed us the signs to look for that indicate a flashover might be about to happen. Toxic furniture... and see that life-size doll over there?" He pointed through the doorway to a creepy-looking doll the size of a ten-year-old child. "They hide that in places where a kid might hide during a fire and then fill the place up with smoke. We get timed on how fast we can find him and get him out."

"So you were here all evening?"

"Until about midnight, when we went over to the bunkhouse for some food and sleep."

"Sleep?"

"We spent Friday and Saturday night out here."

"Sounds more like the Army than firefighter school. I guess that makes sense. Fighting fires is a lot like fighting a battle."

"Yes, ma'am." Seth nodded vigorously. "They even have drills in the middle of the night where we have to get dressed, run out and get a truck ready to go. Or sometimes even go put out a fire."

"Did you have any drills Saturday night?"

"Yep. At about four in the morning we had to put out a vehicle fire."

"One of those?" Kay pointed to the cars in the field.

"The burned-out wreck on the far left. It was blazing by the time we got there."

Kay felt a tingle down her spine.

"Was Deputy Chief Campbell out here Saturday night?"

"Absolutely. He oversees most of our training sessions."

"So he was here for the house fire and then again for the car fire? Does he stay out here all night with you?"

"Oh no. None of the brass does."

"Can I see the car?"

"Sure. Not much to see." They headed over to where the vehicles were lined up. "What exactly are you doing out here?"

"I'm helping the sheriff's office locate a… missing car." She'd almost said "stolen." Better to let him think what he wanted to think. "Where do you get your cars from?"

"Some of them are donations. Others are bought at auction."

"What about this one? It's the one you burned Sunday morning, right?"

"When I saw it, it was already on fire. With the glare and adrenaline, I don't even remember what it looked like before the fire. We always have plenty of cars out here."

Seth was pointing to a dozen cars and trucks. Several were derelicts while others looked almost new.

Kay stared at what was left of the car. It still smelled of burnt rubber and plastic. "Can you tell what make and model it is?" she asked.

"See, there's a little bit of Chevrolet emblem left on the

front," Seth said, pointing to a small piece of metal. "Some compact model, maybe? Here's the VIN number." He wiped at a small metal plate in the bottom left-hand corner where the windshield used to meet the dash. "You take that number and Chevrolet can tell you everything about the car."

"Do you have a pen and a piece of paper I could write it down?"

Seth reached into the cargo pocket of his BDUs and pulled out a pen and small pad of paper. "They tell us to have paper and pen at all times," he said with a grin.

Kay wrote the letters and numbers down, her hands shaking slightly. Everything told her that she was right about what this burned car represented. Of course, if she was right, then all the evidence had been burned and washed away Sunday morning. Still, if the car matched the description of the one that had tried to run them down, and Campbell was involved in an exercise at the academy only a few hours later that had destroyed it, surely that was strong circumstantial evidence.

She thanked Seth as he walked her back to her car. A part of her wanted to ask him not to tell anyone that she'd been out there, but she could tell he was a straight shooter and that would have only aroused his suspicions, leading him to do just what she didn't want him to do. No, she'd take her chances.

Kay drove away from the training facility, trying to figure out her next course of action. If Campbell was the killer, then there had to be more evidence against him. The hard part was figuring out how to focus in on him without tipping him off that she knew he'd killed Alton Singleton.

When Kay turned back onto the main road, her mind was trying to untangle all of the options, and she never saw the pickup truck that passed her. It was her bad luck that the passenger noticed her. If she had looked in the rearview mirror, she would have seen the truck turn onto Dump Road.

Kay rushed home to change for the funeral and to tell Lee what she'd learned.

"They've already left for the church," Ruby told her as Kay headed for the stairs.

When Kay pulled into the parking lot of the church, it was already filling with mourners. Getting out of the car, she kept her eyes peeled for Lee or Jerome. She found them in the sanctuary, working with Lester to put the final touches on the coffin and arranging flower displays around it.

"I need to talk to you," she told Jerome, tugging on his sleeve.

"Sure thing." He let her lead him off to the side where she explained her suspicions about Milton Campbell.

"That's interesting. You got the VIN number of the car?" he asked.

After sending Lester to greet the mourners who were arriving, Lee joined Kay and Jerome in the corner. Kay filled him in on what she'd found.

"When we're done here, I'll pass this on to Sutton." Jerome held up the paper with the VIN number. "He may even show up for the funeral."

"Will he listen to you?" Kay asked.

"He knows the sheriff wants this solved."

"I imagine Milton Campbell will be here for the funeral," Lee said.

"Just act natural and we'll keep an eye on him," Jerome advised. "Is there any chance he knows you're on to him?"

"I don't see how. Unless Seth, the guy at the academy, talked to him," Kay said.

"Then the best thing to do is watch him," Jerome said. "…and be careful."

"I'll tell Lester to keep an eye out," Lee said.

"Where's Alison?" Kay asked.

"She had to go to the restroom," Lee said.

"I'm going to go check on her." Kay looked around. "Which way is it?"

"She went that way." Lee pointed back toward a door on the side of the sanctuary. "I think it's down the hallway on the right."

Kay found the restrooms in a recess with a water fountain between them. Kay opened the door to the women's room and called Alison's name. There was no answer. She looked inside and a quick glance under the two stalls told her that Alison wasn't there.

Worried, she opened the door to the bathroom and was startled to see Milton Campbell standing by the water fountain, looking at her and blocking her way out of the recess.

"I just needed to use the restroom," she stuttered, unable to think of anything else to say.

"Did you use the bathroom at the fire academy?" he said so menacingly that she had to force herself not to shrink back. She felt like she'd walked around the bend in a trail and bumped into a bear. She just didn't know what kind of bear it was. Was Campbell a grizzly that would meet a challenge with an attack, or was he a more timid black bear that could be bluffed? The expression on his face and his clenched fists told her he was all grizzly.

"I've told others." Kay held her ground.

"Told them what? That there is a burned-out car at the fire academy?"

"I got the VIN number and gave it to Jerome," she pressed on. The only way she could see to get out of this would be to let him know that he had nothing to gain by hurting her.

"You never bluffed the other night. That's why you're not any good at poker. So you've told Jerome. What's that prove? That the vague description of the car used to kill Alton Singleton might fit a car that the fire academy used for practice?"

"Yes, you're right. There's nothing for you to worry about." She decided to try to mollify him.

"Where's the money?"

"What?" Kay was momentarily confused by the question.

"Our money. *My* money. Did that cretinous offspring of Dobbs find it?"

"No, no. We don't know where it is any more than you do. Alison doesn't even care about the money. If she did find it, she'd be glad to let you all have it." Kay knew she was babbling, but she couldn't help it. He'd moved closer and, from the look in his eyes, she knew that he was going to hurt her. Maybe kill her.

"Get in the bathroom," Campbell ordered.

Kay thought about her options. Going willingly into the bathroom wasn't one of them. In the whirl of thoughts running through her mind, Kay heard the words of a lieutenant in Vietnam who'd taught her some self-defense moves: *Make up your mind that you're willing to do the most disgusting thing you're capable of to defend yourself. The will to inflict maximum pain is what will save you.*

Kay looked at Campbell's hard, cruel eyes and knew that they were the weak point that she would have to go after. And not just to hurt them. She needed to destroy them if she could.

Campbell reached out to push her toward the restroom door. As he did, she set her feet and prepared herself for the quick and violent actions she would need to take if she was going to live.

"Lee was right. I shouldn't have drunk all that coffee." Lester came striding into the small recess, startling both Kay and Campbell. It was like an old magnesium flashbulb had gone off, breaking the tension between them. Kay shoved past Campbell and collided with Lester.

Campbell turned quickly and shoved both of them against the wall on his way out and toward the door.

"What the hell? You almost made me wet my pants," Lester complained. "I really need to go."

"I've never been so glad to see you," Kay told him. She stuck her head out of the recess and saw Campbell slam his way out of the building. "Go to the bathroom," she told Lester.

"He was threatening you?" Lester asked, finally realizing what he had walked into.

Kay, her legs wobbly from the surge of adrenaline, leaned against the wall. "If you hadn't shown up when you did, one of us was going to end up in bad shape."

Kay pushed off the wall and hurried toward the crowded sanctuary. She caught sight of Jerome and rushed to tell him what had happened.

"He gave you a threatening look?" Jerome frowned. He saw her furious expression and shook his head. "I'm not saying he wasn't going to attack you, but it's hard for me to put out a pick-up order on him based on what you've told me. If he *is* our killer, we have to be careful."

"Careful? I swear the man was going to… I don't know, but it wouldn't have been good." Kay's voice was shaking.

"If he has evidence that we've been going after him for things that don't sound strong enough to warrant our response, his lawyer will have a field day."

"I guess I see your point. The trouble is, my pounding heart tells me this man is dangerous. Like, on-the-edge-of-a-cliff dangerous."

"Sutton's sitting in the back pew. We could go tell him what happened."

"He'll want to know everything, right?"

"Of course. And he's not a quick learner," Jerome reminded her.

"I don't think I can go through the whole story with him right now." She knew that if they tried to explain it to Sutton, the conversation would become adversarial with the investigator coming up with counter-arguments for everything that Kay knew to be true. He could take hours to convince.

Jerome looked at his watch. "The funeral is going to start in a few minutes. I'll go out and talk to the escorts. They can radio in a welfare check for Campbell."

"What good will that do?"

"Campbell's the deputy fire chief. He scans all the emergency radio frequencies; it will let him know that we're on the lookout for him, which should force him to keep a low profile. If he runs from a deputy, that will help establish him as a fugitive."

"He might just go up to the first deputy he sees and convince him he's fine."

"That's okay. That would mean he's managed to calm down enough to act rational. It will also give us his location."

"Guess that all makes sense. Let's get this funeral done so we can get the evidence to put this creep away."

Kay turned to see Lee coming down the aisle. Alison was sitting in the front pew. Behind her were Courtney Webber, Walt Lawson and Victor Pratt. Kay went over and sat down next to Alison. In an urgent whisper, she managed to give the four of them a rough idea about what was going on before the minister went up to the pulpit. They agreed to stay close together and keep an eye out for Campbell.

"What can he do if we stay together?" Lawson said with a shrug.

CHAPTER TWENTY-FIVE

The funeral was touching and heartfelt, with many people coming up afterward to introduce themselves to Alison and tell her how sorry they were about her father.

"Is it me or are there more women than men at the funeral?" Jerome said under his breath to Lee. They were following the pallbearers up the aisle. Lee stifled a snort.

With the coffin solemnly loaded into the hearse and several flower arrangements placed around it, Jerome and Lester drove the hearse slowly from the church. Lee and Kay were in the front seat of the family car, with Alison and Courtney Webber in the back seat. Lawson and Pratt were also driving together in another car.

The bright sky and moderate temperatures belied the grim procession. While rain seemed the natural weather for a funeral, Kay found sunshine to be even more depressing. To her, it indicated the world's willingness to go on without the deceased

After they parked, Lee tried to judge how many people

had followed them to the graveside. He had laid out forty chairs under the big green tent, thinking that would be plenty since there was no family but Alison. Usually, only family and a few close friends made it to the graveside following a large church service. A quick count of the cars lining up in the cemetery proved that Lee's judgment had been spot on.

Lawson, Pratt and Webber all sat next to each other in the front row, with Alison on Webber's other side. Behind them were a number of Dobbs's friends, including Lilly Osbourne and others whose names Lee recognized from the little black book. Lee tried hard not to make eye contact with them.

Wade Sutton sat in the back row. He would stare at Kay for a few minutes before turning to glare at Lee. Lee found himself glad that the man was there. At this point, the more cops, the better, even if they weren't the sharpest knives in the drawer.

Dobbs's plot was at the end of one of the cemetery's internal roads, making it a choice spot. From the tent, Lee could look out over the coffin and down the access road to the main gates of the cemetery. Dobbs was being buried next to his parents and a sister who'd died in her teens. The Dobbs headstones were modest compared to several of the nearby plots, one of which had an actual twelve-by-twelve-foot above-ground crypt. The Dane family had founded the first bank in Lang before the Civil War.

"Dear Alison," the minister began, "it is with deep sadness that you leave your father to rest on this beautiful ground. Yet he is not here. Hubert Dobbs is even now at peace in a gentle land beyond our troubles."

Lee tuned the minister out and looked toward the front gate. He could see Jerome and Lester sitting in the hearse, waiting for the service to end. It was the first vehicle parked at the end of the street nearest to the grave. Lee had parked the family car on the other side of the road, leaving an opening thirty feet wide between the two vehicles.

Lee felt a moment of peace. This was his job and his life. The funeral had gone well, despite Campbell's confrontation with Kay. They'd deal with that later. Right now he savored the view of the coffin, the tent with "Lamberton Funeral Home" spelled out in white letters and the shining hearse.

The sound of a fire engine in the distance disturbed Lee's moment of reflection. The first cold fronts of winter in Melon County always brought a few house fires, with folks using stoves and all manner of appliances that weren't meant for heating houses.

The sound of the siren drew closer. Soon everyone under the tent was looking toward the gate and the road as the siren drowned out the minister.

That's odd, Kay thought. Standing on the other side of the tent from Lee, she watched as the fire engine turned at the gate and came into the cemetery. She knew that something very wrong was happening when the truck didn't slow down. In fact, once it cleared the gate, the engine roared and the red-and-chrome juggernaut picked up speed.

"Run!" Kay screamed.

She put all her weight down on her feet in preparation for getting out of the way of the fire engine that was now barreling toward them. Too late she realized that her high heels weren't going to aid her escape. Both heels sank into the turf, causing her to topple over. The last thing she saw before hitting the ground was Wade Sutton jumping up and turning around. The sound of his high-pitched scream as he saw the fire engine plowing down the road toward them would live in Kay's memory forever.

Trying to get to Alison, Lee tripped over a chair and came down on his previously injured hip, sending a lightning bolt of pain up his side. All around him were mourners tangled in chairs and each other, trying desperately to get out from under the tent. Only a few on the outskirts of the group had much success.

Lee scrambled to his feet and stared as the fire engine kept coming, only fifty feet away from the gravesite now. Then he heard the hearse's powerful Cadillac engine roar to life and everything began to move in slow motion.

The fire engine, with an enraged Milton Campbell at the wheel, was only a few feet from the gravesite when Lee saw the hearse ram into the engine's front end. Physics being what they were, the hearse was no match for the fire engine. The water in the engine's tank alone weighed almost as much as the hearse. The hearse was flung out of the way, but like a cue ball hitting a billiard ball, it had managed to bump the engine enough to knock it fifteen feet off course as it drove off the road. Air brakes screamed as Campbell saw his fate approaching in the form of a large granite crypt. The last word he saw as he flew through the windshield was DANE writ large across the top of the crypt. The fire engine moved the crypt five feet off its foundation before coming to a stop and disturbing three generations of Danes in the process.

In the resulting chaos, Kay tended to the dozen people who'd sustained injuries as they tried to escape, assuring herself that everyone would be fine until the paramedics arrived.

Lee made sure that Alison was okay before he hurried down to the hearse, where Jerome and Lester were climbing out of what was left of the Cadillac. Its entire front end had been sheared away, yet both of them were laughing hysterically, as much out of intense relief as any real humor.

"My legs are rubber," Lester said.

"Sorry about the hearse," Jerome guffawed.

Lee ran his fingers through his hair. "I can't believe I have to be grateful to you for destroying my hearse," he said, managing a small smile as he made sure they were both okay.

Soon the cemetery was crawling with ambulances, patrol cars, deputies and firemen. Injuries were patched up and interviews were done. At one point, Kay overheard Wade Sutton telling the sheriff what actions he had taken to prevent the engine from killing the mourners. She saw the look on the sheriff's face and knew that he wasn't taking in all the smoke that Sutton was blowing.

To Kay's surprise, the sheriff *did* accept her explanation of what had happened. He told her to write it up and give it to Jerome.

By five o'clock, the only people left at the gravesite were Lee, Kay and Alison. The fire engine had eventually been dragged away by a huge tow truck. Lee had stayed to protect his funeral equipment and, if he was being honest, to watch the spectacle. Representatives of the Dane family had come by to survey the damage to the crypt. In a stroke of good salesmanship, Lee managed to talk them into letting him get their relatives new coffins and see to their re-internment in a rebuilt crypt.

"Wow!" Kay said, still marveling at the scene. Then she realized they'd never actually buried their client. "Are you going to lower Dobbs into the ground tonight?" she asked Lee, who was standing arm-in-arm with Alison.

"I wanted to wait for the chaos to move on. If Alison wants, we can do it now. Buck will fill in the hole first thing in the morning."

"That will be fine," Alison said.

Lee hit the lever that released the hydraulics to lower the coffin down to the bottom of the grave.

"I'm glad we didn't have anything worse than some sprained ankles and sore backs out of this," Alison said.

"I think your dad would be too. By all accounts, he was a good guy. High libido, but a good guy," Kay said. She pointed to several stones off to the right of the tent. "Are these your family too?"

"Yes, that's his mother and *her* mother and father."

"That's right. I remember you saying that their last name was Jordan. Didn't you say their surname had been something French before they came over here?"

"Yeah."

Kay pointed at Dobbs's mother's stone. "His mother's name was Mary Jardin Jordon Dobbs. Was Jardin their French name?"

"That's right! I guess my great-grandparents gave her that middle name as a nod to the old country."

Kay was staring intently at the gravestones. "The gamblers said that your father told them the money was buried in the garden… or was it by the garden?"

"Which was why they were all digging up his back yard." Lee looked at Kay "What are you thinking?"

"I picked up a lot of French when I was in Vietnam. The locals all had their *jardins*. Their gardens. Maybe he buried the money next to a Jardin."

Kay looked closely at Mary Jordon's tombstone. Behind the stone were four eighteen-inch pavers. They were a close match for the tombstone, but not an exact match. Kay kneeled down and felt around them.

"Hey, he put an extra key to the store under a paver," Lee said with excitement. "I wonder if…"

The stone on the left shifted as Kay put some pressure on it. She got her fingers under the stone and pulled it up. Beneath it was another stone. That stone lifted easily to reveal a small compartment about a foot deep. Within the stone compartment was a plastic box.

"That can't be a million dollars. It's not big enough," Lee

said, kneeling beside Kay.

Kay pulled out the box and snapped the lid open. Inside was a stack of papers.

"These are instructions and passwords to a Swiss bank account." She held up one of the papers, then another. "Here's one for two bank accounts in the Cayman Islands. There's also twenty or thirty thousand in cash here."

Alison shook her head. "I'm going to give it to Courtney, Victor and Walt. I don't want anything to do with the money."

Lee stood up and hugged her. Over Alison's shoulder, he saw Yin and Yang sitting quietly in the grass, staring at him knowingly.

A week later, with the sheriff happily touting his success in catching a dangerous killer lurking within the fire department, Lee and Kay invited what was left of the gambling ring to Thanksgiving dinner. Ruby and Lester pulled together several wooden folding tables to make a large enough dining table in the parlor.

Ruby spent two days organizing the menu and fixing the food. She created a seating chart that no one dared to change and made Lester dress in his funeral attire to serve the food. Lee knew for a fact that she'd spent at least two hours trying to teach Lester how to serve a formal dinner.

Lee sat at one end of the table with Kay at the other. Jerome and Courtney Webber were on one side, with Alison, Walt Lawson and Victor Pratt on the other. Lee had had to put his foot down to keep Ruby from inviting a random woman to fill out the table.

"I'll confess it feels a little strange to have dinner in here after coming to Bertie's viewing just a week ago," Webber said.

"What feels odd is knowing that Milton was willing to kill all of us for that money," Pratt said.

"I admit I was desperate, but I'd never kill anyone for money," Lawson stated.

"Do we know for sure that Milton killed all of them?" Webber asked.

"I know he killed Dobbs," Lee said. "Once Kay told me about the car, and we knew it was Campbell, I could see what had been right there in front of me the whole time. When we went to the store and looked in the utility room, there was an industrial-size fire extinguisher and all the business inspection notices on the back wall. From the blood on the floor, it was obvious that Dobbs had been facing them when he was stabbed in the back. I think Campbell had decided to kill Dobbs and did it by suggesting they take a look at the inspection notices on his fire extinguisher to make sure his inspections were up to date. While Dobbs was looking at them, Campbell rammed the knife into his heart." Lee reached out and squeezed Alison's hand.

"Looking back, his insistence that he couldn't have started the fire because he was too smart was forced. Captain Marcum, the fire department's arson investigator, told me that Campbell insinuated himself into the investigation and repeatedly insisted that the arsonist was an amateur, but not Ellen Goody," Kay told them.

"He also had a burn on his arm from the fire," Lee explained. "Apparently, he went to the house to look for the money and found Ellen Goody already starting the fire. Campbell struggled with Ellen and killed her. It was too late to stop the fire, so he let it go in hopes that it would cover up Ellen's murder. That's when he got burned. The day I talked to him, he was rubbing at his left arm a bit. At the autopsy, the coroner found second-degree burns on his upper arm."

"I feel bad for his family. I would have thought that a family would have made him less likely to be the murderer," Alison said.

"He was at the age when men can be crazy-scared of failure," Jerome said. "I should have been pointing the finger at him. Those A-personality types are the men who become family killers. They'll murder their whole family to keep from admitting that they're a failure." He turned to Alison. "You don't have to feel too sorry for his wife. She admitted to lying about his alibi for the Goody murder."

"He would have killed all of us." Pratt shook his head and ladled gravy onto his mashed potatoes.

"What about Yin and Yang?" Lester had just come from the kitchen with a platter of deep-fried turkey.

"What about the cats?" Kay said to egg him on.

"You tell them, Lee." Lester put some white meat on Kay's plate.

"That was weird. First the playing card and then the dollar bill they got from… I'm not sure it was right at it… but from pretty close to the Jordan tombstone," Lee said.

"They knew that money was there," Lester insisted, putting a leg on Alison' plate.

"At least they were pointing out that money was the motive." Ruby came in carrying another basket of biscuits. "You need to pay more attention to those two."

"I'll agree those cats are strange." Diplomatically, Lee didn't point out how odd the cats' caretaker was. Ever since she'd started working for his father, Lee had thought Ruby would make a great character in an episode of *The Outer Limits* or *Night Gallery*.

There was no talk of the money—the money that Uncle Sam didn't know existed. Two nights earlier, there'd been a meeting and an agreement had been hammered out. Alison would dole out the money when any of the three needed part of their share. What she wouldn't do was simply dump the money on them. All three admitted that if they had that kind of cash, they'd blow it within a year. There was agreement all around that Hubert Dobbs wouldn't have wanted them to do that. The big surprise had been when all three insisted that Alison accept a good-size chunk of the money herself.

"What are you going to do with the store?" Webber asked Alison now.

"I've decided to reopen it," she said excitedly.

"Do you know much about fixing TVs and radios?" Lawson asked.

"I'm going to make it less a repair shop and more an electronics shop that sells the newest gadgets. Video games, Betamax, VCRs, that sort of thing. I've heard about places renting videos. I may give that a try too. Maybe people would be more interested in buying the machines if they could rent the movies."

"Sure, why not?" Lee's heart was pounding for joy at the thought of Alison moving to Lang permanently. If she'd suggested renting rocks, he would have told her it was a great idea.

"The best part is I can watch all those movies whenever I want," she said.

As everyone was leaning back in their chairs and loosening their belts, Ruby came in from the kitchen. "I hope everyone saved room. There's pumpkin pie for dessert."

Kay and Lee return in:

Memorial to Death
A Mortician Murder Mystery–Book 3

ACKNOWLEDGMENTS

The idea for this new series owes a lot to my wife's own upbringing. When I first met my future father-in-law, he was the only funeral director in a small, North Florida town in the 1980s. My wife has vivid memories of playing hide-and-seek in the casket room, being driven to school in a hearse and being fascinated by the mysteries of the embalming room. I hope these memories add a little realism to this series about a challenging and often misunderstood profession.

Cover Design by Melody Barber
www.aurorapublicity.com

ABOUT THE AUTHOR

A. E. Howe lives and writes on a farm in the wilds of North Florida with his wife, horses and more cats than he can count. He received a degree in English Education from the University of Georgia and is a produced screenwriter and playwright. His first published book was *Broken State*. The Larry Macklin Mysteries is his first series and he released a second series, the Baron Blasko Mysteries, in summer 2018. The first book in the Macklin series, *November's Past*, was awarded two silver medals in the 2017 President's Book Awards, presented by the Florida Authors & Publishers Association; the ninth book, *July's Trials*, was awarded two silver medals in 2018. Howe is a member of the Mystery Writers of America, and was co-host of the "Guns of Hollywood" podcast for four years on the Firearms Radio Network. When not writing, Howe enjoys riding, competitive shooting and working on the farm.

www.ingramcontent.com/pod-product-compliance
Lightning Source LLC
Chambersburg PA
CBHW061532210726
48287CB00006B/1920